What Reviewers Say About Gun Brooke's Books

Sheridan's Fate

"Sheridan's fire and Lark's warm embers are enough to make this book sizzle. Brooke, however, has gone beyond the wonderful emotional explorations of these characters to tell the story of those who, for various reasons, become differently-abled. Whether it is a bullet, an illness, or a problem at birth, many women and men find themselves in Sheridan's situation. Her courage and Lark's gentleness and determination send this romance into a 'must read.'"—*Just About Write*

Coffee Sonata

"In *Coffee Sonata*, the lives of these four women become intertwined. In forming friendships and love, closets and disabilities are discussed, along with differences in age and backgrounds. Love and friendship are areas filled with complexity and nuances. Brooke takes her time to savor the complexities while her main characters savor their excellent cups of coffee. If you enjoy a good love story, a great setting, and wonderful characters, look for *Coffee Sonata* at your favorite gay and lesbian bookstore."—*Family & Friends* magazine

Protector of the Realm

"Brooke is an amazing author, and has written in other genres. Never have I read a book where I started at the top of the page and don't know what will happen two paragraphs later…She keeps the excitement going, and the pages turning."—*MegaScene*

Course of Action

"Brooke's words capture the intensity of their growing relationship. Her prose throughout the book is breathtaking and heart-stopping. Where have you been hiding, Gun Brooke? I, for one, would like to see more romances from this author."—*Independent Gay Writer*

September Canvas

"In this character-driven story, trust is earned and secrets are uncovered. Deanna and Faythe are fully fleshed out and prove to the reader each has much depth, talent, wit and problem-solving abilities. *September Canvas* is a good read with a thoroughly satisfying conclusion."—*Just About Write*

By the Author

Course of Action

Coffee Sonata

Sheridan's Fate

September Canvas

Fierce Overture

The Supreme Constellations Series:

Protector of the Realm

Rebel's Quest

Warrior's Valor

Visit us at www.boldstrokesbooks.com

FIERCE OVERTURE

by

Gun Brooke

2010

FIERCE OVERTURE

ISBN 10: 1-60282-156-9
ISBN 13: 978-1-60282-156-9

THIS TRADE PAPERBACK ORIGINAL IS PUBLISHED BY
BOLD STROKES BOOKS, INC.
P.O. BOX 249
VALLEY FALLS, NY 12185

FIRST EDITION: JULY 2010

CREDITS

EDITORS: SHELLEY THRASHER AND STACIA SEAMAN
PRODUCTION DESIGN: STACIA SEAMAN
COVER ART BY GUN BROOKE
COVER DESIGN BY SHERI (GRAPHICARTIST2020@HOTMAIL.COM)

Acknowledgments

A published writer has many people to thank and acknowledge, which is great because that makes for a less lonely profession.

I owe many thanks to my first readers, whose opinions matters more than they realize: Pol, Maggie, Jan, Wendy, Trish, and Sam. Thank you for all the hours of reading and pondering you've put in. Your feedback has been incredibly helpful.

My publisher, Radclyffe, aka Len Barot, thank you for once again providing an inspiring base for me to grow as a writer. Shelley Thrasher, editor, is my rock, and we work so well together. BSB's graphic artist, Sheri, and I collaborated on the cover. Thanks, Sheri, I love how it turned out! Stacia Seaman's copy-editor/proofreader eagle eyes helped the book be as clean as humanly possible. Then there's all the behind-the-scenes people working for Bold Strokes Books who all help in the process of bringing books to the reader—you guys are great.

On a personal note, I want to mention a beloved spouse without whom I would've starved and despaired during the long and grueling winter of Sweden—Elon. Thanks for all the breakfasts in bed and general encouragement. I also want to acknowledge Malin and Henrik, my children, and my mother, Lilian. Without the therapeutic presence of my dogs, Jarmo and Seven, who faithfully warmed my legs and feet during several months of being bedridden, I would not have fared as well as I did.

Of course, I want to thank my readers for being so faithful and supportive throughout the years. I can't thank you enough. I hope you'll like Fierce Overture.

Dedication

For Sami, my second grandson,
who was born during the time I worked on this novel.

For my mother-in-law, Edith Marie Bach,
who passed away during this time.
She was the best and always treated me like a daughter.
I miss her so much.

Prologue

Two years earlier

Noelle danced to the beat of the music in a breakneck rhythm. She was like a sparkling flame in her short sequined dress as her hips swayed seductively. She grabbed the microphone and yanked it from its stand with a feral toss of her head, her waist-long hair flowing around her with a life of its own.

Helena watched her with more personal interest than she was prepared to admit. Noelle Laurent was the latest addition to Venus Media & Publishing, and it was no small feat to have snagged her from under the noses of her old record company and all the other bidders. Noelle was the hottest young star around, on a steady track to cult status. Helena had not yet had the pleasure of meeting her face-to-face, but was intimately familiar with her voice and performance.

"Happy fortieth birthday," someone purred in Helena's ear as a woman's slender arm circled her waist. "You don't look a day over thirty-nine."

"You crack me up, Myra. Honestly, shut up. I want to listen to this."

"Ah. The scrumptious Ms. Laurent." Myra Hollander, Helena's lover more than twenty years ago and now a good friend, chuckled. "Of *course*, you want to check her out."

"It's business." Helena was lying and she knew it, but she'd never confess that to Myra. Myra knew all about Helena's philosophy when it came to relationships. Short. Sweet. Bye-bye. To be caught gaping like this at a kid more than ten years her junior was embarrassing, which was another reason not to confess.

"Of *course*." Myra opened her mouth to continue, but a quick glance from Helena was obviously enough. "All right. All right. I'll go see a girl about some punch."

Onstage, two other performers belonging to VMP had joined Noelle and they were now slowing the music, moving toward the corner where Helena stood surrounded by friends and employees. The band began to play the interlude to "Happy Birthday," and to Helena's dismay, the trio of young women shimmied down the four steps from the catwalk and approached her.

"Happy birthday, Ms. Forsythe," they crooned.

They stopped right in front of her and kissed her on the cheek, one by one. Noelle was the last in line, and to Helena's surprise she didn't kiss her, but hugged her shyly.

Noelle Laurent was even more breathtaking up close, her complexion damp with perspiration, which only emphasized her scent of citrus and vanilla. Appalled at the deep surge of emotions, which she rationalized as mere lust, Helena stepped out of reach.

"Thank you, ladies. Now, don't let me hog you. I think the audience wants more of you." She could tell that her standoffish response to the public display didn't bother the first two girls, but Noelle's golden eyes seemed to lose their sparkle and turn into a muted dark brown.

"Anytime, Ms. Forsythe," the first of the young women said, and winked before she reentered the stage area. The second one merely giggled and waved at the crowd as she followed suit. Noelle stood as if frozen and looked like she wanted to add something.

"I'm so thrilled to finally meet you." Noelle seemed reluctant to return with the other two, who had already begun a wild dance along the catwalk toward the stage.

"And now you have." The corners of Helena's mouth had never felt so rigid. She tried to smile politely, but couldn't. She didn't need a mirror to know how arrogant she looked. Her reaction shocked her. Even if she normally didn't mind living up to her reputation as the company bitch, she was always civil and professional. What about Noelle triggered this weird reaction? Helena shrugged inwardly. Maybe the fact that she'd never cared much for birthdays?

"Sure." Noelle pivoted so fast, Helena stepped back when Noelle's long hair whipped through the air. She jumped up on the catwalk, ignoring the people who offered their hands for support. Grabbing the microphone, Noelle let her voice dominate the rest of the song, outstaging the other performers by a mile.

Helena knew from a business point of view that VMP had struck pure gold when they signed Noelle Laurent. On a personal level, Helena had no idea why she was certain that she should keep her distance.

CHAPTER ONE

Helena plowed through the busy corridor at VMP's headquarters with an ease born of confidence and familiarity. It didn't hurt that a mere look at her solemn expression scattered the junior staff in all directions. Occasionally an intern too eager to get out of her way would literally hit the wall.

Her office on the top floor of the American Standard Building was decorated to fit the original building. Helena loved it and normally entered the vast room with a feeling of anticipation. Today was different. She was not looking forward to dealing with yet another spoiled pop diva while still jet-lagged after her flight back from Europe two days ago.

"Anything significant come up while I was in London?" Helena asked briskly as she passed Wanda Mayer, her assistant.

"David Boyd called. Said he has something urgent to talk to you about."

"Noelle Laurent's producer?"

"Yes. He doesn't sound too happy."

"Really? Well, better return his call. Give me two minutes." Helena walked into her office. Yellow roses stood in a blue vase on the coffee table in the sitting area of the room. Helena's mother had started the custom decades ago, which Wanda continued. She had worked for Helena's mother's assistant, who had groomed her meticulously until she took over.

Stopping in front of the vintage oak desk, Helena remembered exactly how her mother had looked behind it. Stern and goal-oriented, Dorcas Forsythe had been a woman in a man's world when she took over after her husband became ill during the seventies. When Helena finished boarding school, she'd begun to work with her mother, eager to please and to learn how to become as poised and ambitious.

Helena sat down at the desk, pulled her laptop from her black leather briefcase, and docked it with her desktop computer. As she waited for the call to David Boyd to go through, she updated the files she'd worked on while on her business trip to the London office.

"David Boyd for you on line one, ma'am," Wanda said over the intercom.

"Thank you." Helena pressed the button in question. "Helena Forsythe. What's up, David?" Helena barked her question, making sure she sounded as impatient as she felt.

"Sorry to disturb you, Ms. Forsythe, but we have a bit of a situation." David Boyd seemed apologetic, but also stressed and concerned.

"What kind of situation?" Helena pulled up Noelle Laurent's dossier, and a picture of the strikingly beautiful singer filled her computer screen.

"Noelle is causing trouble. She was impossible to deal with when we met to plan her second release. Come to think of it, she already seemed disgruntled when we recorded her first album for VMP. Makes you wonder how she treated her producers when she cut her first eight albums for those other labels."

Helena browsed through some photos of the tall, curvaceous soul-pop star. With a voice that could move mountains, and enough sex appeal to mesmerize an arena full of fans, Noelle Laurent was apparently completely spoiled and truly represented the new "brat pack" in the music business.

"What did she do?"

"She walked out on us. She's never done this before, and it concerns me. Could be she's preparing to lawyer up and risk breaking her contract, for all we know."

"But you're not sure?"

"No. She just stormed off with that big dude of hers in tow. Morris something. I have to say he became a bit unstable at one time during our...altercation."

"You mean her bodyguard? What in blazes did you do, David? Just what kind of *altercation* are you talking about?"

"Nothing, really. Thor tried to get her to stay by blocking her—"

"And the bodyguard made you all look like fools when he simply guided our little diva out of there."

"Eh, yeah." David sighed. "Pretty much."

"And what exactly provoked this bit of drama?"

"Noelle has written a bunch of songs and now she wants to record them. We tried to tell her those songs weren't her, you know. They're the deep kind of songs. Not at all what her fans are looking for."

"How did she respond?"

"Like a true diva. She probably sees herself as the next Alicia Keys. What worries me even more is that Noelle seems to think she's earned the right to change the contract."

"Oh, she does, does she?" Helena grimaced as a headache began to squeeze her temples. "What the hell. I'll handle it."

"Thanks, Ms. Forsythe. She's being impossible."

Even if Helena could understand his frustration, something prissy and overbearing in his tone made the idea of a rebellious Noelle Laurent understandable.

After Helena hung up she asked Wanda to join her, explaining the situation. "Schedule a meeting with Noelle Laurent and her agent today. Make it clear that if she doesn't show up, I'll consider her in breach of contract."

Helena thumbed through the newspapers and some of the magazines that Wanda had stacked on her desk. The second magazine featured a full spread about Noelle Laurent, focusing on her wardrobe onstage, which showed more skin than fabric. The author asked the readers to go to the magazine's Web site and discuss if Noelle's outfits were too outrageous for her younger fans.

Helena shook her head. Noelle's clothes weren't any worse than other pop star's; she merely filled them better. Frowning at how she kept staring at the picture of Noelle, Helena closed the magazine, uncomfortable about the direction her mind had taken her.

❖

Adjusting her deep purple shirt, Noelle made sure she looked as businesslike as possible, given her outrageous hair and hourglass figure. She'd minimalized her makeup and pulled her long, black-and-blond hair into a severe bun at the nape of her neck. The phone message from Venus Media & Publishing headquarters via Brad, her agent, had sounded ominous, but she was ready to stand her ground. She had paid her dues by doing everyone's bidding over the last decade. It was time for a change.

Noelle sat down at the island in the kitchen, where her mother was making breakfast just as she had when Noelle was little. Her mother had worked two jobs back then, but always managed to cook for her girls before she sent them off to school.

"Can I help, Mom?"

Her mother's raised eyebrows telegraphed her surprise. "With what? Breakfast? Don't be silly. I'm almost done."

"We're big girls, Mom. Almost," Noelle added, with a quick glance in her younger sister Claudia's direction. As the second youngest of the five sisters, Claudia had quickly established her role as the family's diva. She had never showed any sign of getting out of the "terrible twos."

"What's eating you?" Claudia plopped down on a stool next to Noelle. "And what's with that outfit? You look like you're going to church."

"And good morning to you, too." Noelle regarded her sister calmly. Claudia was seventeen going on forty-five, more cynical and acerbic than anyone at her age should be. "I'm on my way to a meeting. And you?" Claudia was dressed in a silk nightgown worthy of a movie star from the forties and tossed her hair in a way that would make any professional hair model envious.

Claudia had already lost interest in what Noelle had to say and reached for the plate of pancakes. "Mine?"

"No, your sister's. Didn't you hear what Noelle said? She has to go to a meeting."

"She's not the only one who's busy. I'm off to school." Claudia's anger seemed to always be simmering just beneath the surface.

"Dressed like that?" Noelle knew better, but couldn't resist needling Claudia.

"Ah!" Claudia twirled and left the kitchen.

"Sorry, Mom." Noelle dug her fork into the syrup-infused pancakes, not about to let Claudia's antics get to her. She was nervous as it was. Being summoned to see Helena Forsythe was like being called to the principal's office, something that had happened only a few times when she was in high school. Always the shy and proper student, Noelle had felt she'd failed her parents miserably the few times she got into trouble. Being the oldest of five girls wasn't easy. *Thank God, they're not all as temperamental as Claudia. Or as ungrateful.*

"You seem far away." Reba sat down with her own plate after she placed the remaining pancakes in the oven to stay warm.

"I'm worried, Mom." Noelle hadn't meant to be so candid, but she was so rattled that not even her mother's comfort food could distract her. "I have to go see the CEO at VMP. She's called the Dragon Lady on her best days, and I'm not looking forward to this. She doesn't like me."

"What? What's not to like?" Reba looked aghast at the possibility of someone not appreciating her firstborn. "What's wrong with this woman?"

"Oh, Mom." Noelle chuckled. "She just doesn't. I met her once, at her birthday party two years ago, and she blew me off for no reason. Totally cold. Treated me like air. I don't know what I did to her then, but I know why she's mad at me now."

"And why is that?" Reba's fork was halfway to her mouth. "Don't tell me she has a problem with your songs? Surely she has to appreciate the fact that you're evolving as an artist. As a performer."

Claudia entered the room, pulling on a pink sweater. "She probably thinks Noelle is stuck-up and conceited." She glanced around the countertop. "My pancakes?"

"Oven. And don't talk about your sister that way. She pays your way to that fancy school and supports all your expensive habits."

"Mom—"

"It could change in a heartbeat, so we better stick together and support *her*." Reba didn't budge. "Apologize."

Claudia obviously knew better than to cross her mother when she sounded so authoritarian. "Sorry, Noey." She looked at Noelle from under her thick bangs. "I can be rather shi—I mean, I can be a bitch in the morning."

"And that's just to warm up, huh?" Noelle smiled to take the sting out of the tease. Claudia was a pain and could be insufferable, but she was seventeen. *I never had to struggle in a famous sibling's shadow, so what do I know about how it affects her?* "What do you say we hit the mall tomorrow morning?" Claudia would recognize the olive branch.

"Sure. Guess we could take the kid."

"Kid. Thanks." Fifteen-year-old Laurel, low-key and the brightest student of the sisters, sat down and accepted a plate from her mother. She propped her head up with her hand and began to munch on her pancakes. "I wouldn't mind going. I need stuff for school."

"For school?" Claudia rolled her eyes theatrically, clearly finding her stride again. "I'm going to shop for clothes and makeup, and get some of the latest CDs. You'd think that stingy bi—" She glanced at her mother's quickly darkening face. "You'd think that woman at VMP would give you all their music as a courtesy. You're supposed to be their biggest star."

"I'm one of their bestselling artists. There's a difference, Claudia."

"Still."

"I'll tell her you said so." *Not.* "I'm out of here. Thanks, Mom." Noelle rose and carried her plate over to the sink.

"Here. Take a few pancakes to Mr. Morris." Reba handed a plastic box to Noelle. "He spends a lot of time waiting for you. He must get hungry sometimes."

"Wish me luck." Noelle gave her mother a quick kiss and waved to her sisters. "Later." *Off to the dragon's lair.*

❖

"The receptionist downstairs called. Noelle Laurent is here," Wanda informed Helena over the intercom.

"Thank you. Tell her to come right in." It would take Noelle at least five minutes to cross the large reception area and take the elevator up. Helena began to tidy her desk, but then relented, letting the magazines, papers, and folders flood her desk as usual. She was normally a bit of a neat freak, but her office usually overflowed with documents and work-related items, especially when she'd been on a business trip.

Helena rolled her shoulders, the constant tension in her neck dissipating some. She was happy with the meetings in London, even if she'd been distracted and succumbed to jet lag and fatigue more than usual. Declining several offers from VMP's London branch execs to take her out for dinner in the evenings, Helena had opted for long baths and tried to relax and rejuvenate in her hotel room. But her soreness and malaise still persisted here in the U.S. Not even playing with her dog,

Soledad, and taking her for long walks along the beach seemed to help. Soledad had pressed against her leg as they strolled instead of running around like possessed and jumping into the water. She seemed to sense Helena's ambivalence.

"Ms. Forsythe?"

A husky voice with a timbre that made Helena shiver interrupted her thoughts. Noelle Laurent stood just inside the door, a large Prada Fairy Bag slung over her left shoulder. Dressed in a dark gray business suit over a purple silk blouse, she looked impeccable, in spite of her extreme hair. Its restraint in a low bun today couldn't hide the fact that the top layers were dyed white-blond, contrasting wildly with the blue-black hair underneath.

"Welcome. Please, have a seat. Your manager not joining us?"

"I thought he was here already. Maybe he's stuck in traffic."

"Perhaps. Can I offer you anything to drink?"

"No, thank you." Noelle walked on ridiculously high-heeled pumps over to the leather visitor's chair, shook Helena's hand, and quickly let go. She sat down while opening her bag. "Brought my own." She held up a deep red thermos. "Mom's chamomile tea."

"Really?" Helena had already risen and now stepped over to the counter where a state-of-the-art coffee-center machine stood ready to provide her with any hot beverage she could possibly desire. She pressed the buttons for black espresso and returned her attention to Noelle as the machine ground the coffee beans. "I received a call from one of your producers. Not going so well with the new album, is it?"

"If you mean I'm not ready to repeat the previous album, I guess you're right." Noelle crossed her legs and brushed away invisible lint from her pants.

"You've signed a contract, and we have a deadline."

"I'm not debating that. I just don't want to sound exactly the same or sing exactly the same songs as I did on the last one."

"Which was tremendously successful." Helena forced herself to sound gracious, refusing to let her annoyance with Noelle show. *Sugarcoat them, if that's what it takes.* Her mother's voice permeated Helena's thoughts. *Whatever it takes to get them to sign on the dotted line. Just do it.*

"Yes. But, been there, done that." Noelle bent forward, showing off her décolletage, deliberate or not. "The thing is, I know I'm capable of so much more. Of sharing so much more with my fans. I can't see myself singing happy-go-lucky pop songs my whole life."

"Nothing wrong with pop music." Helena spoke shortly, dreading a long song and dance interspersed with words like "creativity," "inspiration," and "culture."

"Never said there was." Pausing, Noelle seemed to look for the right word. "What I'm trying to say is…I've worked with several producers over the last decade, including David and his crew, always eager to please and be whatever they needed me to be. I've been so grateful for the chance of a lifetime, never quite sure I deserved it. But now"—Noelle lifted her shoulders in a barely noticeable shrug—"I've finally reached my limit."

"Your limit. Can you elaborate?" Helena sat down behind her desk, balancing the small espresso cup.

"Haven't you ever felt like you've come to a point where you just can't do it anymore?" Gesturing emphatically with her hands, Noelle gazed at Helena with serious, dark eyes. "When it's so important that you follow your heart, nothing else matters?"

Helena couldn't believe that she, who'd stared down the most intimidating old foxes at numerous board meetings, would feel so cornered by the look in Noelle's eyes. Annoyed, Helena thought Noelle needed a lesson in boundaries—as in when not to cross them.

"This isn't about me," Helena snapped. "You've signed a contract that ensures VMP two albums of your trademark music style. We didn't sign you to experiment with your fan base, and if you want to do that, you'll have to wait until you've fulfilled your obligations to us."

"How can you run a recording company and not be interested in your artists' creative growth and development?" Noelle looked both hurt and confused. "I've proved myself and brought my *huge* fan base to VMP time and again. You talk about two albums. Don't forget the six number-one hit singles on the Billboard list, just from the previous album alone. Also the three songs I've recorded for the soundtrack of the new Diana Maddox movie. And come to think of it, you've bought the rights to eventually rerelease the albums I recorded while on the two previous labels. I've fulfilled every single aspect of my contract so far, down to every dorky way to promote it that you've sent me on."

"Dorky?" Helena could hardly believe her ears. "What the hell are you talking about?"

"I know I have fans of all ages, but honestly, what did you think you'd achieve by having me as a guest star on *Barney and Friends*?" Folding her arms, Noelle glowered at Helena.

"Oh. Well, that was a bit ridiculous." Helena groaned inwardly at the idiot PR person who'd thought of that.

"Right."

"But that doesn't mean—" The intercom beeped and Helena pressed a button. "Yes, Wanda?"

"Mr. Brad Haley is here to join you and Ms. Laurent, ma'am."

"Show him in, please." Perhaps he'd be able to talk some sense into Noelle, though Helena doubted it.

"Noelle! Ms. Forsythe, how great to see you again." Brad Haley strode across the room, extending his hand to Helena, pumping hers happily. "I'm sorry I'm late. Total gridlock. No, worse. A parking lot." He sat down, at Helena's suggestion, and patted Noelle's shoulder while getting comfortable. "So what are we talking about? Fill me in?"

"Your client doesn't want to fulfill her contract with us." Helena spoke curtly, feeling edgy and not about to mince words.

"A mere misunderstanding, I'm sure." Brad never lost his broad grin. "Honey, what's going on?" He turned to Noelle.

"I'm not trying to dodge my contract. I'm ready to start recording, but they want me to sing the same mindless songs I've been performing for ten years."

"Which is what your contract stipulates." Helena reclined in her chair, forcing herself to keep her hands neatly folded rather than drum her fingers on the desk.

Noelle straightened. "My contract stipulates that I deliver two albums in the soul genre."

"Soul *pop*." Deliberately making her voice steely and unforgiving, Helena saw how her tone affected Noelle. Her perfect eyebrows knitted and her eyes became slits as Noelle took on the challenge.

"Soul music has many faces." She spoke in a low voice, but her anger was obvious in the way she held her chin and regarded Helena with narrowed eyes. "If I can't grow and develop as a singer, a performer, then what's the use? Why should I put so much hard work, so many hours into sounding exactly the same, album after album?"

"Because you do it so well, and because that's where the money lies," Helena said quickly.

"It can't be all about the money! Music is so much more than that."

"You knew what we expected when you signed the contract." Helena didn't wait for Noelle to answer, but turned to Brad. "And I'm sure you've informed your client of this more than once?"

"I'm right here," Noelle said sharply. "No need talking about me like I'm not."

"Noelle, a contract is a binding document." Brad was clearly trying to soothe her, but instead he came off sounding condescending. "We've discussed—"

"For heaven's sake, Brad. I know what a contract is and what signing it means. Let's get something straight. You work for me. You do my bidding. You find out my goals, wants, and needs, and you do your best to make them all happen."

It wasn't hard to read between the lines. Noelle was obviously saying, *Make it happen, or you don't work for me anymore.*

Brad cleared his voice, but never lost the shimmer in his smile. "Now, now," he said. "I'm sure we can reach consensus on this matter."

"I'm not so sure," Helena said. "Noelle seems pretty set on changing genres, and the producers are concerned about her lack of interest in the work they've put into finding new songs for her to choose from."

"Trust me, they offered the same song, over and over again, so it couldn't have been that hard on them." Noelle stood, slinging her Prada bag over her shoulder. "Since neither of you will listen to anything I say, I'll leave you to it to figure things out. Brad, call me when you have something positive to say."

Noelle's lower lip seemed to tremble as she donned her big sunglasses, but she certainly didn't hesitate when she rattled off her bitter words and swept through the doors.

"I've never seen Noelle like this," Brad said, adjusting his tie. "She's usually such a sweet little thing."

"Are you blaming her behavior on me?" Helena tapped her chin. "Not so good from a negotiation standpoint."

"No, no, Ms. Forsythe. I never meant to imply that." Brad looked shocked. "Noelle has never had anything but good to say about VMP and its management until now."

"'Until now' being the operative words." Helena pressed her palms against her desk and rose from her chair. "You know my opinion. And even if Ms. Laurent thinks she can throw a temper tantrum and have her way just because she's a superstar, she's way off. If she decides to not listen to reason and break her contract, the penalties will be severe. And even if she thinks all the record companies would welcome her with open arms, she might just think twice. She's not the only superstar out there, and people hold on to their money these days."

"Just give her time to cool off. I'll talk to her, and if I need to, I'll contact her mother." Brad stood and extended his hand. "Noelle will come around. I'll see to it."

Something in the man's voice made Helena wonder what means of persuasion he intended to use. There was something about Brad Haley she didn't like, and the way he treated Noelle and talked about her made her uncomfortable. It was one thing that Noelle had decided to go all creative and explore—something she should do on her own time and dollar—but Brad's overbearing manner was not the way to dissuade her. This approach was something he seemed to have in common with David Boyd.

Helena said good-bye coolly to Brad and sat back down at her desk. The relationship between Noelle and her manager wasn't her problem, as long as Noelle honored the contract. Browsing through her latest e-mail messages, she couldn't get the image of Noelle's look of anger and hurt out of her mind.

"Home, please, Morris." Noelle curled up in the backseat of the limo. Morris had scrutinized her with darkening eyes when she returned to the foyer where he patiently waited for her. He knew her so well, and no sunglasses in the world could hide her true emotions from him.

"You all right?" Morris glanced at her in the rearview mirror.

"I'm fine."

"Not true," he muttered. "What did that moron agent say this time? Or was it the Forsythe woman?"

"Both. Never mind that. I have to go home and prepare for Friday evening. I can't worry about what these money-loving barracudas think."

Noelle tried to focus on her upcoming mini-concert on Friday, when she was supposed to sing at a charity function. Annelie Peterson, publisher and Hollywood producer, had approached her personally. Annelie also ran a nonprofit organization for, among other causes, battered-women-and-children shelters.

Deciding to take the leap, Noelle had not asked Annelie to go through her agent, but made the arrangements herself. She intended to sing her own songs, welcoming the chance to try them out on a live audience without having the Forsythe woman or Brad interfering.

Just thinking about Helena Forsythe made her press her lips tightly, not letting any rude words escape. Raised to not curse, to always be well-mannered and humble no matter what, she still found it easy to follow her gut reaction and agree with the people who referred to Forsythe as a company shark and a four-star bitch.

Admittedly, Helena had been just as larger than life as she'd been at her birthday party two years ago. *And just as disdainful.* She filled the room as if she was physically much larger than she actually was, Noelle guessed Helena to be around 5'5" tall, about four inches shorter than her. Though Noelle always wore six-inch heels, Helena's presence was such that Nicole was always left with the impression that they were the same height.

Helena's throaty alto voice was probably a real asset when it came to chewing someone off at the ankles or scaring her business opposition to death. But surprisingly, Helena's golden brown hair, cut just beneath her jawline, looked like silk, and the soft colors of her makeup not only lent her a classic beauty, but also softened her features.

"We're here, Noelle." Morris pulled out of traffic and stopped outside the condominium complex. As a doorman hurried toward the limo and opened the door, a scattered group of paparazzi buzzed around the vehicle. Noelle made sure her sunglasses were safely in place before she exited the car.

She hurried through the small crowd to the sound of whirring cameras and voices calling for her attention. The doorman ushered her into the building and she tipped him generously. As she rode the elevator up to her condo, she did her best to look happy, to not alert her sisters or their mother to anything amiss. She had promised her father that she would look out for them and never forget where they came from, and a promise was a promise.

CHAPTER TWO

Noelle tucked her sheet music into her folder and double-checked her appearance in the mirror. She looked a little pale, but she could easily remedy that with something from her sizable beauty box, which she always carried with her. Her long black dress hung in its protective bag on her bedroom door, which now opened as her mother poked her head in.

"You ready, darling? Morris has already tapped his watch four times."

"As if that helps." Noelle wrinkled her nose. "I'm never late. I just always cut it close."

"There never was a truer word." Reba glanced at the briefcase. "So you're going with your own material after all?" She looked concerned now.

"Yes." Noelle didn't want to get into a discussion, or she'd lose her nerve.

"Why now, when you're in the middle of a minor crisis at VMP?"

"Because I really want to sing these songs to a live audience and…" She shrugged.

"I don't want you to think I'm not being loyal, but what would it hurt to give in and do one more album in the same style as before?" Reba touched Noelle's arm gently.

"That's not the issue." Noelle didn't withdraw her arm, but she did grow tense. "I've sung these songs for ten years and dreamed for *ten years* of doing other things, other songs, my songs. That's a long time. I've earned this chance."

"I see. I've never thought about it like that." Reba caressed Noelle's cheek and hugged her. "Get going. You'll do great."

"Thanks, Mom."

In the limo, Noelle hummed the melody of her opening song, hoping she wouldn't forget the words or screw up some other way, since so much depended on the outcome of her performance. Not when it came to her career, but for her self-esteem. Her self-confidence was pretty shaky right now, since nobody at work had expressed any true interest in her thoughts and ideas. Occasionally, her producers allowed her to change a word or even a phrase, but this...this would be a baptism by fire.

❖

At least eight hundred people mingled in the conference hall of the Hilton. The chatter was deafening, but Helena was used to large groups and had hosted enough shareholders' conventions to not feel intimidated. After adjusting her mauve see-through shawl, she tucked her pearl-embroidered purse under her arm as she descended the stairs. At the bottom Annelie Peterson, whose nonprofit organization hosted this charity function, greeted her warmly.

"Helena. So good to see you." Annelie wore an ice blue evening dress that perfectly matched her eyes. Her long blond hair was swept back in an intricate French braid, with small tresses curling around her neck. Without her usual austere expression, she seemed much more approachable than she had several years ago.

"Annelie, you know I wouldn't miss any of your projects." Helena stood on her toes and kissed Annelie Peterson's cheek. Annelie had been her friend ever since they collaborated in creating the famous Maddox audio books. The books about Diana Maddox had become a huge overnight success, and Annelie had then taken yet another step and produced two movies about the illustrious lesbian criminal investigator. After a stormy courtship, Annelie ended up marrying Carolyn Black, who played Diana Maddox. Now Helena gazed around, looking for the beautiful actress. "Where's Carolyn?"

"At the studio. She's running late, but should be here any minute. She's looking forward to meeting you. Be forewarned, though. She's not happy about you missing our wedding." Annelie winked at Helena, then smiled at the next guest waiting in line. Helena kept walking and braved the crowd. She had set her eyes on a waitress with a tray of champagne flutes and soon was close enough to snag a glass for herself.

"Good God, Helena, you that thirsty?" a familiar voice said from behind.

"Of course, Myra." Helena turned around and greeted her former friend. "And yes, I've had quite the week coming back from London, so I'm very thirsty."

"Don't tell me your superstars are driving you to drink?" Myra sipped her own champagne.

"No. Well, they just might if I let them. It would be hard to find a more self-centered bunch."

"Aw, come on. You love juggling celebrities and earning all that lovely cold cash."

"I wish!" Helena nodded in passing to a few business acquaintances. "Everyone's had to tighten their belt these days."

Myra grew serious. "VMP isn't in trouble, is it?"

"No, we're fine. So far. Like everyone else we need to be smart, though."

"Ain't that the truth. Speaking of your superstars, I noticed that your prize possession is performing."

"What? Who?" Helena looked over at the stage where a grand piano was faintly lit.

"You didn't know?" Myra looked surprised. "Noelle Laurent is the poster girl for this particular charity. She's appearing in a few minutes."

"No, I didn't." Afraid she'd chip a tooth if she clenched her teeth any harder, Helena willed herself to relax. "Then again, I can't keep up with everyone's schedule. That's impossible when you run one of the largest labels in the U.S."

"Ah, don't be humble. VMP is *the* biggest label. Period."

Helena shook her head. "Have you been reading *Forbes* magazine again, Myra?"

"It's my substitute for a little black book," Myra said, and winked. "Never know when the 'richest, most powerful' list will come in handy."

"You calculating bitch." Helena gazed affectionately at her friend.

She and Myra hadn't spoken for a couple of years after their breakup. Myra had actually been quite heartbroken after Helena dumped her, but once they cleared the air, they'd found an easygoing friendship.

"You bet." Myra looked over Helena's shoulder. "Looks like the show's about to begin."

Annelie entered the small stage and stopped by the microphone. After checking something over her shoulder, she turned back and greeted the audience.

"Thank you for attending our annual charity function for the Key Line AIDS Foundation. I couldn't be more thrilled to introduce one of our brightest stars in the sky of popular music, Noelle Laurent."

Applause thundered between the walls as the lights lowered in the room and increased onstage. A curtain fluttered on the left side of the stage and the light homed in on a lithe woman dressed in a long, sleek black dress that revealed her bare shoulders. The black and blond hair was brushed away from her face in a long, low tail, and her only jewelry was a pair of sparkling diamond earrings. Helena held her breath as Noelle sat down at the piano. What was she doing? Where were the sing-back tracks, the dancers and backup singers?

Noelle looked down at the keys before she slowly raised her hands and began to play. The audience was now completely silent, seemingly as mesmerized as Helena was. She was shocked when Noelle began to sing.

> *The reflection in my mirror,*
> *Is this what others see?*
> *Those who go dead silent when I enter*
> *And laugh behind me when I leave.*

With her amazing voice, Noelle told the story of a shy, lonely girl. Instead of the usual roaring lioness who prowled the stage as if stalking prey, Noelle sang every word with naked honesty and a raw emotion that made Helena take a step back, seeking cover near some large plants. Hiding in the shadows, she stared at the revelation that was Noelle, illuminated by an unforgiving spotlight where she sat at the grand piano. She swayed with the intensity of the song as her fingers danced over the keys. Helena tried to remember if she'd ever known

Noelle could play the piano, let alone this well. The arrangement was beautifully done and not overly complicated.

No matter what, I won't surrender.
I made a promise late last night.
I may have miles left on my journey,
But I'm prepared to stay and fight.

Noelle's voice carried easily across the hushed crowd. She sang the refrain one last time and slowly ended with a few wistful chords. After an initial dead silence, the audience drew a simultaneous deep breath before they unleashed their applause. Helena clapped until her hands hurt, and around her, other people did the same.

"God, who knew she could sing like that?" a woman to her left said to her companions. "Young Noelle Laurent obviously grew up."

"Sure did." The man to her left nodded emphatically. "Oh, good, she's not done."

Noelle began to play her second song, this time with a completely different theme and set in a minor key. At first, she hummed the melody softly, lulling Helena into assuming everything was all right. When she went on to sing the lyrics, she yanked Helena back into reality with her first words, making her flinch enough to spill some of her cocktail.

If you think I'll buy a fast "I'm sorry,"
Such empty words don't work on me.
Try giving me a cold, cold diamond,
I'll show you how cold I can be.

It was like a typical "angry young woman" song, but Noelle's voice, and the authenticity with which she sang, turned it into a razor-sharp criticism of anything superficial. *Is that how she's been treated? Is that her reality?* Helena moved toward the stage without really noticing how she nudged people out of the way. She wanted to see Noelle's expression up close; she needed to know for sure, somehow, that these were her own true words and not speculation on Noelle's part. Helena stopped five yards from the stage, still able to hide behind two rows of spectators.

Noelle was hammering the bitter tones on the piano now, and tears, probably of fury, hung like crystals from her eyelashes. Then the music changed again, sent Helena's feelings on a different track as Noelle played softly, her voice low and with a beautiful tremor.

The song rang out with a painfully strong chord, and the audience awarded Noelle with more loud applause. When she rose from the piano stool, people cheered and called her name over and over. Noelle looked like she couldn't believe how her songs were received. Clutching the microphone hard enough to whiten her knuckles, she thanked the audience for their response.

"I have never sung my own songs in public before, and I was really nervous, thinking maybe I'm the only one who likes them."

The audience laughed and several people raised their voice. "We love them. And we love you too, Noelle!" a young man close to Helena shouted.

"Thank you. I love my fans too." Noelle's beauty was nearly otherworldly as she blew a kiss in the young man's direction. "I want to finish with a song that's a little more cheerful. I hope you'll like it. It's called 'One Day.'"

Noelle sat down, this time on a tall chair, and someone handed her an acoustic guitar from the shadows behind her. She tried a few chords and then began to play a wistful but happier song about dreams for the future. Helena wondered how autobiographical the words were and if Noelle realized how transparent she made herself.

I don't think it's too much to ask
For lifelong love and happiness.
A soul mate, and a best friend too,
Someone to help me fight the blues.
So if not right now, or right away...
Then—one day!

Helena thought the stomping and cheering would never end. Noelle finally left the stage after taking a bow five times. Shell-shocked, Helena was beginning to think Noelle had psychic abilities. Several of the phrases she'd sung, and certainly the meaning that was clearly between the lines, could have been picked from Helena's own life.

The first song reminded her of her first awful months at boarding school as an eleven-year-old. She'd gone from being abysmally shy to ruling the school in a couple of semesters. She learned a valuable life lesson when she figured out that young peers eat shy, polite girls for breakfast. Her mother had used Helena's transformation as evidence that boarding schools were a fantastic way of fostering your child into becoming a go-getter and a powerful force. Soon Helena was chairman of several extracurricular clubs at her school and graduated in the top two percent, even being elected Best All-Around Student. Dorcas had made it clear that anything less was unthinkable.

"That was amazing. She's sure come a long way, creatively speaking," a familiar alto voice said, jolting Helena back to reality. Twirling, she found Annelie standing right behind her. "Noelle's fantastic. Congratulations on having her in your stable, Helena."

"Thanks." Helena returned the hug Annelie had just given her. "You sure know how to throw a party. Looks like a huge success."

"Thank you. Carolyn said—" Annelie gestured apologetically. "Sorry. That bell's calling me. Got to go be the hostess for a bit as we're moving into the banquet hall. You're seated at our table so I'll see you there."

"All right." Helena began to walk toward the huge double doors, hoping to avoid the large crowd that would soon get the same idea once Annelie announced that dinner was being served. She glanced over at the now-dark stage, inwardly hearing the pensive, intense tones and the haunting words of Noelle's songs. *She caught me off guard. That's all.*

CHAPTER THREE

Noelle stood trembling in the conference room that served as her dressing room, her breath coming in short gasps. *They cheered! They actually cheered.* She had struggled to pick her strongest songs, and the mere idea of playing a musical instrument in public had also strained her nerves. As she had sat down in front of the grand piano, her hands shook so badly she had serious doubts about accompanying herself.

A blond man who had introduced himself earlier as Gregory Horton, Annelie Peterson's assistant, approached her. "Ms. Laurent? This way, please. It's time to join Ms. Peterson and her company at the head table."

"Thank you, Gregory." Noelle took her beaded evening purse and walked from the room ahead of him. Outside, people hurried toward the banquet hall, but several approached her.

"I love your new songs," a young girl said, beaming. "I could relate so much to the first one. I used to be really shy."

"Thank you. How sweet of you to tell me this." Noelle shook her hand.

"When do you plan to record these?"

"I don't know yet. I'm about to start a recording session, so we'll see."

"I've got all your CDs, so no matter what, I'll know whatever you come up with will be great." The girl looked so starstruck Noelle decided she better leave before they ended up blocking everybody.

"Enjoy your evening. Thank you." She nodded to the girl and her party and followed Gregory, who guided her to the head table.

Everyone's glances and curious stares felt like fingers against her skin, and she wondered, as she often did, why she never became used to being under scrutiny. Early in her career her mother had cautioned her to develop an emotional armor during public appearances, to help her retain her privacy and ultimately her sanity. However, Noelle had never mastered the ability to keep a healthy distance. Unkind remarks and critiques that seemed more personal than constructive still devastated her.

"Here you go, Ms. Laurent." Gregory stopped at a round table. "Do you know everybody?" He gestured toward the six men and women.

"I know some." Noelle gazed around the table and extended her hand to Annelie Peterson.

"Noelle, you were amazing. I can't thank you enough for donating your time and talent to our charity." Annelie rose to kiss Noelle's cheek. "You've met my wife, Carolyn, right?"

"Only briefly, at an awards show years ago. Hello, Carolyn. It's great to see you again."

"You too." Carolyn Black shook her hand firmly, her blue-gray eyes piercing, but warm, as she studied Noelle. "Your voice is something else. I was only able to hear the last song, but I loved every second of it."

"Thank you." Noelle had seen Carolyn Black in several productions on both the big and the small screens, but hearing her famous, throaty voice in person was impressive.

"And of course Helena Forsythe doesn't need extra introductions either." Annelie motioned to the woman sitting with her back to Noelle.

Wondering how she could have missed Helena, Noelle struggled not to flinch as Helena patted the chair next to her. "Have a seat, Noelle. I agree with the previous speaker, you were wonderful tonight."

Every bit as distinctive as Carolyn's, Helena's voice created goose bumps on Noelle's arms. *Say something!* Noelle fought to break out of her temporary daze at seeing Helena here.

"Noelle?" Helena touched her arm briefly, which made her shudder again.

"Yes. Of course." Noelle sat down abruptly, nodding at the other three who sat at the table. "Nice to meet you all."

Gregory took the last empty seat, placing his arm subtly around a pretty young brunette. After the final introductions, Noelle remained quiet and listened to the conversation around the table. Helena glanced her way every now and then, and Noelle tried to think of something to say.

"Annelie tells me you've recorded three of the songs for the Diana Maddox movie soundtrack." Carolyn leaned sideways to let the waiter remove her soup bowl. "I'm thrilled, since that will encourage the younger generation to embrace our characters."

"Our latest statistics reveal that the younger generations are just discovering the Maddox books, the audio books in particular, and the movies are a big part of that," Annelie said.

"To add music by someone with Noelle's popularity and star quality is a smart move," Carolyn said.

"As much as I'd like to take credit for being the genius, the honor goes to Helena," Annelie said. "I called her six months ago, and she didn't hesitate when I asked who among her many talents she recommended to put this soundtrack on the map."

"I remember that." Carolyn pointed her fork at Helena. "You should have heard Annelie that weekend. I don't know who she was praising to the skies more, you or Noelle."

"Noelle's the one with the talent. I'm just a desk jockey who shuffles paperwork around."

Noelle glanced at Helena, trying to gauge her sincerity. Oddly enough, Helena looked completely serious.

"The songs from the soundtrack were great, very rewarding to perform." Noelle chased a mushroom around her plate, anything to avoid looking directly at Helena. "I loved the style and the lyrics."

"Speaking of that," Gregory said, "the lyrics you sang tonight felt very personal. Are they autobiographical?"

Noelle nearly hiccupped, though she'd been prepared for such direct comments. "Eh, yes. Not literally, and not everything, but I've felt most of the emotions I sang about."

"Surely no one ever bullied a beautiful young woman like you?" The woman who asked looked baffled.

"No, not bullied exactly. A lot of people envied me in high school, though."

"God, high school can be hell on earth," Annelie said with a disdainful expression.

"My high school years were fantastic, but middle school wasn't exactly heaven." Helena placed her right hand on Noelle's backrest.

"Yes, middle school wasn't much better." Annelie nodded thoughtfully. "And bullies don't need a so-called reason to do their thing. They persecute a target for any number of twisted reasons."

"They sure do." Helena tapped her glass with her French-manicured nails. "You did a good job on the lyrics, Noelle, and I was impressed with how well you play both the piano and the guitar. I feel silly that I didn't know that about you. You need to take these songs back to the producers and we'll renegotiate. I'm sure we can work something out."

Noelle wanted to leap to her feet and shake Helena's hand, make her promise, make her give her statement in writing on a napkin, or whatever, but she remained calm and merely thanked her. "I'll tell them you said so," she said, making sure Helena knew she planned to test her sincerity.

"So they picked on you, hit you, even?" Gregory's date asked.

"They never beat me, but envy can disguise itself in many ways." Noelle shrugged with one shoulder. "I didn't attend my ten-year reunion, though, so perhaps they hurt me more than I thought."

"Their loss," Carolyn said, winking. "I bet a lot of them were disappointed you weren't there, and some were relieved, knowing you'd outshine them. Living your life well and being happy, that's the best revenge."

"Thanks, that sounds good to me." Noelle was very conscious of Helena's arm, which grazed her back every now and then. Was Helena aware of the possessive gesture, or was Noelle the only one seeing it that way? *Is she showing her superiority, or that she's bought me for an obscene stack of dollars?* Noelle thought of easing in the opposite direction, but didn't want to cause a scene.

"I don't see how anybody could have a problem with you now, for any reason. I could listen to you forever," Gregory's date gushed. "Will you go on tour soon?"

"Eh, no, not any time soon. I have one more album to record before I'm ready to hit the road again. I just finished an international tour nine months ago."

"Tours demand a lot of the artist." Helena finally let go of Noelle's chair. "I saw a few of your shows, and the way you give it a hundred ten percent, every time, is spectacular."

"I'm allowed to live my dream, to do what I love, and people pay a lot for a ticket to these events. The least I can do is give it…what was it? A hundred ten percent." Noelle didn't take her eyes off Helena; suddenly it was important that Helena understand. "It's not only my work ethic. I mean, it's more a sense of gratitude. Tons of youngsters out there dream of a break like mine and a career similar to mine. Most will never get any closer to it than going to a concert."

"Quite refreshing to meet someone so successful who is also humble." Carolyn raised her glass. "Let's toast both Annelie and her charity function, and Noelle for donating more than mere cash to it." Carolyn lifted her glass of white wine. "To Annelie and Noelle."

Blood infused Noelle's cheeks. She hoped her relatively light makeup hid the embarrassing pink, but wasn't sure it did. If she'd worn her flamboyant stage makeup, she could've blushed a deep crimson without anyone having a clue. She murmured a faint thank you and sipped her water.

She never drank alcohol in public, a rule her mother had enforced when she was in her teens and which made a lot of sense later. "You're never on your own time when you're out in public," Reba had said. "You're always Noelle the superstar, whether you want to be or not. Everything you do, say, wear, or endorse shows up on the Internet instantly, and in the papers and gossip magazines shortly after."

"That sure sucks," Noelle had complained, eager to spread her wings and party with friends like everybody else her age.

"I know it does. But you have one thing you'll always be able to call your own. Something that nobody else can touch, not even your nagging old mom." Reba made a funny face. "Don't look so suspicious. I mean your *thoughts*, girl. Those are yours, all yours."

"Noelle? Oh, my, where did you escape to? Didn't mean to startle you." Helena's soft touch on Noelle's arm had made Noelle jump, pulling her into the present at record speed.

"Sorry, yeah, got lost in thought. You were saying?" Noelle tried to focus on Helena's face instead of her hand, where it still rested on her arm.

"If you're not busy next weekend, would you come to a get-together at my house in the Hamptons? I'm having guests that I think you'd like to meet, and I know they'd enjoy spending time with you."

Taken aback, Noelle couldn't think of a single excuse, even if she'd wanted to make one up. "I look forward to it."

"Good. I'll have my assistant e-mail you a map. Why don't you come Friday evening? That will give us all of Saturday and most of Sunday."

"Sounds good." Noelle wondered if she sounded as lame as she feared. *Who's acting starstruck now? I feel like the principal has invited me to tea.*

"Settled, then." Helena let go of Noelle's arm with a quick movement, as if she'd just realized where she'd kept it for the last few minutes. Noelle furtively glanced at her arm to try to spot something that could explain the tingling sensation that lingered. Her arm looked perfectly normal, but the feeling remained for several long seconds.

❖

Helena tried to sneak out when photographers lined up to take the promotional pictures. They were already snapping away, and she hated the purple and green dots before her eyes that the flashes caused.

"Over here, Helena," Annelie said, loud and clear over the noise. "You're a major contributor. I want you right here."

"Damn." Helena glued on a smile and stepped over to Annelie, who stood lined up with Carolyn half in front of her. To her right, Noelle stood patiently waiting, her fingers loosely laced in front of her. Tall in her high heels, she gazed down at Helena, looking almost amused.

"You're not too fond of this part, are you?" Noelle looked completely relaxed, her famous beaming expression in place.

"Not really." Helena stood next to Carolyn, which placed her half in front of Noelle.

"Move back, please. Closer together." A bright-eyed photographer ushered the twenty-some people toward the far wall. Helena had to maneuver twice to avoid getting stepped on, and suddenly two hands were on her upper arms guiding her.

"Whoops. Don't fall, now." Noelle kept her hands on Helena's arms a few seconds longer.

Holding her breath, Helena felt the warmth of Noelle's hands along her back. When someone in front of Helena stepped on her toes again, Helena tried to not crowd Noelle but had to, to save her feet. Now she enjoyed more than Noelle's body heat; this time she felt the entire outline of Noelle's front pressed against her back.

Noelle's scent was intoxicating too, a fruity combination mixed with something dark and sweet, like an expensive port. Helena felt momentarily light-headed, either because she was pressing harder against Noelle or because she was dizzy, but she certainly hadn't reacted this way in years, if ever. *She's not even my type. And she's in VMP's stable. Holy hell, I don't need this.*

Helena willed herself to remain where she was, pressed up against the much-taller Noelle. She thought she heard Noelle gasp, but wasn't sure. When the photographers finally let them go, Helena said good-bye as fast as she reasonably could.

"I'll see you next Friday, then, Noelle."

"Thank you. I'm looking forward to it." Noelle appeared sincere and was still smiling widely for the benefit of the photographers, but the quick flutter of her eyelashes told Helena that she didn't feel as casual as she sounded.

CHAPTER FOUR

The cast-iron gates opened without a sound, letting the limousine through, and as Morris drove up to the main house, Noelle studied the park surrounding them. Maples, birch trees, and an eclectic collection of statues and other artwork intrigued her. The lawn was immaculately mowed, and the low hedges framing the landscaping looked like someone had used a carpenter's level to trim them.

The house was even more impressive. White, with tall columns, the two-story building had an ocean view and its own beach. The sun was setting behind her and the windows reflected the golden glow, sparkling like amber. Morris pulled up by the wide steps that led to the double front doors.

"Thanks, Morris." Noelle waited patiently for him to round the vehicle and open the door for her. She sometimes forgot and let herself out, which made him scold her. She knew he opened it for safety reasons, for one time an overzealous admirer threw his arms around her, pushing her back into the limousine. He had nearly followed her into the car, but Morris had shown that his size didn't affect his speed. Grabbing the young man by the collar, he handed him over to the security guards at the club Noelle was about to attend.

As Morris helped her out, Noelle glanced up the stairs where Helena was waiting for her just outside the door. Dressed in tan chinos and an off-white cashmere sweater, she looked as elegant as always. Noelle smoothed her red straight skirt and made sure her cotton blouse was tucked in. "Morris, I can manage from here. I know you want to get back to Manhattan, so go ahead."

"Let me take your bag—"

"I'm fine. Your sister's birthday's too important to miss. They even delayed the dinner so you could make it. I overheard." Noelle checked her Rolex. "You still have time if you leave right away."

"But—" After Noelle glanced at him sternly, Morris gave in. "All right. I'll be back Sunday afternoon. Thank you."

"See you then." Noelle punched his sizable biceps affectionately.

"Noelle. Welcome." Helena met her halfway down the stairs, cupping Noelle's shoulders before she kissed her cheek. "Hope the traffic wasn't too bad."

"No idea. I napped." Noelle tried to find her bearings. The soft touch of Helena's lips against her cheek lingered, and her own shortness of breath puzzled her. "Thank you for inviting me. Your house is wonderful. I bet its history is exciting."

"Actually, you're right. A theater producer built the oldest part of this house a century ago. The previous owner claimed that more than one of his adoring actresses haunts the place." Helena shook her head. "Come on. Let me show you your room. Then, if you want, I'll give you the grand tour." She walked ahead of Noelle up the stairs to the double doors, moving effortlessly and oozing that commanding presence that captivated Noelle.

Inside, a blue Persian rug on a dark hardwood floor, together with antique Chinese urns, created a cool, yet inviting atmosphere. A semicircular staircase led up to the second floor, and Noelle admired the craftsmanship of the wood railing and the huge crystal chandelier hanging from the tall ceiling. "What a beautiful house, Helena. I really like the colors."

"Thank you. A friend of mine is an interior designer. She did most of the rooms. The house was rather run-down when I bought it ten years ago." She turned right at the top of the stairs and walked halfway down the wide hallway. Opening a door, she guided Noelle inside. "I hope you'll be comfortable here."

Noelle took in the pale green walls, the four-poster bed, and the leather love seat in front of a fireplace. "It's wonderful. Thank you. I'll be very comfortable, I'm sure."

"Excellent."

"Am I the last to arrive?" Noelle didn't hear any other voices in the house.

"Oh, the girls from Chicory Ariose won't arrive until tomorrow morning. They're driving down and wanted to avoid Friday rush-hour traffic."

The news that she was the only guest made Noelle gulp. Annoyed at feeling nervous all of a sudden, she adjusted her features into a bland expression. "I look forward to meeting them."

"They're thrilled to get the chance to meet you. Mike's a huge fan, so I'm told."

"Mike? They're bringing their husbands?"

"Not exactly." Helena looked amused. "Mike is short for Michaela. No husbands."

"I see." Noelle didn't want to let on that she really didn't understand at all.

"Well, I'll let you freshen up. I'll be downstairs in the living room. Just take your time." Helena began to walk toward the door. Suddenly she stopped and turned. "That reminds me. Are you afraid of or allergic to dogs?"

"Neither."

"Good. I have a very friendly Labrador named Soledad. She's outside at the moment, but be prepared. She's very affectionate. And I mean *very*."

"Good to know." Noelle relaxed for the first time. "I love dogs. I always wanted one, but I like big dogs, and having one has never been practical since I live in Manhattan." She wrinkled her nose and laughed. "I never wanted to be like Paris Hilton or Britney Spears and carry a poor little Chihuahua as a live accessory."

Helena joined the laughter. "I hear you. I would probably step on such a small dog. I'm used to Labradors and German shepherds. I've always had a dog ever since I finished school." Helena walked out into the hallway. "Oh, I forgot." She pointed to the other side of the guest room. "That door leads to the bathroom. I'll see you in a little while, then."

"All right. Thank you." Noelle closed the door behind Helena and took a deep breath. Though Helena was petite, her charisma was practically tangible. "The woman nearly leaves a vacuum when she's out the door," Noelle muttered. Helena's gray eyes, so clear and probing, made her feel under scrutiny.

What did Helena really think about her? Not only as a singer and performer, but as a person. Did she see her as the spoiled mega-diva, who threw tantrums when she was challenged, to get her way? Or was it possible for someone like Helena, a seasoned corporate shark, to see beneath the surface? Shaken, Noelle realized that she really wanted Helena to approve of her, to understand that there was more to her than most people saw. When a pessimistic inner voice kept whispering that most people didn't take the time to look past the surface, Noelle sighed and accepted its wisdom.

In the bathroom, Noelle glared at her reflection. She wasn't sure why she'd dressed up before she left the condo. Maybe in pure defiance. The short skirt, the sleeveless top with sequins and glitter in a crazy pattern, and the six-inch heels all emphasized the person she'd been for the last decade. It was a safe disguise of sorts, but not exactly comfortable. Noelle stepped into the shower and set the temperature to as hot as she could tolerate, then turned the knob in the opposite direction until the cold water prickled her skin and she couldn't take it anymore. Her teeth clattering, she wrapped herself in a bath towel.

A glance in the mirror showed that her makeup was smudged. She got her toiletries, grabbed a makeup-removal wipe, and rubbed it all off. She replaced only the mascara and added some peach lip gloss, allowing her natural latte-colored skin to breathe. Frequent facials kept her complexion flawless, but letting her face rest from the makeup was also key. Noelle brushed her wild mane of hair back and wrapped a scarf around it to keep it from her face. Taking her cue from Helena, she dressed in her favorite Calvin Klein jeans and a simple white T-shirt. Blue espadrilles completed her outfit, and checking her watch again, she realized she'd been stalling long enough. *Time to face the music.*

❖

Helena scratched Soledad's head and watched with affection as the Labrador placed a paw on her thigh, looking adoringly at her. "No, you're not getting any more treats right now, you spoiled little princess."

Soledad cocked her head and pulled her ears back, going for a sad expression.

"Sorry, big girl. You just had chicken in the kitchen. Mrs. Baines is such a sucker for those brown eyes."

"Sounds good to me." A voice from the doorway made Soledad

jump halfway out of her skin with happiness, and she bounded across the living room toward Noelle.

Helena shook her head, afraid something might be wrong with her sight. This wasn't the same person who'd stepped out of the ridiculously long white limousine earlier. Instead, a freshly scrubbed young woman dressed in regular clothes now hugged Soledad, ruffling her fur as she squirmed in pure delight. Noelle laughed, the first true, joyous sound Helena had heard from her.

"You charmer." Noelle nuzzled the top of Soledad's head. "You can wrap anyone around that paw of yours." Not only was Noelle barely recognizable, but her voice had changed into the soft accent typical of her home state. "Want me to scratch your ears? No? Your tummy? I see. All right, then." Soledad tossed herself onto her back, displaying herself the way only a very trusting animal did. "She's wonderful." Noelle looked up at Helena, her eyes glittering.

"She's the worst suck-up." Helena found her voice unusually husky and cleared it, feeling far too self-conscious. "Don't let her trick you into giving her any more treats. She'll end up weighing a ton."

"I won't." Noelle patted Soledad one more time and rose from the floor.

"Dinner will be ready soon. Mrs. Baines, my housekeeper and cook, is finishing it right now."

"Okay. Thank you." Though Noelle had seemed so at ease with the dog seconds ago, she now looked shy and unapproachable.

Did she think Helena ate little pop singers for breakfast or something? Helena hadn't expected Noelle, famous for being a flamboyant sex symbol, to look this—well, this young. She searched her memory. Was Noelle thirty yet? No, twenty-nine. *Thirteen years younger than me.* Disturbed at the direction of her thoughts, Helena wanted to wipe her suddenly damp palms on her chinos. What did their age difference matter? Noelle wasn't her type and probably wasn't gay anyway. "What can I get you to drink?" Helena asked abruptly.

"Um," Noelle said, hesitantly, "some white wine, if you have any."

"Dry, sweet?"

"Sweet, please."

Kicking herself mentally, Helena could tell that she was making Noelle even more ill at ease. She made an effort to let up, giving Noelle an apologetic look as she poured a glass of Husch Vineyards Chenin Blanc for Noelle. "This is a nice one, I think."

"Thank you." Noelle sipped it carefully and nodded. "It's very good. Not *too* sweet."

Helena poured a glass for herself. "Ah, here's Mrs. Baines now."

"Dinner is ready, ma'am." The housekeeper motioned toward the dining room.

"Excellent."

Helena introduced the two women, and Noelle put her glass down and shook hands with Mrs. Baines, something that obviously surprised but also seemed to please her. "I'm so happy to meet you, ma'am."

"Do call me Noelle."

Helena stared at her normally grounded and matter-of-fact housekeeper. Mrs. Baines actually blushed. "Noelle. I'm Alice." Her rosy cheeks made her look ten years younger.

Helena groaned inwardly. *Alice? I've never even bothered to remember her first name.* Helena had thought Noelle was the arrogant diva. *Seems I've won first prize on that one. Holy hell.*

Mrs. Baines guided Noelle to the dining room, fawning over her as if she was her long-lost daughter. Not about to interrupt her housekeeper, Helena stayed in the background until Noelle was seated to her left at the long cherrywood table. Sitting down, Helena studied the interaction between the two while Mrs. Baines served the starter dish.

"I'll be bringing in the main course in a little while. Bon appétit!"

"She's great." Noelle tasted the soup. "Oh, wow, and a fantastic cook."

"She is."

They ate in silence for a moment, Helena's gaze constantly drawn to Noelle's face, hands, and outrageously dyed hair. The muted light from the chandelier cast highlights on the blond strands and created mysterious shadows on Noelle's face. Her lips were full and looked soft, no makeup trick behind them, apparently. Her mother's mixed heritage was evident in Noelle's soft, slightly wide nose and her almond-shaped eyes. A deep hazel with golden speckles glimmered in the light from the chandelier.

"So, you really liked my songs?" Noelle asked so suddenly that Helena nearly dropped her spoon. She managed to get a grip on it before it sank into the soup, and Helena realized that Noelle had finished her soup while Helena had mostly stirred hers.

"I did." Helena took a bit of the fragrant bread, hoping Noelle didn't realize she was stalling.

"The audience seemed to like them too." Noelle gazed at Helena with those amazing eyes, as if probing hers for answers.

"Your lyrics are very personal. I have a question. Or, rather, I have two questions. Are they autobiographical?"

"Yes." Noelle didn't hesitate.

"Do you realize how much of yourself you're sharing with your audience?"

"Yes." Noelle placed one hand on the table between them, palm up, as if pleading with Helena to understand. "It's sort of the point. I want to sing about real things, or things that I've experienced and that matter to *me*. I don't mind the songs I've recorded before. In fact, I'm proud of all of them, and those songs have provided me with a fantastic career. I'm financially independent and I can take care of my mother and sisters. I just don't want to sing somebody else's lyrics, somebody else's view on things."

"It's risky to change genres. Your audience loves you for what you've given them so far."

"It's easy to sell the fans short." Noelle looked sad. "I really believe that they'll hear the truth in my words and the honesty I try to convey when I sing. Try to understand, Helena. I don't want to sing *only* soul-pop. Surely there's room for both genres."

"I hear what you're saying, Noelle." Helena nearly reached out and took the vulnerable hand that rested between them. "I do. Here's the deal, though. Today, when the economy is what it is, even solid companies like VMP have to be careful. Your records sell incredibly well, you know that. You're the most successful performer of your generation. Of all current performers, actually. I know Hollywood has approached you and that you've received several scripts. From what your agent told me, you haven't found anything appealing, but acting might also be a good way for you to stay current, to keep your place in the audience's mind."

Noelle began to look frustrated. "The scripts they send me are all about wannabe pop singers who eventually make it, one way or another. Why would I want to play something I've already lived? It's kind of 'been there, done that.' You see?" Noelle sighed. "I want to write more songs, write about what I know, and what I'm learning, and about things I'm trying to understand. Some people think I'm pretty superficial, and who can blame them? Most of the lyrics I've sung so far rhyme. 'Heart/apart,' 'love/above,' or 'cry/sigh/die.'"

Helena had to laugh at the self-deprecating words and the funny face Noelle made at the end of her outburst. Noelle stared at her for a moment and then joined in.

"That's pretty bad, I mean the rhyming." Helena shook her head, still chuckling.

"I know. And that's not the worst of them." Noelle grew serious again. "I'm not being snobbish. I'm not knocking the old songs. My fans love them, and I'll sing them as long as they want to hear them, but if I can't evolve as an artist, I might as well pack it up. I'll lose the spark." She said the last part with sorrow and completely without self-pity.

"I see." Helena looked down and noticed that Mrs. Baines must have been in the room while they talked and switched their plates, because her wonderful Indian chicken dish was now in front of her. *Am I losing it here? How could I miss that?*

Cutting the tender chicken into smaller pieces, she spoke carefully. "I think these new songs of yours can have an audience, if they're all the same quality as the ones you sang at the charity function. Especially your female fans that grew up with your records."

The young men who drooled over Noelle probably wouldn't see the charm in her new style, generally speaking. She didn't want to voice that opinion out loud, but Helena knew the business, particularly the demographics for the major music genres. The males who were fifteen to twenty-five loved Noelle's hot dance moves, her sex appeal, and her sensual charisma onstage. They would hardly recognize her the way she looked now.

But I do, and I like it. A lot. The truth hit her out of nowhere, and Helena quickly reeled in her libido. It had been too long since she'd been on a date, or even looked appreciatively at another woman. That must be it. She needed to get laid. *Or laid to rest.* She chuckled inwardly at her own acerbic joke.

"So there's a chance I can record them?" Noelle's eyes lit up as she touched Helena's hand briefly. "Really?"

"I'll think about it and discuss it with the producers. Maybe they can exchange a few of the songs they've lined up for your best ones." Helena's skin tingled where Noelle's fingers had brushed it. The feeling was unwelcome, to say the least. Even if Noelle were her type, Helena never confused her business life with her private affairs.

"Thank you. I hope they see it our way." Noelle's features softened as she spoke shyly.

Mrs. Baines served ice cream and strawberries, something that gave Noelle obvious pleasure. Helena found she enjoyed watching her guest's blissful expression as she finished her dessert.

"I'm planning to take Soledad for a walk," Helena said, trying to break out of the hypnotic mood Noelle's beauty placed her in. "Would you like to come, or are you too tired?"

"I'd love some fresh air, thank you. You have a beautiful garden. Or should I say park?"

"Thank you. I guess it'd qualify as a park." Helena shrugged. "My gardener had to hire two part-time guys to help him maintain it."

"I can see why."

Helena dabbed the corners of her mouth and rose. "Let me grab a jacket. See you outside in five minutes?"

"Sure. I'll just go find Mrs. Baines. Dinner was great. Thank you." Noelle waved, a funny little gesture with her fingertips, and walked toward the kitchen. Muted voices and then a hearty laugh from Mrs. Baines confused Helena even more. Noelle hadn't turned out to be anything like she'd pegged her to be. Whereas Helena had expected a true high-maintenance diva, she'd found a shy woman, twice as sensual as she was onstage.

Sure, Noelle was sexy as hell. Her body could elicit a wet dream in a half-dead person, but her appeal was more than that. The way Noelle looked at Helena, her eyes barely blinking as she listened to every word, was mesmerizing in itself. She seemed to absorb every word, storing them as if they were riddles meant to be solved. Noelle looked like she found everything fascinating, as if she was not in the least bit blasé.

Helena was increasingly certain she was losing it. Noelle was about to prove her wrong, from what it looked like, and Helena took pride in never being wrong. She wanted to cling to her image of Noelle as a spoiled brat, someone who lived a superficial life of parties and shopping, but instead she was respectful, caring, and soft spoken…and so stunningly beautiful, she would drive the straightest woman in the world insane with desire.

Helena dashed to her dressing room and quickly found her favorite cardigan. She had to button it three times because she kept misaligning the buttonholes. I'll just have to keep a cool distance from Ms. Laurent. Helena descended the stairs, and only when she reached the bottom did she realize how hard she clung to the railing. Oh, yes, that's really cool. Sighing at herself, Helena walked outside to test her strategy in how to handle Noelle.

CHAPTER FIVE

S oledad! Get back here." Helena called after her dog, which chased a squirrel along the hedge. "Silly dog. Leave the poor animal alone."

Amused, Noelle saw the pout clearly visible on Soledad's face as she returned to her owner. Sighing, the dog looked pleadingly at Noelle, as if asking for backup. "No, no, your mom is right. No chasing squirrels," Noelle said, shaking her head. "You scared him."

Helena patted her left leg and Soledad obediently stayed glued to her side the rest of the walk. "So, what were you saying earlier? No pets for you, Noelle?"

"I wish I could have a dog, or possibly a cat, but I travel so much." Noelle inhaled the crisp evening air. "I suppose if I lived like this all the time, it'd be possible."

"You always stay in Manhattan between tours?"

"No. I try to spend as much time as I can in my house in Miami. I love it down there—the slower pace, the culture, and of course the climate."

"Miami?" Helena looked surprised. "I would've thought you'd keep a house in Texas."

"I have very few ties to Texas these days." In fact, Noelle didn't like to go back to Austin, where painful memories of her father and his difficult last years always surfaced. "My mother and two youngest sisters are living with me in Manhattan, and the other two are off at college."

"Which you pay for." Helena held up a hand. "Sorry, didn't mean to sound like I've snooped around. It's rather common knowledge."

"Yes. I take care of them. I promised my dad…" The unwelcome memory of her father's deathbed made Noelle pause. "And I do it gladly."

Helena stopped walking and Soledad immediately sat down next to her. "I've never seen you this way. Your shows and your music made me view you quite differently. You're an enigma, or should I say a chameleon, the way you can switch between your stage persona and your private one."

"Really?" Noelle clasped her hands behind her back, feeling self-conscious. "I thought someone like you, who works in the entertainment industry, would realize that my stage persona is a role I play, probably since the music I've performed so far kind of demands it. Did you expect me to be that person twenty-four-seven?"

"No, when you put it like that, of course not." Helena looked vaguely chagrined. "I must sound really dense, but the difference between how you appeared when you came to my office with your agent not long ago, and now, is also obvious."

"I see." Helena was right. Noelle had acted differently when she tried to negotiate with Helena, fighting for the right to record her songs. Dressing the part, Prada bag and sunglasses, she'd made sure Helena knew she was dealing with a star. Noelle glanced down at herself. She sure didn't look like a star now. Perhaps that was a mistake. "I hope I haven't disappointed you. I'm pretty ordinary when I'm just me."

"Oh, Noelle." Helena eyes warmed. "You're anything but. And no, I'm not disappointed. How could I be? You're turning out to be much more interesting than I ever gave you credit for." She bit off the last word and suddenly turned around, starting to walk back toward the house.

Noelle followed, as did Soledad, and didn't know how, or if, to comment on Helena's cryptic remark. "You're not quite what I expected either." That didn't come out the way Noelle intended, and Helena's curious glance made her want to inhale her words and swallow them. "I mean, you're the CEO of an empire of companies, and…" Noelle struggled to find the right words. "I guess that intimidates a lot of people."

Helena stopped again, this time stepping closer to Noelle, who drew a deep breath at the intensity in Helena's narrowing eyes.

"Do I intimidate you?" Helena folded her arms across her chest, raising her chin.

"You did, once." Noelle figured that when Helena's voice sank an octave like that, she'd better stick to the truth.

"But not anymore?" Low and reverberating, Helena's voice sent curious tingling sensations along Noelle's arms. Goose bumps appeared in their wake, and Noelle pressed her tongue hard against the roof of her mouth when her breath caught as well. What was it about this woman, so unlike anyone Noelle had ever met—so chic, so commanding, and so stunning?

"No. Yes. Maybe a little," Noelle said. "I don't know."

"Ah." Relenting, Helena continued to stroll toward the house. "Either way, I'm glad I'm getting to know this side of you. It actually helps to have a more rounded, three-dimensional image of you."

"Thank you. I think." Noelle muttered the last words, hoping Helena didn't hear, but a quick glance in her direction said otherwise.

"You're welcome." Helena jogged effortlessly up the stairs and opened one of the double doors to let Soledad in. "I don't know about you, but I'm ready for bed." She faltered, and Noelle thought she saw a faint pink come and go on Helena's cheekbones. "Mind if I take you on the grand tour once our company arrives tomorrow?"

"No, not at all. I'm tired too. Thank you for dinner and for the walk." Noelle passed Helena in the doorway, a bit taken aback by the fact that Helena didn't move to let her pass. Inadvertently brushing against Helena, Noelle detected her fresh scent of something fruity, with a trace of musk. She inhaled deeply and suddenly her stomach fluttered. Confused, she walked to the stairs. "See you tomorrow, then." Her words tumbled over her lips way too fast.

"Sure. Good night." Helena stood motionless in the doorway, her eyes firmly locked with Noelle's.

"Good night." Noelle escaped up the stairs to her room. Inside, she stood in the middle of the room with her fists clenched. "What the hell was that?" she murmured. Her heart was pounding and her palms were damp. A mirror on the far wall showed her reflection. Noelle frowned as she studied her image. *I look ready to bolt.* Forcing herself out of her inertia, Noelle pulled off her T-shirt and tossed it on a chair. She dug around in her bag for one of her old, way-too-big T-shirts, nearly washed to pieces. *Guess Helena would assume I sleep in satin negligees and wear slippers with swan's down around the house.* Noelle chuckled, got ready for bed, and crawled under the covers.

The bed was heavenly—soft enough to cushion her but firm enough to support her. Noelle buried her face in the large pillow. Curling up, she closed her eyes, then opened them immediately when a vivid image of Helena's face appeared. Noelle tried to settle down against the pillow again. Willing herself to relax, she yawned and closed her eyes once more. This time it took about five seconds before Helena's face showed up.

"What's going on?" Noelle had no idea why the vision of Helena Forsythe would upset her so. They were getting along much better, and Noelle had a faint hope that she'd be able to record some of her own songs. Why would the sight of Helena, even in her imagination, rattle her so?

Determined to not let it bother her, Noelle grabbed one of the many pillows in the bed and held it close to her chest as she closed her eyes a third time. When Helena's face unsurprisingly flickered behind her eyelids, Noelle resisted the urge to open them. She hugged the pillow close and let the memory of Helena's voice and scent engulf her. More tired than she'd realized, she soon gave in to the irresistible urge to fall asleep.

In her pre-dream state, Noelle felt soft hands stroke her hair, tuck it behind her ear. Certain the hands belonged to Reba, she glanced up at her mother, but gasped when she looked into Helena's steady gaze. "What are you doing here?" Noelle murmured to the dream image. "Why do you invade my nights all of a sudden?"

"Shh. Just sleep." Helena's voice sounded far away. "I'll be here when you wake up."

"All right." Noelle felt the hands in her hair again, and this time she was certain it wasn't her mother's touch. Gentle fingers massaged her scalp in slow, sensuous circles that made her toes curl. Eventually the touch became lighter, only to disappear as Noelle allowed sleep to claim her completely.

❖

Helena and Soledad walked up the stairs to her master bedroom suite. The dog settled into her leather-upholstered basket with a contented sigh, and Helena continued into the bathroom, where she ran the shower. She could still feel how Noelle had brushed against her in the doorway and couldn't understand why she hadn't moved out of the way. She had stood there, as if rooted in place, not giving Noelle much choice but to slide against her in order to pass. *I'm such an idiot. She's probably thinking I'm either an old horny bitch, or, if she's as innocent as she seemed tonight, she simply thinks I'm acting weird.*

She stepped into the shower, gasping as the hot, prickling water hammered at her shoulders. Knowing it was futile, Helena tried to wash the feeling of Noelle off her skin, scrubbing with her favorite body salt but, of course, she couldn't. Her mind overheated, she began to picture Noelle in bed, her hair loose around her shoulders, perhaps sleeping in the nude.

Furious, Helena rinsed off the salt and began washing with her olive oil–based soap. The silky feel didn't do much for her peace of mind, and she stepped out, reaching for a bath towel. She briskly dried herself and blow-dried her hair.

Soledad was snoring sweetly when Helena was ready for bed. Slipping under the covers, she reached for a folder that sat on her bedside table and flipped through the financial report with less than her usual keen interest. Helena reclined against the pillows, the folder falling from her hands onto her lap. Her mind insisted on reminding her just how exquisite Noelle's full breasts felt against her body. With her impossibly small waist, Noelle had hips and breasts that made her breathless. *I'd have to be a zombie, for heaven's sake, to not respond to her beauty. She may not try for sexy when she's not performing, but she can't hide that blatant sensuality.*

Helena tossed the innocent folder on the floor. She glared at it, but decided to leave it where it was until morning. She pushed the pillows aside and stretched out on her stomach, which was her favorite sleeping position. Burying her face in the crook of her arm, she squeezed her eyes shut. She refused to allow her treacherous body to trick her into seeing Noelle as anything other than a business associate. No way would she ever fall for a straight woman again.

No way.

CHAPTER SIX

H elena! You look wonderful." A woman with chocolate brown hair swept back in a soft twist walked up the stairs and grasped Helena's hands. "It's been too long."

"Well, who would've guessed that you'd start a girl band at your ripe age?" Helena embraced the woman before turning to Noelle, who stood a bit to the side while watching three women climb out of a black minivan. Their driver was hoisting bags from the trunk, the youngest-looking woman helping him. "Noelle, this is Manon Belmont, an old friend. We met at boarding school, and even if Manon was only a student there for two semesters, we've kept in touch."

"Noelle, this is an honor." Manon extended a hand. "I know about your fantastic career, of course, and Mike has been completely incoherent at the thought of meeting you ever since we started out early this morning."

Mike? Noelle looked down at the driver, who was lining up eight bags and what looked like instrument cases outside the minivan. She had thought Mike was a woman, and though she had fans of all ages, she was surprised that the correct and distinguished looking man in his late sixties would be *that* into her music.

"Eryn, stop fussing over your guitar and come say hello." Manon impatiently waved at a tall woman with blazing red hair kept in a loose braid.

"I'm coming, I'm coming." Eryn took the steps two at a time and wrapped an arm around Manon. "Helena, love your place." She winked and shook hands with her hostess.

"And this is Noelle."

"Who needs no introduction." Eryn greeted Noelle just as warmly. "Love your voice, Noelle. Great to meet you in person."

"The pleasure is mine." Noelle felt a little less shy than normal around the easygoing redhead.

"You girls okay?" Eryn said over her shoulder.

Noelle gazed down at a fourth woman exiting the car. The tall, dark woman, who seemed the youngest of the four, was assisting her, placing a white cane in her right hand. *Talk about not needing an introduction.* Mezzo-soprano Vivian Harding was world famous. Nobody in the U.S., or the world, had been able to avoid reading about the opera singer's personal tragedy. When she had announced that she was retiring from the international opera scene, the tabloids were full of speculations as to why. And when it became public knowledge that she was going blind, she had surprised the music world again, this time by returning to the stage as a member of the experimental, improvisational group Chicory Ariose.

Reaching them, Vivian Harding now pulled off her sunglasses and squinted at Helena. "Nice to meet you again, Helena." She kissed Helena's cheeks. "Mike says this place is as impressive as the Dodd Mansion."

"It is. The park is fantastic." The fourth woman, tall and with spiky blue-black hair, grinned. "The ocean view as well." She looked over at Noelle and blushed. "Oh, hi."

"I take it you recognize Noelle Laurent?" Helena hugged the dark girl quickly. "Noelle, this is Mike Stone."

Ah. So this *is Mike.* "Hi. I think this house is great too. Can't decide if I prefer the park or the ocean view."

"Hi, Noelle. I have all your CDs." Mike still looked flustered. "And the DVDs of your shows." She was obviously a fan, but she wasn't gushing or crowding Noelle, which was unusual.

"I'm flattered." Noelle wished she could say she'd heard them play, but she hadn't.

"How about we go inside? The stairs are getting a bit crowded, and Ben obviously wants to carry your bags in." Helena ushered everyone inside except Mike, who went back to the car where she grabbed two of the bags.

Noelle hesitated for a second, not wanting to appear presumptuous, but followed Mike and took two of the other bags. "Here, let me give you a hand."

"Oh, you don't have to do that, ma'am." Behind her, Ben sounded appalled.

"Don't worry. I'm happy to help."

"Thanks." Mike looked appreciatively at her. "That's nice of you." She didn't have to add that it was unexpected. Noelle was used to being treated like a spoiled diva, not because she was, but because that was how the press usually portrayed her.

"No problem." They carried the bags into the hallway, where Mrs. Baines was waiting for them with a bellhop cart.

"There's an elevator at the end of the corridor over there," Mrs. Baines said, and pointed to the north corridor. "Saves you from dragging it up the stairs."

"Why, thank you, ma'am," Ben said, and bowed.

Mrs. Baines looked at him under a raised eyebrow. "Hmm. You're welcome." She hurried to the elevator. "I'll show you to your rooms."

She guided them to three rooms across from Noelle's. Apparently, the women planned to share, which confused Noelle since at least twice as many guest rooms were available along the corridor. Ben placed the bags in their rooms before he kissed Mrs. Baines's hand and thanked her again. Mrs. Baines murmured something unintelligible and disappeared down the stairs.

"Ben. You flirt." Mike grinned.

"Can't help myself when I see a beauty who apparently can cook too." Ben looked innocent and Noelle had to join in the laughter. "See you girls later." He disappeared into his room.

"Great digs." Mike opened one of the suitcases and rummaged around. "Here. I...I hope you don't think I'm being too forward." She handed over a CD.

"Absolutely not." Noelle examined the case. It was Chicory Ariose's first CD. "I can't wait to listen to it."

"There's no rush. I just thought you might be a bit curious. It's done well for a non-mainstream genre." Mike colored faintly. "Not anywhere near how well yours do, naturally."

"I'm hoping to switch styles a bit, so who knows in the future?" Noelle wasn't sure if talking about her hopes and plans might jinx them.

"Really?" Mike regarded her with keen eyes. "That sounds exciting."

"Not sure it's *that* exciting to anyone but me." Noelle played nervously with the CD case. "But I hope it will be."

"If a person writes what's in their heart, it resonates with people. My friend Eryn, she's a writer, and for years she worked at a local newspaper and finally hated it. Now she's a successful novelist, probably because she writes what she cares about and her passion shows." Mike looked kindly at Noelle. "That's possibly why we've been moderately successful with our first album. Since we improvise, it's very honest. Not always brilliant. I mean, you can be unfortunate and catch us on a bad day, but it's always honest."

"Now I'm even more curious." Noelle meant it. "In my career, which songs I sing, and when, has been very calculated, almost to an extreme. When I started writing for real last year, suddenly this new music, new tones and melody strands, just surfaced. Guess I put a lid on them for a long time to solidify my career."

"Nothing wrong with trying to make a name for yourself, and goodness knows it's hard in this business." Mike opened another suitcase. "Just want to hang up Vivian's suit before it looks too bad."

So she was sharing the room with Vivian. Noelle had assumed the opera singer would rather room with Manon Belmont. A socialite with a strong concern for the underdog, Manon came from old money. Her foundation was famous worldwide, and Noelle remembered donating money to it during a TV-commercial drive.

"Guess we better join the others before they send out a search party." Mike grinned. "They probably think I'm hogging you."

"Hey, I don't mind." Noelle felt comfortable with Mike, though she normally didn't make friends easily. Being famous, bordering on iconic, didn't exactly encourage true, trusting friendship. Mike, on the other hand, seemed impressed with Noelle, but not in a fan-worship kind of way.

They walked downstairs where the rest of the women sat in the living room, with Helena pouring coffee for them. "Coffee, Mike? Noelle?"

Mike eagerly grabbed a mug, but Noelle said, "No, thank you. Could I have some orange juice instead? I'll be completely wired if I have more coffee."

"Sure. I'll call Mrs. Baines—"

"No, no. I can manage." Noelle walked into the kitchen, where Mrs. Baines managed to look affronted and pleased at the same time.

"I could've brought it to you, ma'am. It's my job."

"I know. I just figured that with six women to wait on, you'd be busy." Noelle raised her glass. "I don't mind getting my own drinks."

"All right, then. You may enter my kitchen, then, anytime." Mrs. Baines sighed and shook her head. "Just don't try to cook."

"I promise. Trust me. I'd be doing everybody a favor by staying away from the stove." Mrs. Baines's chuckle followed Noelle out of the kitchen.

Back in the living room, the only free spot was next to Helena on the love seat. Noelle sat down, clinging to her glass, and tried to look more casual than she felt. Her left thigh touched Helena's gabardine-clad leg, and Noelle had to force herself not to jerk sideways to avoid the faint contact. Soledad rose from Helena's other side and sat down next to Noelle, keeping her from shifting. Noelle's leg tingled and the sparkles eventually spread to her belly.

Finally, Helena moved and broke the connection. Noelle glanced furtively at her and thought she saw a quick frown, but unsure of what she thought she'd seen, she focused on Vivian's beautiful voice as the opera singer retold an anecdote from their road trip.

"…and I was dozing off in the backseat next to Mike, when all of a sudden I hear Ben cursing up a storm. You know, he's always such a gentleman and I just couldn't understand what was the matter. I nudged Mike to get her to see if she could help him, and that's when she started laughing."

"I did not!" Mike nuzzled Vivian's cheek, clearly trying to hide her mirth. "I was giggling, possibly. Not the same thing."

"Semantics, darling." Vivian ran a finger along Mike's cheek with a loving gesture, an expression of adoration on her face. Vivian had to be in her mid fifties, and Mike at least twenty years younger. Were they a couple? Then Mike took Vivian's hand and kissed the tip of the well-manicured finger.

"Oh. Anyway, where was I?" Vivian said. "Oh, yes. By now, Manon was stirring behind us, and Eryn was complaining that she wasn't sitting still. Ben was still muttering up front and Mike was *giggling*." She paused, adjusting the huge beads of her long freshwater pearl necklace. "I have a strong voice and decided it was time to make myself heard, so I called, 'Ben, what's the matter? Do you need help?'

"He didn't answer at first. Then I heard a faint, 'I wish.' By now I think Mike was getting curious. She unbuckled her seat belt and came to the front of the van. And those giggles of hers became laughter, no doubt about that." Vivian chuckled.

"As it turned out, our Ben was drinking some coffee from his thermos mug, and apparently he'd tried to close the lid, so it wouldn't go cold, right after he took a sip. His beard got stuck in the mug's closing mechanism, so he was driving down the highway at sixty-five miles an hour, holding on to the steering wheel with one hand and trying to dislodge the thermos cup from his beard with the other."

"It had completely attached itself and it hurt," Mike said. "I had to help him, and then when I was telling Vivian and the others about it, we laughed so hard he nearly pulled over and made us walk the rest of the way."

They were all chuckling now, and Noelle relaxed marginally.

"The poor man, having to put up with the four of you for hours on end." Helena wiggled an elegant finger at them. "Remember, he's got to drive you back. Don't antagonize him."

"Ah, he'll be fine. Ben knows we love him to death," Eryn said, placing her empty mug on a side table. "We'd be lost without him, literally. And Perry and Mason would mourn."

Before Noelle could ask who Perry and Mason were, Helena nodded. "Ah, the precious little pups. How are they, Vivian?"

"Amazingly well. They're still at Dodd Mansion, though. We didn't think they'd enjoy the trip, since it's for only a couple of days. Otherwise, we take them with us when we can."

"Perry and Mason are Vivian and Mike's Great Danes, Noelle," Eryn explained. "They're brothers and so friendly. Right up there with that one." She motioned toward Soledad, who still sat next to Noelle, almost glued to her right leg. "She seems quite taken with you, Noelle."

Noelle nodded and patted Soledad's head. The dog licked her fingers quickly and Noelle gently gripped Soledad's chin. "You kissing me, huh?"

"Who can blame her?" Eryn teased.

"Behave, Eryn. You're making Noelle blush," Mike said.

"Hey, I wasn't the one hogging her upstairs for so long." Eryn stuck her tongue out, clearly pulling Mike's leg. "Boy, who's blushing now?"

Mike shook her head at Eryn. "Don't mind the writer over there, Noelle. She's got no manners."

"Ha!" Eryn turned to Manon, who'd watched the exchange with an amused look. "I've got manners, don't I, sweetie?"

"I'm sure you do," Manon said. "One of these days we'll all get to witness them."

"Manon!" Eryn gasped, her eyes twinkling. "You brat. Don't agree with Mike. She's insufferable if you encourage her."

All four members of Chicory Ariose used different terms of endearment so freely. Noelle saw Manon tug Eryn's long red braid with a look of affection on her face, her eyes softening. Glancing at Helena, Noelle thought she saw a glimpse of longing, or was it envy, pass over her features. Her eyes narrowed and she seemed to press farther into the backrest of the love seat. She turned and looked at Noelle, suddenly appearing gentle.

"What a crew, wouldn't you say?" Helena gestured toward her friends, palms up. "You can tell that they know each other well."

"Yes." Just how well wasn't entirely clear, but the fact that they were sharing rooms...rooms with queen-sized beds, Noelle just remembered. Of course. Cursing herself for being so dense, she realized that the Chicory Ariose members were divided into two couples. Two lesbian couples. *It's none of my business, and it doesn't matter one bit.*

But Noelle wondered about her own naïveté. Working in the entertainment business, she was used to and entirely comfortable with having gay, transgendered, and transvestite colleagues and friends. She'd taken part in a TV special with the best drag queens in the business, one of them doing a better "Noelle" than she did, she claimed afterward. In retrospect, she'd felt more comfortable around the gay guys than the hetero ones, and told herself it was because they didn't see her as a sex object, as someone to conquer. The lesbians she'd encountered so far had never shown any particular interest in her, not overt anyway, and Noelle had always assumed it was because they knew she was straight.

But I never knew if I was straight, did I? She had never liked sex all that much—the messiness, the smell, lying there under a guy while he grunted and carried on. Noelle had blamed her natural shyness, at first, then the fact that the macho rappers her agent and her previous label encouraged her to date were too rough sometimes.

Was I so easy to manipulate that I just went out with the "right" guy whether I was interested or not? Her agent had told her that she had to stay current in the tabloids to keep her career going, if she wanted to keep providing for her mother and sisters like she'd promised her father. *I was so young and not very street smart.* Noelle didn't kid herself that she was all that much smarter now, but these days she knew better than to let anyone pick her dates. *It's been years since I was on a proper date…and even longer since I went to bed with anyone.*

"Noelle?" Helena's throaty voice reached her eventually, and Noelle's cheeks warmed when she noticed six pairs of questioning eyes, including Soledad's.

"Yes?" Noelle looked pleadingly at Helena, hoping she wouldn't direct anymore attention to Noelle's distractedness.

"Vivian was wondering if you'd participate in an improvisation session later today."

"Oh. Sure. Absolutely." Relieved, Noelle cleared her throat. "I'd love to, Vivian, if you think I can contribute."

"Are you kidding?" Mike said quickly. "Your voice would match Vivian's mezzo-soprano in a fantastic way, I'm sure."

"All right. I'm in." Noelle slowly relaxed as Mike and Eryn chattered about the possibilities, but suddenly she felt Helena's hand on her knee. The touch burned through her chinos and made her tremble.

"You all right?" Helena murmured. "You seem flustered."

Flustered? Noelle was having a hard time breathing, and her heart was pounding so loudly she was certain it could be heard across the room. "I'm okay," she whispered, glancing between Helena's face and her hand on her knee. Heat permeated her skin around the area, and she tried to convince herself that she was overreacting.

"You sure?" Helena squeezed Noelle's knee, probably for emphasis.

"Yes." Coughing embarrassingly, Noelle pulled back a little.

Helena let go of her knee as if she'd burned her hands on an open flame. She looked uncomfortable for a fraction of a second before the professional mask slammed into place again. "Very well, ladies. I'll go check on lunch, and after that, I'll give you the grand tour. Unpacking and freshening up might be on the agenda before we eat, though?"

"You took the words out of my mouth, Helena." Manon rose and left the room hand in hand with Eryn.

Mike stood and helped Vivian up. "See you later, girls," she said, winking at Noelle. Vivian let her white cane click back and forth on the floor as she and Mike followed Manon and Eryn.

"I'll…I'll take Soledad for a walk." Noelle knew she was running, but she couldn't face Helena right now. *She must wonder what the hell's wrong with me. All she has to do is pay me any attention or touch me, however briefly, and I'm incoherent and stuttering. Great. Perfect initial negotiation position.* Noelle stood and Soledad, having heard her name, was already ready to go.

"Thank you. She'll like that." Helena's slight frown showed that she was probably aware of the not-so-subtle stall. "Lunch should be ready in half an hour or so."

"I'll be back before then." Noelle walked toward the door. Even without looking, she knew Helena was watching her. *Even her gaze is like a touch.*

Outside, the crisp air helped Noelle get a grip on herself. Her heart rate slowed and she struggled to put things into perspective. Helena was unlike anyone she'd ever met. She was also the one who could make her dreams about her songs come true. Of course Noelle would be sensitive to Helena's approval.

As Noelle followed Soledad across the lawn, she tried to quiet the persistent inner voice that kept asking what her physical response to Helena's touch had to do with any of it.

CHAPTER SEVEN

Helena sat alone on a small leather couch while the other five women rummaged through the musical instruments on the other side of the room. Next to her, Ben was munching on the snacks Mrs. Baines had provided. The marble coffee table was filled with sliced vegetables, potato chips, beef jerky, fruit, dips, and drinks, enough to feed half of the Hamptons.

"I had no idea you had a private studio," Manon said as she plugged in the Roland keyboard. "Do you play?"

"No, I'm sorry to say." Helena reached for a piece of cucumber. "Whenever I throw a party or host a function, sooner or later, someone asks one of my artists to perform. I relented about two years ago and bought some instruments and other equipment."

"Some instruments?" Eryn snorted. "These aren't just 'some instruments.' These are top-notch." She'd brought her own electric guitar, her beloved Stratocaster, but was now strumming a Godin with a flamed maple top. "Mmm, like the sound of this."

Manon was playing a scale on the Roland that reminded Helena of the sound of a bubbling brook. The contrast of the elegant woman to the state-of-the-art modern instrument made the impact even greater. *Guess that's one reason their concerts are always sold out.* Helena knew she'd found a unique wondrous constellation of musicians two years ago when she signed Chicory Ariose. Her advisers hated the name of the group and claimed it needed to be changed into something less tongue-twisting. The four women refused, and Helena thought the name grew on you and made the group stand out. On the verge of becoming a household name, Chicory Ariose was booked solid for the next year.

Noelle stood a little to the side, examining a set of microphones. She hadn't said much since her walk with Soledad. Lunch had been fun, and she had laughed along with everyone else, but as soon as she looked at Helena, Noelle's face became blank. *She's acting like she's afraid of me or something.* Helena didn't know why that thought made her stomach twitch painfully.

Normally she found it useful for people to fear her. Intimidation had its possibilities, and certainly in her position she couldn't be too touchy-feely. Helena took pride in being stern but fair. The music industry was cutthroat, and if you slacked even a bit, your competitors were waiting nearby to take you down. Still, it did bother her that Noelle had clammed up so much and became rigid around her.

"You all ready, girls?" Mike sat behind a set of digital drums she'd brought with her. "Who wants to start? Eryn?"

"Okay, why not? Let's start with something soft and smooth like this." Her fingers slid over the Gobin's strings and a sound that induced pictures of crying angels in Helena's mind echoed throughout the basement. After Eryn coaxed unnervingly beautiful sounds from the guitar, she nodded to Manon, who began to play a tantalizing loop of silvery tones that quickly darkened to the lowest growl. Mike's drums encouraged this direction with a suggestive beat. Discreet and low impact, it followed rather than led.

Vivian joined in, a wordless, soft chant that grew into a crystal-clear tone. Eryn's guitar followed, hit the exact tone and kept it, as if challenging her friend. Vivian let her voice sink an octave, using her impeccable technique to inject more feeling.

Helena settled back and simply enjoyed the performance, feeling unusually humbled. She closed her eyes for a moment and let the musical instruments and the famous voice create patterns in her mind. This was Chicory Ariose's true gift. They could take you to another place merely by improvising and using their talents and their love. It took trust, Helena surmised, like free-falling, to perform this way.

Another voice, low, vibrant, and full of sultry sensuality, made Helena snap her eyes open and sit up. Noelle stood next to Vivian, with Vivian's hand on her shoulder, singing into another microphone. Her eyes were closed and she rocked a little as she used her voice in a manner Helena had never heard her do before. Tiny hairs rose on Helena's arms, and she couldn't take her eyes off Noelle. She still wore a simple white shirt and jeans, her hair falling freely around her shoulders, almost to her hips. Her voice was as different from Vivian's as water from fire, but they complemented each other. Trained and harnessed, Vivian's mezzo-soprano cut like a knife through the air with perfect tones and technique. Noelle's husky, sexy voice floated through the room toward Helena like a seductive temptress, beckoning her. Animalistic at times, and angelically sweet at others, Noelle's performance stunned Helena into complete silence and immobilized her.

"That young woman is quite something," Ben murmured next to Helena, breaking her out of her reverie and making it possible for her to breathe. "She's amazing."

"Yes." Helena tried to force more words past her struggling vocal cords, but all she could do was swallow painfully so she wouldn't choke on her cucumber.

The women played and improvised for about fifteen minutes before Mike let the drums close the performance. Everyone stood completely still for a few moments, until Eryn walked over to the singers. "Girls, you take my breath away," she said, wrapping an arm around each of them. "Vivian, you were brilliant, and Noelle, I have to ask you, where did that come from?"

"I…I don't know…" Noelle had a weird expression on her face, like she was shell-shocked, and for the first time since her walk, she actively looked for Helena. "I just kind of went with it."

"You sure did." Mike joined them and gently kissed Vivian on the lips. "You never cease to give me goose bumps, Vivi. And Noelle, you sure can sing."

"Thank you." Noelle acknowledged Mike's compliment but turned her gaze back at Helena right away.

Feeling as if something big and fast had hit her, Helena stood on slightly wobbly legs. She was not ready to interpret her own reaction on a personal level. She was still trying to fathom that her pop-star diva had held her own next to a world-famous opera singer. Helena would deal with the fact that every hair on her body stood on end and her inner organs melted another day. "You were wonderful," she said, meaning all five of them, but her eyes were locked on Noelle. "Amazing."

"Think we could have you as a guest star on our next CD?" Mike asked casually, looking taken aback at Noelle's sudden solemn expression. "Oh, I didn't mean that we should piggyback a ride on your fame. I just meant, it'd be fun to actually get some of this magic recorded." Mike looked unhappy, probably thinking she'd stepped in it with both feet.

"It's not that, Mike," Noelle said, hurriedly, "not that at all. I'd be happy to do something like that with y'all. It's just that I'm, well, I'm kind of negotiating to do stuff of my own and it's a bit—" She stared darkly at Helena. "Sensitive."

"Helena?" Manon looked at Helena under raised eyebrows. "Would that be against VMP policy? For us to collaborate, I mean?"

Feeling annoyed at being put on the spot, especially by a savvy businesswoman like Manon who ought to know better, Helena frowned. "As lovely as the idea sounds, it's nothing we can or should discuss now."

Mike acted like she wanted to object, but she only shook her head, muttering something indistinguishable. Manon glanced knowingly at Helena, who wondered if her friend could see right through her. *And if she can, what does she see? A confused lesbian with a chip on her shoulder?* Helena shifted her gaze to Noelle, who stood quietly, her eyes void of emotion. Wanting to reach out to her, reassure her, Helena raised her hand, only to jerk it back when a sharp ringing tone shattered the silence.

"Sorry. That's mine." Noelle dug into her pocket and pulled out a cell phone. "Excuse me." She stepped out of the room and ran up the stairs.

"Obviously someone important," Eryn said. "Boyfriend?"

"Who knows?" Helena was aware that her voice sounded harsh. "It's not my job to keep track of Noelle's private life."

"Stand down, *ma capitaine*," Manon interjected, looking a little worried. "I'm sure Eryn didn't mean to annoy you."

"Sorry, Eryn." Helena had the good sense to know she had overreacted.

"She's a stunning young woman. Would be weird if she didn't have a flock of eager young lads after her—or lads of all ages." Eryn winked. "And another of young women, of course."

"As I said, I haven't the faintest." Helena fought to remain calm. "Noelle is almost thirty, and she doesn't need a chaperone."

Eryn made a funny face. "If you say so, Helena."

Noelle picked this time to reenter the room, looking bemused. "That was my mother. My sisters want to borrow the limousine and Morris tomorrow evening. There's apparently a concert somewhere in New Jersey that they *have to* go to." She seemed ill at ease as she turned to Helena. "I hate to impose, but may I stay until Monday?"

"Sure. No problem." Helena's heart thundered at the thought of them being alone in the house except for Mrs. Baines. "You may stay as long as you need to."

"Oh. Thanks." Noelle hesitated, then briefly touched Helena's arm. "I appreciate it. Morris will be here early Monday morning."

"You're a kind big sister," Vivian said warmly. "Not everyone would be so generous."

"My sisters would've nagged my poor mother to death if I hadn't let them have the limo. Especially Claudia. She has an iron will, that kid."

"I hear you." Eryn sighed. "As one of three girls, I know what it's like to try and keep the peace. Nowadays we get along famously, but when we were younger... Oh boy, it was no picnic, not for us and not for our parents either."

"Any siblings, Helena?" Vivian asked. "I was an only child."

"Me too," Helena said. "I was off to boarding school when I was ten. That sort of gave me tons of sisters. Manon was one of the nicest ones, though quite shy."

"I was. I hated boarding school. I was fourteen and just wanted to go home." Manon's eyes darkened. "Helena was a genuine leader already back then, even if she was a bit younger than me, and she made sure everybody treated me well. I was still the outsider, though, and once I was allowed to go home, I was home-schooled." She turned to Noelle. "What about you?"

"I'm the oldest of five girls. Two are in college now, and two live at home with my mother and me." She looked wistful. "We lost our father when I was nearly twenty, but at least I had him that long. My younger sisters were just toddlers when he became ill, and we hoped he'd recover." Noelle's voice trailed off and her eyes grew shiny. "He never did."

"Oh, Noelle, we didn't mean to bring up sad memories." Eryn wrapped an arm around Noelle. "I'm so sorry."

"It's okay. It's been almost ten years now."

"But memories can still hurt." Manon looked seriously at Noelle. "I know."

Helena remembered how broken Manon had been when she came to the boarding school, ghostlike and fatigued after losing her twin brother to the reckless driving of a man found guilty of DUI. Even at age twelve, Helen had possessed an innate ability to judge a person's character. *Until now?*

Helena looked at Noelle, who still stood close to Eryn. Noelle was constantly surprising her, or rather yanking the rug out from under her feet. Helena didn't appreciate being kept on edge like this. As a seasoned CEO of a vast conglomerate of companies with VMP as its crown, she hadn't gotten where she was today by allowing anyone to throw her repeatedly. *And I'll be damned if I'll change now. If there ever was a time when everything depended on me sticking to my guns, this is it.*

"Yes, memories can hurt," Noelle said quietly. She looked directly at Helena, her eyes unwavering. "That's one of the reasons we have music. For its healing qualities."

"Amen to that," Vivian said. "Music and love, nothing like them." She stroked Mike's arm.

"So I'm told." Uncomfortable, Helena acted deliberately casual. "Why don't we go upstairs and see what Mrs. Baines has whipped up for us. Another healing power. Food."

"Or carnal pleasure," Eryn said, and winked.

"There is that." Mike wiggled her eyebrows, looking at Noelle as she spoke. "Not to forget."

To Helena's surprise, Noelle blushed and averted her eyes briefly. Wondering what the two youngest of this group had talked about when they carried the bags up, Helena walked up the stairs to the dining room where Mrs. Baines had just finished setting out a dinner buffet. Something told Helena she shouldn't ask Noelle about Mike's mysterious comment, but Mike might be more approachable.

As they sat down to eat, Noelle ended up on Helena's left. Noelle's fresh scent, combined with something reminding her of autumn apples, wafted toward her. Inhaling deeper than she intended, Helena felt her midsection tremble. Noelle's hair acted like it was a live entity now that it was free from any restraints. When she rose to help herself from the buffet again, it floated through the air toward Helena and landed on her arm like a soft caress. Shivering, Helena developed a full-body set of goose bumps. *I can't believe this.* Clinging to her utensils, she prayed nobody had noticed, only to look up in time to catch Manon's knowing glance.

Damn.

CHAPTER EIGHT

H ave you noticed the way she looks at you?"

"What?" Noelle nearly dropped her glass of wine.

"Helena." Mike propped her hip against the patio railing, looking kindly at Noelle.

"What do you mean? She doesn't look at me. She's hardly said a word to me all evening." Realizing how revealing that last part could be, Noelle clenched her jaw before she made matters worse.

"Exactly." Mike looked like a lawyer who'd just heard a judge respond "sustained" to her objection. "Helena has tried very hard not to talk to you, or look at you, *all evening*." She regarded Noelle expectantly.

"That's what I said."

"No, no. You misunderstand. She's *tried.* That doesn't mean she's succeeded. As soon as she thought you weren't looking, she's devoured you with her eyes."

"Oh, Mike." Noelle didn't know whether to laugh or be angry. "You're making this up. Helena doesn't look at me. She doesn't have a reason to unless it's because she's annoyed with me."

"Uh-huh. Well, that's where you're wrong. I don't know how alive and kicking your gaydar is—"

"My what?" Of course Noelle knew the term, but it wasn't really possible to be certain about a person's sexual preference unless they told you, was it? Stalling, she frowned. Though Mike was gentle, she was clearly on a mission.

"Gaydar. Don't tell me that you, who work among the best and the most famous in the gay world, haven't heard that word before."

"I have, but if there is such a thing, I don't possess it."

"I'll say, or the glances you and Helena keep sending each other would make a lot more sense to you."

"What are you getting at?" Noelle wasn't sure she wanted to know. Her heart was pounding hard enough to actually damage her breastbone.

"I'm not trying to be nosy or meddle in anything that's not my business." Mike sounded sincere, and her blue-black eyes were kind as they gently probed Noelle's. "But it'd be a shame if you didn't act when you could, just because you simply didn't know."

"You're confusing me." Noelle really was at a loss. "What is it I don't know?"

"You must realize that Vivian and I are a couple, that we're lesbians, right?"

"Yes. I kind of figured that out. You're cute together." Noelle meant it. The elegant, flamboyant opera singer and the tomboyish, down-to-earth Mike seemed to complement each other well.

"Thank you." Mike looked genuinely happy. "And it's no secret that Eryn and Manon are another couple."

"I figured as much."

"What do you think of Helena, when it comes to sexual orientation?"

"Eh…" Noelle ran out of air, and trying to draw her breath, she had to confess to herself that she had heard it mentioned a few times, but paid no attention to the rumors. The grapevine had whispered that VMP's CEO was a take-no-prisoners stone-cold bitch, a hard-nosed businesswoman and a lesbian. Feeling awkward when anyone tried to gossip about Helena's private life, Noelle had deliberately tuned them out. She wasn't doing so for any angelic purposes. She hated gossip and the rumor mill that flourished on the Web and in magazines about her and the hunks the media tried to pair her with, so she tried to walk the walk when it came to her own conduct. "I heard someone mention it, but rumors are rumors, and in our business they can be lethal. If Helena is a lesbian, that's her life, her concern."

"True, but she's just made it yours by the way she looks at you. See? A method to my madness…I mean logic." Mike briefly touched Noelle's shoulder. "I don't know about you, what you've figured out about yourself and so on, but take it from someone who fell head over heels in love with a woman who was supposedly straight and quite a bit older than me. I recognize the signs."

"You do?" Noelle squeaked. "What signs?"

"How you blush. Hold your breath when she talks to you or merely looks at you with those piercing eyes. How you wipe your palms on your legs and moisten your lips. How you have to leave the room for a little while sometimes, when it all gets overwhelming."

Feeling sucker-punched, Noelle wanted to rebut all of Mike's observations, but she simply didn't have enough oxygen to speak.

"Please, Noelle, don't freak out. I know how overwhelming this must seem." Mike looked worried now, probably rethinking her idea of having a heart-to-heart with Noelle on the patio.

"I'm not freaking." Noelle managed to get the words out and even sound normal. "It's not that I haven't thought about it over the years. Especially lately."

"Yeah?"

"Yeah." Noelle sighed, twirling a hank of hair with trembling fingers. "I've even written some song lyrics about possibly being attracted to women." Seeing Mike's eyes light up, she held up her hand. "No, no, no. Nothing that I can share yet. My lyrics are really personal, not all of them are meant to be performed." Her mood darkened. "If Helena had her say, none of my own songs would ever see the light of day."

"Not true," a husky voice interrupted from the doorway. Helena stepped outside, joining them with a nearly finished glass of red wine. "We'll negotiate further this upcoming week, but I would never say never."

Praying that Helena hadn't overheard everything Mike and she had said, Noelle felt her heart speed up again.

Mike seemed to be worried about the same thing and said, "I better go see if Vivi needs me."

Noelle sipped her wine twice. "I'm glad you still think that about my next recording. Still, from experience, I know better than to celebrate until everyone's signature is on the dotted line."

"Clever. That's more than some of the new young people right out of business school know." Helena lounged against the railing the same way Mike had just done, only much closer, and when Helena gently touched Noelle's arm, ripples traveled along nerve endings Noelle had previously been unaware of, making her shiver.

"I—eh, I…" Feeling stupid for not being able to piece two words together, Noelle cleared her throat again. "I didn't mean to sound ungrateful."

"You didn't." Helena had raised her glass again to sip her wine when the wind caught Noelle's hair, wrapping them both in a blond-black cocoon.

"Oh, damn." Helena sounded as out of breath as Noelle felt as she tried to free herself from the misbehaving locks. Several of them had become tangled in the buttons of Helena's shirt.

"Here. Let me." Noelle stepped closer, eager to free Helena. Her fingers trembled as she fiddled with the buttons, and it didn't help that she inadvertently brushed against Helena's breasts with the back of her hand several times. Unsure if she really heard Helena gasp, Noelle was close to tears from the pounding of her heart and the weakness in her knees.

"Talk about getting caught in someone's yarns." Helena looked bleakly up at Noelle.

"I'm so sorry." Noelle tried to smile back, but her lips felt even fuller than usual, blood-filled and super-sensitive. "I should've tied it back before I came outside."

"No harm done." Helena gathered the part of Noelle's hair that they'd managed to free from the buttons, holding it away from them. This, in turn, forced her to step even closer to Noelle, to keep from tugging painfully at the curls, which created even less space between them for Noelle to work herself free.

"It's like silk. I thought the dye would make it coarser." Helena's unexpected words made Noelle stop working.

"You thought about my hair?" she asked before realizing she had actually spoken.

"I confess. It's hard not to. It's one of your trademarks, and when I saw it loose for the first time, up close and personal…granted, not *this* close and personal." Helena's chuckle, deep in her throat, made Noelle inhale sharply. "When I saw it loose, I used to think it was too over the top, you know? Too much? But I don't anymore. It's beautiful, just like you."

Warmth, no, *heat*, permeated Noelle's body in seconds. She'd trembled for all sorts of reasons around Helena all day, and now, standing this close with her hands caught between them, she stopped when heat totally infused her. Her heart still thundered in her chest, and her breath was still shallow and fast, but her hands were steady as she disentangled the last strands from Helena's blouse. "There. Done. You're free."

"I am?" Helena didn't let go of Noelle's hair. Instead, she did something so incredible and unexpected that Noelle's knees nearly buckled. She slowly raised the hand holding the long, wild strands of hair and inhaled their scent. "I suppose I am." She let go and took a step back, clearly to be out of reach. "There. It's late. I'm off to bed, and I think the others are on their way upstairs as well."

"Bed. Yes. I mean, good idea." Biting hard on the tip of her tongue to stop it from causing more trouble, Noelle had to endure another chuckle from Helena.

"Very good idea." Helena stepped back and allowed Noelle to walk inside ahead of her. The living room was empty, and Noelle continued directly toward the stairs, wanting to hide in her room and try to forget how idiotic she'd just been.

"Sleep tight, Noelle," Helena said, remaining at the bottom of the stairs. "I'm just going to let Soledad out one last time before I turn in."

"Night, Helena." Noelle spoke quickly and had to force herself not to run up the stairs.

In her room, she rushed into the bathroom and turned the shower on. Tearing off her clothes, she tied the untrustworthy hair back and stepped under the spray set to whip hard against her skin. "I need to get a little savvier if I'm ever going to be able to negotiate with Helena Forsythe," she muttered.

She paid her agent good money to negotiate for her, and normally she trusted him to do that, but in this case, that wouldn't work. Her songs were personal, so she needed to show Helena something strong and personal, which meant not running away from her when things got…well, weird. Noelle frowned at the word. It hadn't been weird on the patio. It had been many things—confusing, mind-blowing, arousing.

Arousing. The truth hit hard, and Noelle stopped soaping her suddenly oversensitized skin. Standing so close to Helena when she was wrapped up in her long hair had been all of those things. That's why she'd run into the shower—to wash any evidence of her arousal away. Noelle looked down at her full breasts, her nipples hard and tightly puckered. Farther down, her sex pulsated, swollen and almost too sensitive to touch. Grabbing the extra showerhead, Noelle set it to a cooler temperature and rinsed herself between her legs. Even that turned out to be almost too stimulating, and turning off the water, Noelle stepped out, wrapping herself tight in a large terry-cloth towel.

She slipped nude into bed in the moonlit room and pulled the covers up, holding on to them just beneath her chin. The queen-sized bed seemed larger, and lonelier, than before.

CHAPTER NINE

The second jam session went even better than the first. Sitting on the couch, Helena was glad to see that Noelle had found new confidence and that Vivian showed her a few exercises and breathing techniques that produced a more rounded vocal quality.

Noelle beamed as she hugged Vivian, thanking her. "My voice has never sounded like this, no matter how I worked with my voice coach."

"That's the difference between classical training and training geared toward popular music." Vivian gently tugged the closest section of Noelle's double ponytail. "I'm not saying that to sound snobbish. They're just different."

Vivian's affectionate gesture redirected Helena's thoughts to last night, when she stood wrapped in Noelle's fragrant hair masses. The memory was so sensual that her breath caught in her throat. Grateful she was well out of earshot, she deliberately drew a few deep breaths to control her rampaging libido. *I'm acting like a schoolgirl with a crush on my idol, damn it. Snap out of it!*

"I'll practice these exercises." Noelle was still talking with Vivian. "I like how they help me reduce my vibrato. I've always struggled with that. Overusing a vibrato like I tend to do is a bad habit."

"Vibrato, when it's called for, can be beautiful and add to the feeling you want to convey," Vivian said. "However, I agree that when overdone, it becomes...eh, annoying, for lack of a better word."

"That's just what it is. Annoying," Noelle said emphatically.

Eryn played an ear-piercing chord on her guitar, which made them all jump. "So what do you say, ladies, should we do one more? A short explosive one?"

"God, woman." Vivian gasped, pressing a hand between her full breasts. "You'd think I'd be used to you doing that by now." She shook her head and scolded in Eryn's direction. "I'd spank you if I could actually find you."

"Promises, promises," Eryn said in a singsong tone. "I might ask Manon if she'd do it for you. If I'm lucky." She winked at her flustered partner.

"Eryn. You're being outrageous." Manon raised a warning eyebrow.

"And the compliments keep coming." Eryn began to play a slightly more muted riff. "But you lo-o-o-ve me."

Helena studied Manon, the woman most similar to her in age, social and financial status. Manon was looking at Eryn with the softest of eyes, clearly adoring everything about her, even her outrageousness.

"I do." Manon spoke quietly, but Helena could tell from the expression of everyone up on the small stage that they heard her. Eryn blew her a kiss between two chords, and Mike began a steadily increasing rhythm on her drums.

Noelle looked at Helena, the gold speckles in her huge eyes glittering like a wordless challenge. The link Helena felt when she met Noelle's open gaze was totally new. It connected with her stomach and resonated throughout her system. Noelle opened her mouth and began to sing, creating nonsense words, like an Eastern chant. Vivian nodded approvingly and placed her voice just two notes above. She followed Noelle effortlessly, and the powerful voices, combined with the musical instruments accompanying them, made Helena shiver. She congratulated herself for signing Chicory Ariose, and not only for the money they would bring VMP.

A group consisting of four accomplished women who happened to be not only lesbians, but couples, was one in a billion. Her expertise in the media and music business told Helena that the four women could easily cross over to mainstream. In a sense they already had. Now it was up to Helena and the group's manager to help them reach the big audiences. They were already lined up for interviews on the *Today Show* and *Live! with Regis & Kelly*, and by Leno and Letterman.

Manon wasn't thrilled about the exposure, but compared to how uptight she'd been two years ago, she was much more relaxed. Her love for Eryn had changed everything. The topic of love always made Helena cringe, and she quickly refocused on the jam session, which didn't help, since Noelle looked positively stunning when she danced to the rhythm and sang in deep, nearly guttural tones. Vivian ended the session with a perfect tone, reminding Helena of a lark, soaring to the sky and slowly disappearing from earshot.

Before Helena realized it, she was applauding hard enough for her palms to sting. "Amazing. Absolutely amazing. If you're up for it, Noelle, we should bring your agent on board and negotiate for you to make a guest appearance on their CD."

"You think I can contribute something worthwhile?" Noelle's voice had an odd catch.

"Of course. If you can do something like this in the recording studio, the outcome will be fantastic." Helena squinted as she tried to figure out why Noelle didn't seem as interested as she was yesterday.

"I'd be happy to work with Chicory Ariose any day." Noelle squeezed Vivian's hand, who in turn raised Noelle's to her lips and gently kissed the back of it.

"We're the ones that are honored, *dolce amica.*" Vivian turned her unseeing eyes toward Helena. "If you can make this happen, we will all be in your debt."

"Ah, that's all right," Noelle said, looking embarrassed. "You'd be doing me a favor, Vivian. I don't know if Mike told you, but I'm trying to switch gears a bit and am writing my own songs. A bit more serious and…well, I wouldn't say deeper, but sort of, anyway. So working with you would show my audience there's more to me than soul-pop and dance music."

"Your own songs?" Eryn stepped up to Noelle and Vivian. "Oh, can't you sing one for us? And no, Mike didn't say anything."

Noelle looked both pleased and apprehensive. "Thanks. I mean, I'm not sure. You really want to hear?"

Helena tried to gauge if Noelle was acting coy or if her shyness was real, but there was nothing false in the reddening of her cheeks or the way she bit her plump lower lip.

"Absolutely, are you kidding? We'd love to."

"Oh. Okay." Noelle hesitated for a second. "Is it all right, Helena?" She wiped her hands on her jeans.

"Sure. Why not?" Helena wasn't sure at all, because the songs she'd heard Noelle sing were so revealing. Still, if Noelle wanted to open her heart and soul to her new friends, perhaps it was a good idea.

"I'll accompany myself on the Roland," Noelle said, and Manon rose, patting the stool.

"Here you go."

"Thanks." Noelle sat still for a moment, as if mentally browsing her songs. "This one is called 'Moonstruck.'" She played a few chords to get a feel for the keys. "I wrote this last week, and I'm still learning to play it, so please forgive me any mistakes."

"Don't worry. Just play." Manon briefly touched her shoulder and walked across the room to sit down next to Helena. Eryn and Mike stayed next to Noelle, looking ready to join in.

Helena forced herself remain calm, not knowing what to expect from Noelle. The fact that she'd written the song recently made her wonder if it tied into some of their issues. The title didn't suggest so, but she was beginning to expect the unexpected from Noelle.

Where do I go from here,
When everything is strange and new,
And you are standing there.
It's hard to understand
Why things just can't remain the same
And be the way they were.
Moonstruck, I hang by your every word.
Though I don't know where this will lead me,
Bewildered and angry, still I'm spurred
To learn and grow, hoping one day you'll see me.

Helena listened to the words, which hit home with astounding force. Was this how Noelle perceived her? Like someone who didn't see her? Didn't believe in her? *Have I ever given her reason to feel that I do believe in her?* About to resort to her normal haughtiness when feeling she was under attack, Helena heard something in Noelle's sensuous voice, something hopeful and vulnerable, that made her listen to the rest of the song with a more open mind. The song was about someone going through changes, who had met someone who challenged her at every corner. Since Helena was quite sure the song was autobiographical, it was easy to imagine that the person who provoked all the conflicting emotions was her. Feeling Manon gaze her way a few times made it clear that the message wasn't lost on her either.

Mike and Eryn joined in the next refrain, playing softly with Noelle, which seemed to emphasize the heartfelt words. Noelle had been honest in her lyrics, though the part about being moonstruck disturbed Helena because Noelle didn't reveal if she idolized or was romantically interested in her.

Everyone applauded when Noelle played the last chord.

"Noelle, that was amazing!" Mike rose from the drum set and rushed over to hug her. "What a beautiful, *beautiful* song."

"Thank you." Noelle blinked against tears forming at the corners of her eyes. "Thanks, Mike."

Vivian joined Mike and kissed Noelle's cheek. "Beautiful only begins to describe how you performed it. You invited me into your heart. Very rare feeling."

"I agree," Eryn said, placing her guitar in the stand on the floor behind them. "That song is a keeper."

Manon was still sitting next to Helena. "She's avoiding you. You better reassure her ASAP."

"Nah, she's just talking to the others. She knows I think her songs are good." Helena wasn't ready to face Noelle just yet. Not sure if Manon knew she was stalling, Helena rose and busied herself over by the side table, pouring herself a glass of sparkling water. Reconsidering, she filled a second glass and, digging deep for courage, walked over to Noelle, handing it to her.

"You look a bit drained." Helena raised her glass. "Here's to yet another great song."

"Really?" Noelle moved her glass back and forth between her hands. "You liked it?"

Helena heard the unspoken question. *Did you understand it?*

"Yes, Noelle. I liked it, and it wasn't hard to figure out who you had in mind." Cringing at her presumptuousness, she carried on. "I've given you a bit of a hard time, I know. Trust me, I'm working on things."

Noelle lit up. "Thank you, Helena." Her voice was soft and her lips looked so luscious and yielding—

"You're welcome." Helena interrupted her own train of thought, angry with herself for being so easily distracted. *And single-minded.* Before anyone spoke, Helena motioned toward the door. "I know I sound repetitive, but believe it or not, it's time to eat again." She was making excuses, but the way Noelle affected her threw her for not only a loop, but a whole series of emotional somersaults.

"Yeah, well, I don't mind that type of repetition," Eryn said, beaming. "We'll be hitting the road soon, and I'd love to sample more of Mrs. Baines's gourmet cooking."

"Spoken like a true bon vivant." Manon wrapped an arm around Eryn's waist. "I couldn't agree more."

It dawned on Helena that she would be spending the rest of the day alone with Noelle. And the night, an evil little voice inside her mind reminded her. Helena huffed, drawing curious glances from Mike, who was passing her. Forcing a pleasant expression, Helena told herself she could harness her emotions and play the perfect hostess for another twenty-four hours.

She simply had to.

CHAPTER TEN

The evening air was chilly, but the gas patio heaters made it possible to have dinner outdoors. Noelle had stood by the pool, even contemplated swimming a few laps in the heated water, but somehow, wearing her black swimsuit in front of Helena would feel too revealing, emotionally as well as physically. She had now pulled a thigh-long cardigan over her jeans and T-shirt, anticipating the evening to be colder than it was.

Mrs. Baines slipped back into the kitchen, politely declining Helena's offer to join them for dinner.

"Guess that was a bit of a faux pas in her eyes," Helena said as she gestured for Noelle to sit opposite her. "She's worked for families out here in the Hamptons all her life. I doubt if any of them asked her to join them."

"Still, I bet she appreciated it." Noelle sat down, uncomfortable being the target of Helena's clear eyes. "Some of those families probably treated her like part of the furniture. I've seen that happen."

"So have I. I detest it. My mother used to say, 'Always treat the service people well. You never know when you'll have to rely on them to save the day.'"

"Guess she had a point, your mother." Noelle began to eat. "If you start treating everybody as if you're entitled, you forget your humanity and, in my case, where you come from."

"Entitled to what?" Helena stirred her soup, scrutinizing Noelle's face.

"Entitled, period. I see that a lot too. It's not what my parents taught me. They loved us, despite hard times, and showed their affection in a million ways. At the same time, they taught us never to expect a free ride." Noelle scooped up a slice of carrot and chewed it thoughtfully. "That's where I've failed with my two younger sisters, especially Claudia. They were so little when Daddy died, I guess both Mom and I have tried to compensate for his absence a little too much. Mainly when it comes to Claudia. She's a brat."

"Like letting her have the limo and the bodyguard to go to a concert."

"Yeah, sort of." Noelle averted her gaze. "I'm sorry to have to impose on you an extra night."

"No, no, I didn't mean it like that. It's great that we have a chance to talk without anyone to disturb us." Helena stared at her. "We need to address some things before we go back to New York."

Tensing, Noelle put her spoon down. "I know." She became rigid, trying to brace herself. Helena was the embodiment of casual elegance, from her golden brown hair to her pale blue button-down shirt, dark brown chinos, and boat shoes.

"I've given this a lot of thought. You should pick your two strongest songs and we'll add the tracks to the new CD," Helena said encouragingly.

Noelle's heart didn't contract, as it should have. Her blood flow seemed to back up against her lungs, making it impossible to breathe. Disappointment shot through her, and she realized she'd had her hopes up after the jam session and after performing the deeply personal song earlier. Helena apparently didn't get it, and fury mixed with sadness. Noelle straightened, knowing how her own hazel eyes now possessed an amber glow. She'd heard enough times from her sisters that her eyes turned yellow, like those of a stark-raving-mad dog, when she became angry enough. She was certainly angry now. In fact, angry didn't begin to describe it.

"That's not good enough. I won't do it." Noelle spoke clearly, using every vocal technique she knew to keep her voice from trembling.

Helena flinched. "What? I thought that's what you wanted?" Her lips narrowed into a fine line. "What now? Some more demands that VMP has to heed before you're satisfied?" Clearly, Helena was becoming angry too.

"No. No new demands. You just don't get it, do you? You don't *listen.* I've told you over and over why I need to do this, what I'm prepared to sacrifice in order to follow my heart."

"And I've told you that good business sense—"

"We're not on the same page here. We're not even on the same *planet*, the way I see it." Noelle had forgotten all about her food. "If I add one or two songs to an album of happy-go-lucky, bouncy soul-pop songs, they'll look like something temporary, something quirky. I've poured my heart and soul into these songs, and if I record them, they won't be a parenthesis. I want them center stage."

"Damn it, Noelle, you may have poured your heart and soul into them, but I risk a lot of money if I let you stray too far off the beaten track. I don't know if you've noticed, but the country—hell, the *world*—is in a recession."

"Don't patronize me. So you don't think my fans will buy something that isn't my same ol', same ol'." Trembling now, Noelle didn't intend to back down. She wanted Helena to tell her the truth.

"It's a stretch to think you'd be able to attract the same listeners."

"Because deep down you hate the songs." Noelle knew she sounded childish, lashing out that way, but at this point, she could care less. "You sat there during the jam sessions and when I played my song for Mike and the others, and you thought, 'As long as I can get her to endorse Chicory Ariose and give their CD a sales boost, I'll sit here and clap at her pathetic little songs—'"

"Stop it! I never thought any such thing and you know it."

"Oh, come on, Helena." Noelle lowered her voice. "I'm the company tits-and-ass factor, right? I appeal to a certain demographic that won't bother with the fact that I have a brain and a *heart*! From day one, especially on day one, you've made sure I knew how little you think of me."

"What are you talking about?" Helena frowned.

"Your birthday party, remember? You were so friendly to every single person there—friends, colleagues, performers—until I came up to greet you. Didn't you think I'd noticed the way you looked at me?" Noelle shook her head. "I was so happy to be there, to finally meet you in person. I saw a person that I wanted to emulate because you were so together, so accomplished and successful. I never imagined you could also be so cold and calculating."

"That's enough." The low growl in Helena's throaty voice made

Noelle clamp her mouth shut. "You're exaggerating and putting words in my mouth. You know you affect me with your songs. I've never lied to you about that or anything else." Something fleeting, something that resembled remorse or guilt, passed so quickly over Helena's features that Noelle wasn't sure if she'd imagined it.

"Really." Noelle refused to let the tears that burned behind her eyelids run down her cheeks. "Then you shouldn't have a problem understanding that if I were to add any of my own songs, I would want them to be treated with equal respect. Anything else is like disrespecting me, but I wouldn't expect you to understand that." She rose. "I've lost my appetite. Please excuse me to Mrs. Baines." Not even able to look at Helena anymore, Noelle stormed inside the house and ran upstairs. She barely resisted the urge to slam the door to her room, but she did close it quietly and fell against it, allowing the tears to stream freely.

Well, that's that. Not only have I burned my bridges with VMP, but I've alienated the woman Mike insists might be the one I could finally connect with. Sobbing quietly, Noelle crawled onto the bed, reached into her briefcase, and pulled out a writing pad and a case with pencils and erasers. Drying her tears on her sleeve, she flipped the pad open to a new page and began to hum quietly as she wrote down new words, new thoughts.

Helena remained by the pool for almost an hour after Mrs. Baines carried the nearly untouched food back into the kitchen. She had looked at Helena with obvious concern. "You all right, Ms. Forsythe?"

"I'm fine. Thank you. Good night, Mrs. Baines. I won't need you anymore this evening."

"Should I walk Soledad?"

"Oh. Yes, please."

Mrs. Baines called the dog and went inside with the tray with Soledad following just behind, no doubt hoping for a treat. Helena sat staring at the tea lights flickering in the light green glass candleholders, the flames creating a meditative mood. Noelle had been formidable. Ramrod straight, she'd argued with cast iron in her voice and fire in her eyes. Her outward beauty was enough to take Helena's breath away, but that fire, that unbending strength and belief in her talent and songs impressed her more. Given the choice, Helena would much rather listen to Noelle's own songs.

The minutes ticked by as Helena slowly examined that last thought. She looked down at her linen napkin that she'd crumbled into a wrinkly mess. When had she stopped paying attention to her intuition when it came to business? Her mother had detested Helena's unorthodox methods sometimes, but even she knew to trust her daughter's gut reaction regarding important decisions. *Why did I stop listening to myself?* Had it been when she'd had her last affair with a married congresswoman from D.C., a torrid escapade that lasted two weeks and left Helena with a bad taste in her mouth? It had seemed perfect. No strings attached, no reason to suspect that the temporary woman in her bed would suddenly think it was more than it was.

Then Helena had seen her lover on TV, posing with her husband, three children under the age of fifteen, and their four dogs in front of their home. The reporter had asked the congresswoman what she valued most in life, and she had gone on and on about her family, about nuclear family values, about how she appreciated honesty above all. And the whole time, Helena kept hearing the noises the woman had made when they had sex in an obscure motel outside D.C. two evenings earlier. Helena didn't know it then, but that was the last of her casual affairs. *So is that why I react like I do to Noelle? Am I that frustrated? Is it only sex?*

Slowly getting up, Helena knew she needed another one of her marathon showers. She hadn't thought of her long history of casual affairs in months, not this in-depth, and she felt cold. There was nothing wrong with casual sex, if that was what both wanted. *So where does that leave me, since I don't believe in relationships either?* Back in her bedroom, Helena undressed and walked into the bathroom. She stepped into the luxurious shower stall and let all eight nozzles blast her with hot water. This way she could tell herself that the drops of water on her face weren't tears.

Afterward, she realized she needed to talk to Noelle before things got completely out of hand. If nothing else, this incident had put Helena back on track. *If I'd rather hear* her *songs, I can't be the only one.*

Wearing a nightgown and silk bathrobe, she padded through the corridors to Noelle's room. She had raised her hand to knock when an unexpected sound kept her from following through. Noelle was singing and the lyrics filtered through the door, barely audible.

When I cry myself to sleep
No matter why I weep
My pillows gather all my tears.
Hiding them and all my fears
I hope there'll come a time
When I won't have to cry
Alone.

The sad lyrics, sung with no pathos, just a simply melody, very quietly, ripped at the armor around Helena's heart. She had to talk to Noelle. Her repeated knock abruptly ended the song, and she waited a few seconds.

"Noelle? It's me. Can I talk to you?"

A few seconds without a sound passed, and Helena raised her hand to knock again. The door opened slowly.

"Yes?" Noelle's voice was husky, probably from crying.

Cringing because she had upset Noelle, she lowered her hand. "May I come in?" she asked quietly.

"Uh, sure." Noelle wore the same outfit, making Helena feel vulnerable in her nightgown. Noelle's height advantage didn't help.

"Noelle, I'm sorry." Helena blurted out the words, knowing she sounded as stern as always, but hoping Noelle would hear the sincerity behind them.

"What for?" Noelle kept her hands laced in front of her, looking at Helena with thoughtful, opaque eyes.

"I can be such a bitch sometimes." Helena rubbed the back of her neck and sighed. "Honestly, sometimes I'm more like my mother than I'd care to admit. She was all about the numbers and the bottom line. I used to be able to trust my gut instinct, and…well, it's been a while since I allowed myself to do that."

"What does that have to do with me?" Sounding aloof, distant, Noelle wasn't giving an inch, making Helena feel she was treading water.

"It has everything to do with you!" Helena flung her hands up. "You've infuriated me, worried me, kept me guessing, and yes, embarrassed me, and I can't figure you out."

"No wonder you think the world of me, huh?" Studying Helena with narrowing eyes, Noelle finally showed some emotion.

"That said, you're still the most fascinating woman I've met in a long time, if ever, and I know I've been acting weird. Total confusion will do that to you."

"Confusion? *You* talk about confusion. I've been trying to do all you ask of me, trying to follow you in this dance, and I just can't figure out what I'm doing wrong. I really did think you liked my songs—"

"I do. I love them. I want you to record six of them, and six of your old style on the next CD. Show the two sides of you."

Noelle merely stood there, looking dumbstruck.

"I mean it. Once I stopped mimicking my mother, I saw it so clearly."

"Really?" Noelle whispered.

"Really."

"Why...I mean, what made you change your mind?" Noelle kept blinking, as if warding off tears.

Helena gazed up at Noelle. She'd never seen her look so beautiful, with hardly any makeup, faint shadows under her eyes, and her hair in disarray. Noelle's full lips parted enough for Helena to glimpse the perfect white teeth. When Noelle swallowed visibly, Helena acted on impulse, pushing her gently up against the wall.

"I can't get you out of my mind," Helena whispered against Noelle's cheek as she gently held her in place with both hands on her shoulders. Noelle's breath was labored and she stared at Helena with huge eyes. "I can't stop thinking of you and I can't take my eyes off you as soon as we're in the same room. I know our guests saw it. Pretty obvious."

"Helena..." Her name gushed from Noelle's lips as a soft moan.

"When your hair pulled me in, I was in heaven. And in hell. I stood there, and you accidentally touched me when you tried to free us. All I could do was hope that it'd take a long time for you to untangle your hair from my shirt." Helena squinted, trying to read Noelle's dazed expression. "Do I make you uncomfortable now? Does this make matters worse for you, Noelle?" Helena massaged Noelle's upper arms, sliding her hands up and down the thin cardigan, feeling the toned dancer's body underneath, but still so soft, so yielding.

"No." Noelle spoke in a strangled voice. "No. It doesn't."

"Are you...I mean, have you ever been with a woman?"

"Been with? Oh. I see. No." Staccato, the words came unevenly.

Done talking for now, Helena had to find out. She was risking everything when it came to future collaborations with Noelle, not to mention *any* sort of personal relationship, but she still stood on her toes and pressed her lips to Noelle's. At first, nothing but a sweet, insistent pressure, yet Helena found no available oxygen. Slowly, Noelle's lips softened against hers, and then, by some divine miracle, they parted.

A whimper escaped Helena's throat and she pressed closer to Noelle, feeling the sweet agony of her full breasts and curvy hips against her own, slighter frame. She cupped Noelle's cheeks and tilted her head for better access, deepening the kiss. Helena's heart performed impossible acrobatic tricks in her chest as she tasted Noelle's mouth for the first time. She pushed at Noelle's tongue, reveling in the satiny feel of it against her own, and suddenly—Noelle kissed her back. Her slender arms wrapped around Helena's neck, pulling her closer, and she trembled now as the kiss turned feverish. Helena stroked her sides, wanting Noelle to feel that it was all right, wanting to show how much she—

Helena stopped cold and took a step back. "I—I apologize." She was close to panicking, her intense tenderness for Noelle so new and frightening. Helena had to leave, immediately, and when Noelle reached for her, she backed toward the door. "We both have an early morning tomorrow," she said hastily. "We should get some sleep. Good night."

Heading out, she heard Noelle gasping her name, but she wouldn't—couldn't—turn around. Nearly running, Helena returned to her room where she tumbled into bed after popping a sleeping pill. It took about fifteen minutes before drowsiness engulfed her, and she squeezed her eyes shut, willing herself to sleep. Still, the last image in her mind was that of half-lidded golden eyes gazing at her in complete desire.

Had she imagined it, or had Noelle returned the kiss with an equal amount of fire? Helena sank deeper into the medically induced sleep. No matter what, she wasn't ready for all the damn tenderness.

CHAPTER ELEVEN

Noelle pulled her legs up under her on the backseat of the sleek white limousine. Morris kept checking his rearview mirror, looking worriedly at her, and she tried to look casual, even if her insides were in turmoil. She couldn't blame him for being concerned. After all, she'd called him at four in the morning, asking him to come get her as soon as he was awake enough to drive. Ever loyal, Morris had left his apartment instantly and driven to the Hamptons in record time.

Exhausted from lack of sleep, Noelle slumped back, hiding her closed eyes behind sunglasses. She had gone over last night's events repeatedly and still couldn't make sense of them. It wasn't so much *what* had happened, as her reaction to it. She had been upset with Helena and her stubborn, cold way of reasoning and disappointed that Helena simply didn't understand. When Helena showed up at her door, dressed in her night clothes, freshly scrubbed and smelling of whatever wonderful soap she used, Noelle was at her most rigid and defensive.

Helena's reasoning for changing her mind was still fuzzy to Noelle. Had she really had such an epiphany in the shower that she did a one-eighty just like that? Still, all that paled to what came next. The kiss. The one-of-a-kind, mind-blowing, sweet kiss that had pushed Noelle up against the wall, that she hadn't had a single impulse to try to stop. Helena's lips felt fuller and softer when pressed against Noelle's than they looked. Not sure how the kiss deepened, she just knew it did and she'd found no defense.

Only seconds into the intimacy created by Helena's tongue against hers, any residual wish to stop had evaporated. Noelle experienced the most erotic and romantic feelings possible. Nothing had ever felt that good, she thought, nothing. Helena's slighter frame, with narrow hips and small, soft breasts, seemed alien yet familiar. Her hands, those elegant hands with perfectly manicured nails, caressed Noelle as if Helena could never get enough of her. Noelle couldn't help but compare them to the much larger male hands that had touched her in the past, which had rarely been soft and kind.

After Helena passionately explored Noelle's body, Noelle realized that the thrill this exciting, commanding woman caused was only part of the reason Noelle reacted as she did. Maybe Helena didn't merely desire her. Perhaps she might love her.

Noelle shook her head. She was in deep water to even consider a faint hope of being loved. Of course Helena, who could have any woman she wanted, didn't love her. And she wasn't in love with Helena. Definitely not. She couldn't fall in love with a woman when she still wasn't sure how she could be attracted to someone of her own gender. A small inner voice insisted that she had asked herself many times if she could possibly be attracted to a woman, since men didn't really do it for her. *And now I know, don't I?*

Noelle's cheeks warmed at the thought of how obvious her arousal had been, from her diamond-hard nipples to her damp underwear. Helena must have noticed some of it. *As if my moans and whimpers weren't enough to give me away.*

Back in Manhattan, Morris drove into the underground garage and followed Noelle faithfully up in the elevator. Noelle stopped him when he began to enter with her.

"Hey, Morris, you need to get some sleep. You've gone above and beyond this weekend. Don't think I don't know. I haven't planned on doing anything special today, so you take off and sleep, okay?"

His apartment was in the same building at the lower levels, the section where several of the staff belonging to the condominium owners resided.

"You sure?" Morris looked like he thought she was bluffing.

"Would I lie to you, buddy?" Noelle pushed teasingly at his hard stomach.

"Yes."

"Ah. Well. But not today. Night, night." She waved and opened the door.

A wall of techno music slammed her eardrums. Noelle frowned

at the painful sound and went to look for its source. Her mother was usually not home this time of day. She worked for several charities and was the chairperson of the parents' association at her sisters' prep school. Claudia and Laurel ought to be in class, which one or both of them obviously weren't.

Her sisters were slumped on the couch in the family room with the music at an ear-piercing level and, to Noelle's astonishment, a movie playing on the large LCD TV screen.

"What are you two doing home?" Noelle yelled to drown out the music.

Neither of them reacted, their eyes never leaving the screen. Noelle turned the music off and the sudden silence was a shock. Claudia turned around, at first looking nervous, then annoyed at the sight of her.

"Put the music back on. We were actually listening to that."

"What are you doing home?"

"Are you deaf? We're listening—to—music." Claudia enunciated the words in an exaggerated way.

"Deaf? Well, with that 'music' I might as well be. Quit screwing around. Why aren't you in class?"

"None of your business, sis." Claudia reached for the remote and turned the TV up loud.

Noelle walked over to the TV and turned it off manually. Claudia turned it back on again. "Hey, you're blocking our view."

Noelle was not in the mood to play Claudia's games. Laurel was just as guilty, but at least she had the good sense to look ashamed and embarrassed. Noelle pulled the plug on the TV, which infuriated Claudia even more.

"Can't we even watch a fucking movie without asking the almighty Noelle for permission? You might be the big 'star,'" she said, drawing exaggerated quotation marks in the air with curled fingers, "but you're not our boss."

"I do, however, shell out a neat sum of money so you can attend the school where all the rich and preppy kids go. If you cut class again, you'll find your ass back in public school so fast—"

"Hey, that might still happen." Claudia rose, her voice scornful. "If you insist on recording those stupid, dorky songs of yours, Laurel and I will find our *asses* back in public school anyway, because nobody will ever want to buy them."

Stunned at the vehemence behind the words, Noelle opened her mouth to slam Claudia, but a stern voice from behind forestalled her.

"What is going on here?" Reba stepped inside the family room, hands on her hips.

Claudia paled and Laurel sank deeper into the couch pillows.

"Mom. You're…you're early." Claudia tried a broad smile that quickly faded when Reba only shook her head.

"Why are you two home?"

"We weren't feeling well. Lots of kids are home with stomach flu. Perhaps we're getting it too." Claudia adjusted her face a bit belatedly, clearly trying for a queasy look.

"Don't even try, Miss Claudia," Reba said, her voice lower and her Texas accent more pronounced than usual, which was always a warning sign. "You're cutting class again, and now you've convinced Laurel that it's a good idea. Laurel, I can tell that I don't have to make myself any clearer to you. Go to your room and gather your things. You can still make the class after morning study hall."

Laurel rose and hurried to the door, and Claudia was about to follow her when Reba stopped her just by raising her hand. "One moment, Miss Claudia."

"I can make it back by then too." Claudia looked less queasy and sunnier, now going for a convincing attitude.

"No. You're going to listen to me."

"Oh, Mom. Does Miss Perfect have to listen to you read me the riot act?" Claudia whined.

"I'm not going to read you any such thing. I have a few questions for you, however." Reba sat down opposite Claudia, motioning for Noelle to take a seat as well. "Now, tell me, what did you do this weekend?"

"You know what I did."

"Tell me anyway."

"I went to a concert with Laurel."

"How did you get there?"

"The limo. Morris drove us."

"Who pays his salary?"

"Noelle." Claudia was looking increasingly grumpy.

"Who pays the rent for the penthouse condo?"

"Noelle."

"Who pays for your school?"

"She's already rubbed that in today." Claudia stared at Noelle angrily.

Reba wasn't fazed. "Answer the question."

"Noelle."

"Who paid for the concert tickets?"

"Laurel and I did. We used our own money." Triumphantly, Claudia folded her arms over her chest.

"Hmm. Who pays your allowance?"

Claudia's face fell. "Noelle."

"Who was Morris supposed to pick up when he ended up driving you and Laurel?"

"Noelle." Claudia spoke more quietly now.

"I'm sure you see the trend here. Noelle supports us. She could tell me to get a job, one that pays a real salary, but she makes it possible for me to work five different charities. I've asked her many times if it's still all right. Every time she assures me that it's worth every penny to have me help women and children in need, whole families sometimes. And if I had to get a paying job, I don't have the education to get a very well-paid one, so we'd have to move to the suburbs and register you and Laurel in public schools and your older sisters in community college.

"There's nothing wrong with that option. Tons of kids make do with that type of education and end up doing just fine. Still, this is what you're used to, and this is what you've come to expect, isn't it? And still, *still*, you're ready to throw it all away by taking it for granted and being careless and ungrateful." Reba took a deep breath. "It's time to bring the truth into the open. I know you're jealous of Noelle. Of her fame and success, among other things."

"I'm not jealous." Claudia looked stricken, but she still objected to something Noelle knew in her heart was true.

"You don't have to be, anyway," Noelle said. "You really don't. Fame isn't all it's cracked up to be, and the work is sometimes very hard. I swear."

"You're the perfect child. Mom always sides with you. You can't do anything wrong, and you're always rubbing our noses in the fact that you make the money and are the boss around here." Obviously not realizing she was contradicting herself by sounding very jealous, Claudia sat there with her lower lip now trembling.

"Honey." Noelle sat down by her. "I know being compared to me sucks. People ask you stupid questions. They might make friends with you only so they can meet me. That's just wrong. First of all, you're a stunning, smart girl who deserves to have loyal friends who care about you, and nobody else. Second, you won't be dependent on me and my wallet for the rest of your life. As soon as you've decided what you want to do in life, you will get that education because I promised Dad I'd make sure everyone in the family was all right. The same goes for Laurel and the others. Once you're done with your education, you're on your own. You'll be independent and self-sufficient, and you can be proud of yourself. And I hope you'll be proud of your mom and the rest of your family who's been behind you and cheering you on the whole time."

Claudia looked at Noelle like she'd never seen her before. Her hazel eyes, so like Noelle's, were wide and shiny. "You promised Dad?" She frowned. "What...I mean, when did you do that?"

"When you were seven years old." Noelle looked up at Reba and saw a solitary tear running down her cheek.

"So he worried about me, about us?"

"You and Laurel are the youngest. He was very worried about you growing up without him to fend for you. Since I'd just had my big break and money was starting to pour in, he turned to me. Also because I'm the oldest. He was worried for all of you, and for Mom too. I promised him to keep the family together and make sure you got all the breaks humanly possible."

"Oh, Noelle." Reba sighed and took one of her hands and one of Claudia's. "Hold hands, girls."

"What?" Claudia looked at Noelle's free hand as if it would bite her.

"Please. Humor me." Reba had that look that meant she wouldn't let them off the hook.

"All right, all right." Claudia took Noelle's hand. "See?"

"Good. What were you about to say, Noelle?" Reba asked encouragingly.

"Ah, yes. Claudia, I'm sure you'll still be mad at me many more times." She didn't take her eyes off Claudia. "You're at that age, and don't think I don't remember what that was like. I was a bit of a hothead when you were little. I remember being so mad I pulled Mom's hair."

"What?" Claudia's eyes were nearly bulging. "For real?"

"For real."

"Wow." Noelle wasn't sure if Claudia sounded impressed or shocked. "What did you do then, Mom?"

"Grounded her for a month. She could go to school and to her auditions, but that was it. No friends over, no nothing."

"So much for me being Miss Perfect." Noelle made a face. "Claudia, can we agree on a few basic things that will make life easier for all of us?"

"Okay. What?" Claudia still looked suspicious, though a bit more relaxed.

"School is important. Don't cut class. Respect every family member, especially Mom. And if you get in trouble, no matter what it is, nothing is worse than not coming clean. It's pretty simple."

Claudia looked thoughtfully at Noelle. "All right. Can I add something to that?"

"Sure."

"Now you know that I know who's paying for everything. If I do what you said, can we not have it repeated on a daily basis anymore?"

"Suits me fine," Noelle assured her.

"As long as you *act* as if you remember." Reba kissed both of them on the cheek. "Now, see? I knew there was some truth to this method."

"What method?" Noelle and Claudia asked in unison.

"Holding hands. It's impossible, practically, to fight with someone if you're holding their hand."

Noelle looked down at their joined hands. "Oh, that's devious."

Reba looked delighted.

"And smart."

"You've been to one of those believe-in-yourself lectures." Noelle didn't know whether to moan or be grateful that her mother came home just at the right moment. She decided on the latter.

"I have. Money well spent."

"So since you're the breadwinner here, you're to blame for those lectures she goes to," Claudia said, making a wry face. Her eyes glittered and she giggled contagiously.

"Ah. Yes. Blame me." Noelle let go of her hand. "Hmm. Well, if you make a mad dash, you can just make it back to school in time for…" Noelle glanced at her watch. "For lunch."

"Oh. Okay. I'm off." Claudia rose and hurried into the hallway. Suddenly she poked her head back in. "Eh, how am I going to explain it to Mr. Delgado?"

"I'll e-mail him regarding your absence, and Laurel's too." Reba looked evenly at Claudia. "I won't lie. I'll tell him you stayed home for family reasons."

"Thanks, Mom." Claudia hesitated. "It won't happen again."

"Good. Now go on."

Claudia left and Noelle found herself the only target of her mother's scrutiny. "And what's happened to you during the weekend, honey? You have an expression in your eyes that I don't remember ever seeing." Reba squinted. "Don't tell me you met someone? You did, didn't you?"

"No, Mom. I didn't." Noelle wasn't prepared to discuss recent events with her mother. First of all, she wasn't sure what happened or what the situation with Helena would be like when they met again. Secondly, whatever it was, it was too frail, too sensitive, to stand up to Reba putting it under her maternal microscope.

"You're flushed, you're fidgety—"

"Mom, I didn't meet anyone. It was just Helena, the women in Chicory Ariose, and me. Unless you think I fell for their sixtysomething chauffeur, Ben." Noelle made sure she didn't smile too broadly.

"Hmm. All right. There's more, but I won't pry. Just tell me when you're ready. Far be it for me to meddle in matters of the heart." Reba patted Noelle's hand. "I'm going to get something to eat before I head off to my next meeting. Go rest a bit, honey."

"Okay." Noelle kissed Reba's cheek. "See you later." She went to her master bedroom suite, showered and changed into jeans and sneakers, and hid most of her hair under a baseball cap. Donning huge sunglasses, she grabbed her iPod and headed out. Central Park was always busy, but at this time of day, on a regular workday, it wasn't too crowded. So far, she'd never been recognized in this type of outfit and she really needed to go for a walk. The exercise and fresh air would help clear her thoughts…she hoped.

CHAPTER TWELVE

Helena tore into her office just before lunchtime, her scorching glance making everyone stand at attention. Wanda, her assistant, knew better than to ask any questions and simply handed her a strong latte and a pile of messages, then made herself invisible. Helena grumpily read her messages, tossing them into two different stacks—"can wait" and "can wait longer." She wasn't in the mood to negotiate with full-of-themselves agents or be the arbiter between artists and producers. In fact, she was pretty sure anyone would regret asking her to attend such a meeting, since she'd most likely live up to her worst reputation within five minutes.

"Ms. Forsythe?" Her assistant's assistant poked her head in, looking timid. "Can I trouble you with an office matter?"

Hell, no. "Sure." Helena waved the girl in and tried to remember the name of this new member of the office staff. "Eliza, isn't it?"

"Yes. Well, Elise."

"All right. What can I do for you?"

Elise held out a small box containing dollar bills, mostly fives and ones. "I thought you might want to be in on our present to Mrs. Chen. She's worked here more than twenty-five years, and it's her fiftieth birthday next week."

"Mrs. Chen?" Helena couldn't believe she'd never heard of someone who'd worked at her office that long. "You sure?"

"Yes, ma'am."

"So, she's been with us that long, that's amazing." Helena tried to stall while she browsed her memory.

"And she does a wonderful job." Elise beamed, but then a frown marred her forehead. "It's so easy to overlook the maintenance crew, and some don't even acknowledge the cleaning ladies."

Cleaning ladies? Ah. A little shamefaced for not having bothered to know who cleaned her office, especially since she so often worked overtime and ran into these employees, Helena vaguely recalled a middle-aged Asian woman vacuuming and wiping off shelves. "Mrs. Chen deserves only the best," she said, and added a hundred dollar bill to the pile. "Thank you, Elise."

"Oh, wow, thank you, Ms. Forsythe—"

Wanda stopped just inside the door, looking horrified. "Elise? Oh, goodness, I never meant for you to bother Ms. Forsythe with that. I'm sorry, ma'am, Elise is new and—"

"And I'm happy to oblige. Don't worry about it." Helena waved them both out, finding to her surprise that her bad mood was mellowing and she was able to stop clenching her teeth. She might even be able to address the "can wait" pile.

Helena buried herself in reports, and when someone called an emergency meeting, she went to it, determined not to allow herself to get worked up again. It was ten minutes before she ripped someone's head off, chewed yet another person out, only to turn to a third, ready to do the same. After the meeting, Wanda walked next to her back to the office, giving her several furtive glances.

"Yes, Wanda?" Helena motioned with her free hand for the other woman to speak.

"Eh, are you feeling well, Ms. Forsythe?"

"I'm fine, thank you. Why do you ask?"

"You seem preoccupied and stressed today, not like yourself, actually." Wanda looked genuinely concerned. "Can I do anything?"

Oh, God, I have to be a real treat today, if I surpass my own reputation. Helena tried for casual. "I'm a bit tired. Had company all weekend and not much rest. I promise to be on my best behavior the rest of the day. The rest of the week, for that matter."

"Sounds good, ma'am." Wanda smiled. "I'll hold you to it."

Helena gave a surprised laugh. "All right."

Back in her office, she couldn't take it anymore. She called Noelle's head producer, David Boyd, and asked him if Noelle was in the studio.

"I haven't heard from her in more than a week." David sounded surprised. "Was she supposed to come in?"

"We reached an understanding regarding her album over the weekend, and I was pretty sure she'd be eager to start recording."

"Really? Well, no sign of her here. I'm working on other projects in the meantime."

"All right. Talk to you later, David."

They hung up and Helena flipped through her contacts on her cell phone, found Noelle's number, and dialed. Noelle's cell went directly to voicemail. Helena left a short message, asking Noelle to call her as soon as possible. Unable to focus on the paperwork on her desk, Helena glanced repeatedly at her phone, as if constant monitoring would made Noelle respond sooner. When it did ring, she jumped in her seat, startled.

"Hello, Helena," Manon greeted her.

"Oh, hello. It's you."

"Who were you expecting?" Manon laughed. "Oh, don't tell me. The stunning Ms. Noelle."

How did she know? "Not at all." Helena tried for her lightest tone. "I'm waiting for several business calls." .

"On your private cell? Really?" This excuse obviously didn't fool Manon. "You sound tired, though."

"Honestly, between us?" Helena relented. "I'm at my wit's end."

"I'm listening."

"It's Noelle. Or rather, it's me." Helena groaned. "I kissed her."

"And?"

"What do you mean?"

"Did she kiss you back, or did she object?" Manon enunciated every word carefully.

"She seemed shocked for a second, then she probably was caught up in the moment, because she did respond." *Quite sweetly, actually.* "Then I came to my senses, thank God, and it didn't go any further."

"What do you mean by caught in the moment?" There was a frown in Manon's voice.

"Hey, I didn't get her drunk or anything."

"I never suggested you did."

"She…well, we kind of had a misunderstanding, or a fight, to be honest. I stopped by her room to tell her I had second thoughts." Helena cleared her throat. "I wanted to let her know I was meeting her halfway so she wouldn't go to bed worrying."

"You wanted to make her happy." Manon's voice was soft.

"Yes. I suppose so."

"And then what happened?"

"You're persistent."

"And you're stalling."

Yes. I am. Sighing, Helena settled back and crossed her pump-clad feet on the desk. She had always considered Manon a friend, even if they didn't socialize on a regular basis. After Helena signed Chicory Ariose, they'd reconnected, and Helena had enjoyed being able to talk to someone who not only understood her work as a CEO, but also turned out to have the same sexual orientation. Manon had not come out officially, but did nothing to hide that she was in love with Eryn and living with her. Giving Eryn most of the credit for her new openness, Manon was becoming increasingly comfortable with herself.

"So?"

"She was so lovely, so sexy, when she wouldn't give an inch. I was practically groveling, and she was merely looking down her nose at me, her arms crossed over her chest. I snapped. I mean, I didn't molest her or anything, but I did grab her."

"And kissed her senseless."

"Ha. I think I was the senseless one. I ended up pushing her away."

"How did she look?" Manon asked seriously.

"Shell-shocked."

"Considering the way she stared at you during the weekend, something tells me that she looked shell-shocked because you pushed her away, rather than because you kissed her."

"I can't be sure about that." Helena rapped her fingertips on the desk.

"Of course not. That's why you have to ask her."

Helena shrunk in her chair. "Ask her? She probably has had more than enough of me. I don't quite measure up as the big business CEO, do I?" She pressed her lips together, waiting, certain that Manon would agree.

"Hey, you're human." Manon spoke soothingly. "Don't beat

yourself up. It's counterproductive, trust me. Go find Noelle. Talk to her."

"I'm not sure that's a good idea." Helena backpedaled. "She needs time to figure out what—"

"No, she doesn't. She's had almost all of today, and you're the only one who can answer all the questions she might have. Go find her." Manon sounded so sure, so certain, that Helena knew she wouldn't give up.

"She's not answering her phone. Or she didn't fifteen minutes ago."

"All right. I'll get off so you can call her."

"If you insist." Helena shook her head. "You are persistent."

"And right." Manon chuckled. "Talk to you soon. Eryn said to say hello and thank you for a wonderful weekend."

"Tell her 'anytime.'"

"Will do. Bye-bye." Manon hung up and Helena slowly disconnected. She redialed Noelle's number, but still got her voicemail. Looking up Noelle's data on her computer, Helena dialed her home phone number before she chickened out. Three signals beeped in her ear, and she was just about to hang up when a woman's soft voice answered.

"Hello?"

"Hello. This is Helena Forsythe with Venus Media and Publishing. Is Noelle home?"

"How did you get this number?" The woman sounded suddenly standoffish. "Can you give me any proof that you are who you say you are, and not a member of the press?"

"Proof?" Caught off guard, Helena thought fast. "Well, Noelle stayed with me in the Hamptons during the weekend and met the group Chicory Ariose. Her bodyguard's name is Morris. Eh…she's been writing her own music lately and I need to talk to her about that. I'm not sure she understood when I tried to explain that we want six of her own songs on the new album."

"Really?" The woman's voice sounded marginally warmer and surprised. "I'm Reba, Noelle's mother."

"Can you get in touch with Noelle and have her call me back, or possibly come to the office to see me?" Helena closed her eyes, willing Reba to say yes.

"She's gone out and I'm actually getting concerned, since she apparently didn't take her bodyguard."

"That doesn't sound good." Helena's heart picked up speed. "Any idea where she went? Was she upset?"

"Well, yes, in a sense. She had a terrible fight with her sister, and usually Noelle takes Claudia's jealousy in stride, but something set her off this time. They were in a screaming match when I got home." Reba sighed. "I wonder if she's gone to that place in Central Park she loves so much?"

"Can you tell me where it is? I really need to talk to her."

"She dresses down and wears a baseball cap and sunglasses and goes to the fountain on the Bethesda Terrace."

Helena didn't doubt she'd recognize Noelle anywhere, in any attire. "I'll head over there right away."

"It sounds like your business with my daughter is urgent." Reba still sounded a little suspicious. "She's been very quiet about her new album, even a little depressed."

"I know she has. I'll take care of it." Helena tried to feel as confident as she sounded.

"Thank you."

Helena disconnected her phone, grabbed her jacket from the backrest, and told Wanda she was leaving early. She had to give her assistant credit for not looking too relieved at the news. The cab ride to Central Park was uneventful, unless you counted the fact that her cabdriver recognized her and insisted on repeatedly singing a Celine Dion song from the nineties.

Relieved, Helena left the cab and walked to the Bethesda Terrace, where she saw far too many young people in baseball caps and sunglasses. She rounded the fountain, inconspicuously scrutinizing the faces of the people sitting around it. No luck. Helena decided to expand her search, walking in a bigger circle.

Eventually her gaze fell on a young woman in jeans huddled over a notepad and a pencil. *I knew I'd recognize her anywhere.* Helena stood motionless for a moment, and an unfamiliar feeling of strong affection made her inhale sharply. Noelle couldn't possibly have heard her where she sat, five yards away, but still she looked up. Flinching visibly, Noelle hugged the notepad against her chest and rose. She walked slowly up to Helena and gazed down at her, her eyes nearly invisible behind the dark sunglasses.

"What are you doing here, Helena?" she asked in a low voice, with no audible emotions.

"Looking for you, of course. Your mother told me where to find you."

"She did." It was not a question, merely a statement uttered between stiff lips. "And why is that? What can you have told her that would make her divulge my favorite place to come and be alone and anonymous?" Anger was showing now.

"Because I told her I would be able to fix everything." Helena wasn't used to having to dig deep for courage, but this time, she had to persuade herself to stand still and not run away.

"That's pretty arrogant."

"I can be very arrogant."

"And did my mother buy into that arrogant statement? Well, dumb question. You're here, aren't you?"

Helena raised one shoulder. "Yes, I am. Can we go somewhere and talk?"

"I'm not sure. Nothing public, that's out of the question. Not my place, that's for sure. My mother would hover, my sisters would eavesdrop."

"What about my place? My Manhattan condo is really close."

"Eh, Helena…" Noelle colored faintly.

"I promise you're quite safe." Helena's smile turned self-deprecating.

"I—I guess that's one of the things we need to talk about if we're ever going to be able to work together." Noelle spoke with sadness around her mouth, and Helena was baffled that she could read Noelle's face at all, when she couldn't see her eyes.

"Let's go then. It's only a short stroll." Helena had a strong urge to take Noelle's hand, not sure whether to keep her from running away or if she merely longed for the connection.

"Lead the way," Noelle said, tucking the notepad under her arm and the pencil into her baseball cap.

Helena pointed along Cherry Hill. "That's the way toward Fifth Avenue."

Noelle actually laughed, which Helena saw as an encouraging sign. "What's so funny?"

"I live on Fifth Avenue too, only a short distance from here."

"I know." Helena couldn't wait to get Noelle to herself, to explain everything. She refused to listen to the part of herself that was more interested in carnal pleasures and decided it was time to be selfless and business savvy, and that the two opposites weren't as irreconcilable as they sounded.

Chapter Thirteen

Noelle entered a penthouse condo, not unlike the one she owned only six blocks away. Large rooms with high ceilings boasted panoramic windows that overlooked Central Park. Accepting a glass of white wine, she strolled to the closest window and looked at the familiar view. She remembered when she'd relocated to New York with her mother and sisters, at first living at a less posh address, but loving every moment of it. Shopping, going to clubs, rising on the Billboard charts, it had been a fun, magical time, and perhaps that glamorous sheen had lingered so long, she hadn't figured out how empty her life could feel until it overwhelmed her.

"Noelle?" Helena's voice behind her startled Noelle.

"Sorry. Lost in thought." She sipped her wine.

"Care to share?"

"Nothing interesting. Just stuff."

"I'm always interested." Helena had changed from her power suit to designer navy and white sweats. Her hair looked so soft where it framed her face, and her eyes regarded her with what looked like true concern.

"Thank you." Noelle didn't elaborate further. It mesmerized her to stand this close to Helena again and she was a little apprehensive, since last time had ended in such confusion. Still, Noelle found herself glancing repeatedly at Helena's lips, as if she could still taste them if she focused a bit.

"First of all, I'm glad your mother trusted me enough to disclose your favorite spot in Central Park." Helena motioned for Noelle to take a seat on the couch by the window. She sat down close enough for their knees to touch, which made Noelle tremble inside. Perhaps it had been a mistake to join Helena here. *But if we can't talk things through like adults, what hope do we have to figure out our professional issues?*

"And secondly?" Noelle asked when Helena didn't continue.

"Oh. Right. Secondly, I'm glad you decided to come with me. You hungry?"

"No. Not really." Noelle glanced out the window again. "Truthfully, the other thing that draws me to Central Park is the hot dogs. I had three not long ago."

"Three?" Helena's voice rose half an octave, something Noelle had never heard before. "Where on earth do you keep them?"

"I don't eat them very often, or I'm sure they'd show." Noelle giggled. "You should see your face. You'd think I told you I was doing drugs."

"Just surprised. Hot dogs. Haven't had one in years. Decades!"

"I'm very partial to funnel cake too."

"Now that's something I wouldn't mind." Helena placed a finger on her lips, looking lost in thought. "I—I'm sorry I kissed you the way I did."

"You are?" Noelle's heart contracted painfully. So she was right to suspect that Helena regretted kissing her. "That's all right. No big deal." She spoke fast, carefully placing her glass on the coffee table. She couldn't trust her trembling fingers to hold on to the thin crystal stem.

"No. It is a big deal. You've signed a contract that makes you dependent on me, in a sense. To put you in a vulnerable situation like that isn't fair to you."

"I'm a big girl, if you hadn't noticed, Helena," Noelle said, more sad than annoyed. "A kiss won't kill me."

"My first priority should always be your career and my company."

That last remark stabbed Noelle worse than anything Helena had ever said to her. "I see. Business as usual, huh? Go figure."

"That's how it should be."

"Okay. That settles that." The temperature in the room seemed to sink by at least twenty degrees. "Guess it was overkill to bring me to your place just to tell me that. You could've just as easily sent me an e-mail or explained yourself in your office." She rose from the couch, ready to grab her notepad and leave. She fumbled for it where it sat on the coffee table, but the tears that rose in her eyes blurred her vision and she knocked over her wineglass. It shattered against the marble surface, its contents spilling all over her notepad.

"Oh, God, I'm so sorry." Noelle felt like a prize fool as she tried to keep the wine from dripping onto the area rug.

"Noelle. Noelle, leave it. It doesn't matter." Helena's hands were on Noelle's shoulders, pulling at her.

"I'm so clumsy. I'll pay for it." Noelle wasn't listening. She pushed at the small rivers of wine with her notepad, then gave up.

"Stop it, please, honey. It really doesn't matter. It's just white wine. It won't stain."

Noelle flinched. *Honey?* "But—"

"Really. I mean it. Don't worry about it."

"I'm sorry." Noelle tried to calm down. She had meant to storm out, to just cut her losses, emotional and professional, and leave. The pain still congested her lungs and made her want to run.

"What's this?" Helena picked up the sodden notepad, handing it back to her.

"Nothing. Just doodling." Noelle made sure she sounded gracious, bordering on cheerful, something she'd resorted to all her life when things started to fall apart. Suddenly Helena's arms were around her, pulling her into a tight embrace. Noelle remained rigid for a few moments, then relented.

"Here. Come sit next to me again." Helena spoke huskily, her eyes darkening. "I'm not sure what I said to trigger your flight reflex, but I don't want you to go." She gazed up at Noelle, looking so concerned, so beautiful, Noelle could hardly breathe.

"Helena." Noelle sat down again on the couch. The notepad fell from her hands onto the floor. "I just can't figure you out. Figure myself out. Just when I think you care, you act all businesslike, and when I think that's who you really are, you do a one-eighty. It's—it's confusing!"

"I bet it is. I know just what you mean." Helena was still cupping Noelle's shoulders, rubbing them in small, soothing circles. "I think I'm actually confusing myself."

"What do you mean?" It was hard to focus with Helena's hands touching her. She pushed into the touch, mesmerized. Warm, incredibly soft, and with a tenderness Noelle suspected few people associated with this woman, Helena stroked her upper arms from her elbows to her neck.

"When I still can think, reason like I normally do, I mean, I try to do the right thing. Then all you have to do is look at me and I fall to pieces."

"Look at you in what way?" Noelle tilted her head, squinting as she tried to decipher Helena's cryptic words.

"Like that." Helena slid her fingertips along Noelle's cheek, brushing her thumb across her lower lip. "You look at me with equal parts confusion and desire, and it's damn sexy. You're breathtaking, Noelle, and I don't just mean your physical beauty, which is obvious. It's everything about you."

"So you find me sexy."

"Yes, among other things."

"And I'm really that transparent?"

"I'm not sure you're so transparent. Perhaps I'm just tuned in." Helena pulled off Noelle's baseball cap and gasped when masses of curly hair tumbled out. "Then there's that hair of yours. I'll never forget how it felt when it wrapped around us on the patio."

Noelle would never forget either. "You kissed me." Her words startled her.

"Yes."

"And you regret it."

"Not the kiss itself! Just the way I jumped you." Helena blushed. "That wasn't how I'd planned it."

Noelle stopped breathing. "You planned to kiss me?"

"No. Of course not. What I meant was, I sort of daydreamed about it. You know, as an unattainable thing. For all I know, you're not into women, not really."

"That sounds kind of crazy," Noelle said, trying to make sense of Helena's words. "I mean, yes, I can see why you'd be apprehensive since I've only dated guys. If you were a fan, I could understand the daydream part, but you're not. You're the one in power, the one holding all the cards."

"Is that how you see me?" A wrinkle appeared between Helena's eyebrows. "Person of power, your boss?"

"Well, yes, in a sense." Noelle thought she better be honest now, or she'd paint herself into a corner. "And given your words earlier, that's how you see yourself too. You said, 'You've signed a contract that makes you dependent on me.'"

Helena rubbed her temple, a sudden look of remorse, or perhaps sadness, in her eyes. "I guess you're right." She raised her gaze to the ceiling, as if the beautiful crown molding could provide answers. "Why don't you give your mother a call so she won't worry, and I can call for takeout? If nothing else, we need to hammer out the details regarding your songs."

Experiencing both regret and relief, Noelle nodded. "All right."

"Chinese?"

"Another favorite." Noelle pulled up her cell phone, wiggling it. "I'll call Mom." As she pressed the speed dial for her home phone, Noelle watched Helena leave the living room. If Helena was experiencing any insecurity, Noelle certainly couldn't detect it in her steps as she strode toward the hallway. She walked with her usual dynamic body language, already rattling off the order for food on her cell phone. Noelle wondered how a person could radiate so much presence that a room seemed empty and cold once she left.

Helena pushed the cardboard boxes away, thought better of it, then put all of them on the tray and carried it off to the kitchen. She returned to the room she used as a music room and library with more white wine and handed a glass to Noelle, who sat on a large pillow on the floor. The dim light from outside reflected in the bleached strands of her hair and reflected in her eyes, making them glitter. Helena couldn't remember meeting anyone with such eyes, ever. Big, almond-shaped, and with those unusual golden speckles that seemed to grow in numbers when she was happy or excited.

"Thanks," Noelle said, and took the glass carefully with both hands. She sipped it and placed it on the low table in front of her. Helena curled up in the corner of the love seat, wishing Noelle would sit there with her. *My floor-sitting days are over.*

"Mind if I borrow this?" Noelle gestured to the guitar behind her.

"Be my guest."

"I've written some new songs." Noelle looked at Helena through her eyelashes. "The weekend was inspiring." She made a funny face at Helena's frown. "Nah, I mean that in a good sense. Promise."

Helena doubted it. Bracing herself, she pulled a couch pillow close to her chest. Noelle quickly tuned the guitar and played a few chords. She was sitting with her back against an armchair, her fingers wandering across the strings of the acoustic guitar. At first she merely hummed the melody, her husky voice reverberating against Helena like a caress. After sending Helena a curious, prolonged glance, Noelle began to sing.

Will I be good enough,
Will I endure,
Will I take care of you,
Can I be sure
That I'll be what you need
And not so wild.
My dreams run deep for you,
My unborn child.

The song was filled with such longing and apprehension, Helena bent forward, not wanting to miss a word. Was Noelle longing for children or writing about her own childhood? Either way, the lyrics worked, and when they were delivered with that famous, bluesy voice, they rocked Helena. Noelle looked up at her, looking cautious when the song was over.

"Think it can turn into something, maybe?"

"I love it." Helena spoke softly. "Makes me wonder how much of you is in the lyrics."

"A lot. I love children. I just don't know if the life I lead would benefit a child."

"Things can change, in more ways than one. If you have a child, you can make other priorities. You're financially secure, as far as I know."

"I am. It's something to think about." Noelle rose onto her knees. "I have another song that I wrote in the park today. Join me at the piano?"

"All right." Helena's pounding heart seemed ready to break its mooring.

Noelle sat down at the baby grand piano, patting the wide piano bench beside her. Helena sat and felt the entire length of Noelle's thigh along her own.

"This is a very simple arrangement. I've memorized only the melody and the words, so it might sound a bit choppy. You'll get the idea anyway, I hope." She took a deep breath and startled Helena with a strong chord. "It's called 'Never Before.'"

The melody was dynamic and so was Noelle's passionate voice. The lyrics described the beginning of a stormy but loving relationship. Further into the text, Helena felt her back go rigid as she realized just how deeply personal the song was.

I call her my angel,
Keeping me whole.
I call her my demon,
Invading my soul.
She lives under my skin,
Dwells in my mind,
Warms me and chills me,
Kissing me blind.

After Noelle played the last chord, the women remained sitting next to each other, Helena lost in the scent of vanilla and citrus, something she associated with Noelle by now.

"Oh, Noelle." Helena sighed.

"It's not *literally* about you, the song. It's a lot about how I feel, though." Noelle turned and lightly placed her hand in the small of Helena's back. "Please."

"Please, what?" Helena heard that her own voice was throatier than usual, with a slight tremor.

"Kiss me again?" Noelle was trembling now.

"Are you sure?" Angling her body toward Noelle, Helena pushed her hand underneath the masses of wild hair. "That song may not have been about me, *literally*, but it certainly affected me." She edged closer, massaging Noelle's neck.

"It did?"

"Oh, yes."

"What kind of effect?"

"This kind." Helena parted Noelle's lips with the thumb of her free hand before she kissed her. Noelle whimpered and wrapped strong arms around Helena. The kiss was a lot like the one they'd shared in the Hamptons, but also very different. While Helena had been the aggressor the first time, now the kiss was definitely more equal. Noelle's tongue caressed hers repeatedly, and she held Helena so tight, she almost impaired her breathing. Slowly they let go of each other's lips.

"Oh, God," Helena said breathlessly. "Tell me you felt that too."

"I did." Noelle didn't ask what Helena meant. "It almost hurts to inhale."

"Yes." Helena stood, a bit light-headed, and held out her hand. "Come with me?"

Noelle took her hand without hesitation. "Where to?"

"My bedroom."

CHAPTER FOURTEEN

Noelle clung to Helena's hand, her own palm slightly damp. Hoping Helena wouldn't think it was a total turn-off, Noelle noticed other signs of arousal, some more unexpected than others. By no means a virgin, Noelle still felt completely out of her element when it came to being intimate with another woman. *Not to mention that it's been* ages *since I had sex with anyone.* This thought stirred a rather unwelcome idea, which made her falter on the doorstep of Helena's bedroom. Was this just sex? Did she want no-strings kind of sex, especially the first time with a woman?

Helena turned, raising an inquisitive eyebrow when Noelle hesitated. "You all right, honey?" The soft term of endearment sent sparkles throughout Noelle's abdomen. Helena's expression was an intriguing mix of uncertainty and blatant sexiness.

"I'm—I'm fine." Determined, Noelle stepped inside the bedroom, taking it all in with one glance. Decorated in the popular New England style—dark wood; white, blue, and red fabrics; and soft off-white walls—it was simple yet elegant. A king-sized bed dominated the room, and when she turned around, a fireplace, together with an enormous flat-screen TV, created another obvious focal point.

"You look cold. Want me to start a fire?" Helena's words were innocent enough, but the quality of her voice, low and reverberating, suggested she meant them as a double entendre.

"No. I mean, I'm not cold."

"You're shivering." Helena began to look concerned. She raised her free hand and tucked some of Noelle's hair behind her ear. "Do I frighten you? We can say stop at any time, you know." She gave a one-shoulder shrug. "Despite what my reputation might suggest, I'm only a barracuda in the boardroom, not the bedroom." Helena laughed, a short, slightly cynical sound. "Unless that's what you might want."

Those last words made Noelle gasp. "Really?" She tried to fathom what being a barracuda in the bedroom might entail. Her own sexual experiences had been more about men either worshiping her to a degree that they hardly dared touch her, or touching her far too roughly, as if they needed to prove how tough they were, even in bed.

"Really." Helena gently pulled Noelle into the bedroom and stood well within her personal space. "Noelle, why don't you tell me what you want, or don't want? We can just curl up on the bed and watch some TV if you like, or merely talk. Now, don't get me wrong. I want you. I've wanted you since I first saw you at my birthday party, and I've fought my desire every step of the way. You're not my type. You're supposedly straight, though that song you wrote makes me wonder. In my experience, straight women are often quite curious and not all that hard to seduce, but that's not what I want. I don't want to seduce you and then have you regret it and blame me for the whole thing." Helena cupped Noelle's shoulders. "Tell me what you're thinking."

"There's so much to say, and I don't know how to tell you or where to begin." Noelle swallowed, her throat dry. "All I know for sure is that I really do love for you to hold me. When you do, it's like nothing I've ever felt. Am I bi, or a lesbian, or what? I don't know."

"Oh, honey." Helena's features softened and her lips looked fuller, softer. "Do you trust me?"

"Yes."

"Good. Come lie down with me." Helena pulled Noelle toward the bed. There, she guided her onto the blue bedspread and stacked some of the throw pillows for them to rest against. "Here we go." She settled and motioned for Noelle to do the same.

Noelle joined Helena with a strange feeling that she would wake up any minute from this amazing dream. She lay down, her head resting against the padded headboard. The bed seemed to engulf her, the soft mattress inviting her to slide farther down, something she wasn't comfortable doing just yet.

"Better?"

"Yes."

"May I touch you?"

Nobody had ever asked Noelle that. "Yes." She answered quickly before she changed her mind.

Helena slid an arm under Noelle's neck and pulled her onto her shoulder. "That's it. Just relax for a moment. Just relax."

Under Noelle's ear, pressed against Helena's collarbone, Helena's heart thundered, which was the only sign that gave away her arousal. Oddly enough, this sound comforted Noelle more than any soothing words. Slowly her breathing became even and her eyelids began to close.

"Mmm, doesn't that feel nice?" Helena stroked Noelle's hair. "I'm here. I'm not going anywhere."

Noelle didn't fall asleep, but focused on Helena's scent. Today it reminded her of exotic places—spicy in a gentle way. Without making a conscious decision, she let her left arm slide up and around Helena's shoulder, stroking it gently.

"Mmm. Nice," Helena murmured in Noelle's ear, her hot breath tickling her skin.

"Yes…" Noelle slid her hand up and down the entire length of Helena's arm, feeling the expensive fabric of her long-sleeved sweat jacket. Somehow she urgently needed to feel Helena's skin. Humming almost inaudibly, Noelle let her hand follow the collar of the jacket and slipped inside it. The zipper was only half closed, and the jacket glided off Helena's shoulder easily.

"God." Helena sighed and shifted, angling her body farther toward Noelle.

Noelle kept her eyes closed and found that Helena wore only a tank top underneath her jacket. The loose design allowed her to reach all the way down to Helena's elbow. Softly, Noelle stroked Helena's smooth skin, and then it wasn't so smooth anymore when a multitude of goose bumps appeared.

"Are you cold?" Noelle whispered, reluctantly opening her eyes. "Should I—start a fire?"

"God, you're evil." Helena rose on her elbow, gazing down at Noelle. "Don't you understand what you do to me?" She nuzzled Noelle's cheek, occasionally kissing it.

"I'm touching your arm."

"Oh, yes." Helena moaned against Noelle's temple.

"Tell me what that does to you."

"It drives, no, *you* drive me insane. You know I want you so much, and you still touch me so innocently, so without concern for how much I'm restraining myself." Helena did sound strained, as if her vocal cords were like taut bowstrings.

"I don't mean to." Noelle turned her head as Helena kept nuzzling her, their lips nearly touching.

Helena gasped and latched onto Noelle's lower lip, sucking it in between hers and running the tip of her tongue over it. Noelle whimpered and opened her mouth. Soon the kiss deepened and they explored each other's mouths for what seemed an eternity, but still not long enough.

"Mmm..." Noelle had both her arms around Helena's neck now, wanting her to remain this close. *Closer even. Oh, please, don't stop. Don't let go.*

Helena raised her head enough to speak, but Noelle could feel every word in her half-open mouth, inhaling them.

"Noelle, honey, you're so wonderful." Helena drew a line with the tip of her tongue along Noelle's upper lip. "I want you so much."

"I want you too." Noelle spoke huskily. "Surely you must realize that you drive me just as crazy."

"I'm glad." Helena buried her face in Noelle's hair. "I need to calm down some. I'm burning up."

"Oh, no, please. Don't do that. I need it. I want all that passion." Noelle reversed their positions quickly and Helena gasped again. Surrounded by Noelle's hair, they were seemingly shielded from the world, and Helena moaned as she arched her back.

"Take my jacket off." It was something between a plea and an order.

Noelle unzipped the jacket before she had a chance to reconsider. Pushing it down Helena's shoulders, she took in the pale skin she uncovered, inch by inch. Helena yanked her hands free from her sleeves and pulled off her tank top, now wearing only a white lace bra.

"Take your T-shirt off, Noelle." It wasn't as much an order as a request, almost a plea. Noelle sat up in bed and pulled off her T-shirt, the soft fabric of her white bra unable to hide the fact that her nipples were hard as stones and protruding shamelessly. "Oh, God." Helena groaned as she stared hungrily at Noelle's chest.

"Touch me," Noelle whispered, somehow guessing that Helena wouldn't, unless clearly invited.

Helena slowly raised a hand and cupped Noelle's left breast. She flicked across the taut nipple with her thumb, sending hot sparkles through Noelle's body. They ignited her and created a wave of moisture between her legs.

"Helena." Noelle curled into the touch. Helena continued, using her other hand as well to caress both of Noelle's breasts. Blood-filled and aching, they seemed to strain to break free from her bra. "Undress me?" Noelle asked, out of breath. She wanted to bury her face in Helena's pale neck and just hold on. Something about the way Helena held her, touched her, evoked feelings Noelle couldn't remember ever experiencing before. Sure, she'd been aroused, even climaxed, though not very often. Now she was trembling and couldn't get enough of Helena's hands and lips.

"Lift your arms." Helena sat up next to her and pulled the bra off when Noelle complied.

Feeling her breasts bounce and sway back into position, Noelle was unprepared for Helena's reaction. She cupped both breasts with eager hands and took one in her mouth.

"Ah!" Noelle threw her head back, placing both hands around Helena's head to hold her in place. So this was pleasure bordering on pain. Shaking so much her teeth nearly clattered, Noelle caressed Helena's silky hair. "Don't...don't stop."

"Mmm," Helena said around the nipple in her mouth. Her tongue worked it slowly, maddeningly, and Noelle was uncertain whether her arousal or her frustration was winning.

Letting go of the dark brown nipple, Helena scrutinized Noelle. "You like this?"

"I do. Yes." Feeling bolder, Noelle unhooked Helena's bra with trembling fingers and tugged it off, unwrapping her. Helena gasped when the bra fell into her lap and her small breasts broke free. Noelle looked hungrily at them, desperate to caress them but uncertain how to proceed.

"Please, touch me," Helena whispered, and took Noelle's hands, placing them on her breasts. She pressed them hard against her, and as Noelle massaged their softness, Helena's pink, hard nipples prodded her palms and made her mouth water. "Yes, oh, yes, like that." Helena slid forward and kissed Noelle, deep kisses that Noelle hoped would never end. The way Helena nibbled her lips, teased her tongue, explored every part of her mouth was also new to Noelle. Light-headed, she clung to Helena, one arm around her neck, one hand on a warm breast.

"Breathe. Don't forget to breathe," Helena said against Noelle's lips.

"Helena. Oh, God, Helena." The rampaging emotions and intense arousal were beginning to overwhelm Noelle. Feeling out of control, like ocean waves were crashing over her head, she tried to explain. "I can't…I mean I could never…" She couldn't form coherent words.

"You don't have to." Helena withdrew, suddenly looking sad. "I told you this."

"What?" Noelle tried to figure out what Helena had just said.

Helena wrapped her arms around Noelle and hugged her gently. "You're all right. We don't have to go any further."

"Second thoughts?" Noelle buried her face against Helena's neck, her eyes prickling.

"You mean me? No, but I understand that you have. This is all so new to you, and you don't know me. Not really."

Noelle caressed Helena's cheeks, cradling her face with both hands as she tried to decipher the cryptic words. "You don't want to slow down. I don't want to slow down." She rose on her knees, towering over Helena. Kissing her again with all the passion she'd accumulated, Noelle felt more than heard Helena cry out into her mouth. She inhaled and captured the sound. *I don't know if I'll ever feel this way again, and I need to remember every second of it.*

"Noelle, I thought…I thought you meant you didn't want to—"

"But I do."

Taking command again, Helena growled deep in her throat as she pushed Noelle onto her back. She unbuttoned Noelle's jeans and pulled the zipper down. Without hesitation, she pushed her hand inside, cupping Noelle's sex, her cotton panties the only thing between them.

Noelle moaned and pushed against Helena's hand, unable to comprehend what she was feeling. She didn't care that she was so wet—no, soaked—that Helena had to feel it through her underwear. Noelle was so on fire, she wasn't thinking about her inexperience now; she only knew she wanted to savor more of Helena. Tugging Helena's sweatpants down around her knees, Noelle grabbed her bottom, massaging it for several moments before realizing she'd managed to push Helena's panties down as well, if she had been wearing any at all.

"God, woman." Helena jerked and fell onto her side next to Noelle.

Moving fast, Noelle took off Helena's sweatpants completely. Naked, and so alluring, Helena rested against the pillows, her half-lidded eyes never leaving Noelle's.

"May I look at you?" Noelle asked quietly.

"You can do anything you want, as long as you don't let go." The need in Helena's voice sent Noelle into action.

Gently she parted Helena's legs, wriggling in between them. She wanted to know not only what Helena looked like, but also her scent, her taste, and what pleased her, what drove her wild. Exploring Helena with her eyes, Noelle soon followed with her fingers. The female softness, the musky scent of Helena's arousal, and the way she sounded when Noelle touched and caressed her was beyond anything Noelle could've dreamed of. When she bent to lick a trail around Helena's belly button, she heard a soft cry. Noelle reveled in the feel of Helena's smooth skin, the slight sheen of perspiration, but most of all, the sounds emanating from Helena's throat.

Eventually, Helena began to pull at Noelle, tugging at her for full body contact.

"Not fair," Helena murmured, and grabbed Noelle's jeans. "You're seriously overdressed." She pushed the jeans down Noelle's legs. "Oh, God. That white cotton is damn sexy." Helena purred. "But these have to go too." She pulled down the panties, leaving Noelle just as naked.

"Oh." Helena stared at Noelle for so long, she was beginning to cringe.

"Something wrong?" Noelle finally asked.

"What? Oh, no, no, no." Helena rested her cheek in her hand, lying alongside Noelle. "I've always found you beautiful, but this… you're beyond beautiful, Noelle."

Used to compliments, both genuine and exaggerated, Noelle had never heard anyone speak with such honesty. "I never thought you'd be interested in me. Or want me."

"You couldn't be more wrong." Helena's expression turned

dangerous as her eyes narrowed and glittered beneath dark eyelashes. "I'm burning up. I want you so much."

"Then take me." Brave words, but Noelle nearly regretted them even if she truly meant them. What if Helena found her to be nothing but a major disappointment? Harsh words from a couple of guys nagged at the edges of her memory.

"I will." Helena kissed her while spreading her legs. "And I can see that you're nervous, honey. Don't think I don't understand."

"Just nervous that I'll be a clumsy fool." Noelle tried a smile, but her lips wouldn't cooperate.

"Never." Helena aligned herself with Noelle, who moaned at the contact between breasts, stomach, and hips. "Wrap your legs around me." Helena undulated softly against Noelle, who pulled her legs up, shivering as she exposed herself to Helena.

Helena pushed a hand down between them, spreading Noelle's folds. "You're so wet. Oh, honey, and so am I. I can't wait. I want you so much," Helena said in her throaty voice. Noelle would remember this for the rest of her life. The searching fingers, the burning sensation between her legs, but most of all, the feeling and look of awe on Helena's face when she pushed her fingers inside Noelle for the first time. Gently, but without hesitation, she filled her, curled her fingertips, and let the rhythm begin that would be Noelle's undoing. Helena's thumb carried out its own dance, strumming Noelle's clitoris, much like Noelle had played the guitar only moments ago. Something began to build between Noelle's legs, something that expanded quickly into a nearly unbearable pressure.

"M-more." Her throat was so dry, Noelle could hardly speak.

"Please, honey, touch my breasts?" Helena pushed herself up a bit on her elbow.

"Like this?" Noelle rolled the unbelievably hard nipples of Helena's breasts between her fingertips, all the time squirming against her with her hips.

"Yes. But harder. Pinch me."

The words thrilled Noelle and more moisture pooled between her legs, making both of them even more slippery. Noelle tugged at Helena's nipples, tried to establish a good rhythm, but it was difficult since her orgasm was looming at the horizon, nearly frightening her.

Whimpering louder, she wasn't sure if she was fighting to reach it or keep it at bay.

"You're so close, honey. Just let it come. Come for me, Noelle. I'm here. I won't let you fall."

The staccato words made Noelle lose cohesion in her joints. Weakly she clung to Helena and then a dam burst inside her. A burning sensation, turning into molten metal against her sensitive tissues, created luminescent patterns on the inside of her eyelids as she squeezed them shut.

"Ah!" Noelle bucked against Helena, unable to keep her hips still. "Helena...Helena..."

"Here. I have you." Helena rocked her gently, her own body shivering. "You're so responsive, honey. So utterly gorgeous and absolutely stunning when you come."

Noelle hid her flaming face at Helena's neck. "I am?"

"Yes."

Noelle caught her breath, then rolled them over, pinning Helena, who gave a very gratifying gasp. Still reeling from her own release, Noelle didn't want Helena to think she was completely inept. She wanted to feel and hear Helena experience the same pleasure. "Tell me what you enjoy." Noelle looked intently into dazed gray eyes.

"Anything you do—"

"Teach me." Noelle slipped her legs between Helena's and gently rolled her hips.

"Oh. All right. Like that. Your lips on me." Helena frowned. "But you don't have to."

"I know." A new surge of arousal inside Noelle startled her as she slid down Helena's body, making her spread her legs wider. Once she reached her sex, it seemed like the most natural thing in the world to kiss her there, much like they'd kissed each other's lips before. This was Helena, the woman she... Noelle stopped that line of thought before she acknowledged the potential depth of her feelings. She focused on giving Helena pleasure. Latching onto Helena's sex, she used her tongue and her fingers, reveling in the sensations, the taste and feel of Helena against her. Helena writhed beneath Noelle, called out her name several times, and finally, she clawed the air for Noelle, who crept up, one hand busy between them, holding Helena tight with the other.

"Noelle!" Helena curved her back, moaning her name several times. "What...oh, God." She shivered uncontrollably, clinging to Noelle, who reached for one of the cashmere throws at the bottom of the bed. Cocooning them in the blanket, Noelle held Helena with all the tenderness that flooded her chest. Helena had climaxed in her arms, squeezed her fingers like a precious silk glove. Happy and proud, Noelle closed her eyes and listened to Helena's breathing slow, become even.

"Noelle, honey?" Helena sounded drowsy. "Please. Stay the night."

A tiny ray of light penetrated Noelle's heart. She had half expected to have to get dressed and leave soon. "I'd love to." She nuzzled Helena's cheek and hair, unable to stop touching her. Helena's contented sigh assured her that she didn't mind.

CHAPTER FIFTEEN

Helena watched Noelle leave the bed and head for the bathroom. They had made love throughout the night, and still she felt a pang of desire when she studied Noelle's naked backside. Her mind whirled with the scattered memories of soft skin and sexy whimpers. She had virtually devoured Noelle, once she realized she was the most responsive lover she'd ever been with. *Lover. Oh, God.* Suddenly, Helena struggled to inhale. The idea of having someone like Noelle in her life, in her bed, exhilarated yet frightened her. *She's so much younger. Thirteen years, and I can't be sure she's really gay, can I? Plenty of bi-curious women out there who end up returning to male lovers once their curiosity has been satisfied.*

Noelle crawled back into bed, a drowsy smile on her lips. "Morning." She kissed Helena's neck and let her lips paint a hot trail down to her shoulder. "What time is it?"

"Eight-thirty, I think."

"Ah." Noelle stroked Helena's hair back, hovering over her. "You're so beautiful."

"In the morning, at my age?" Helena knew her laughter sounded forced.

Noelle frowned. "What do you mean, your age?"

"You look stunning no matter what hour of the day. I, however, don't have that luxury anymore. I'm pretty sure I look pale, a bit haggard, and my hair a total mess."

"Helena, what's wrong?" Noelle sat up and, for the first time since Helena helped undress her, she covered her naked breasts with the bedsheet.

"Nothing. Nothing's wrong. Breakfast?" She was close to panicking since Noelle seemed to have a sixth sense regarding her.

"Sure." Noelle's voice trailed off, and Helena knew she was confusing the hell out of her.

"I'll just grab a shower first." Helena hurried into the bathroom where she stopped in front of the mirror, not recognizing the woman staring back at her. Her hair was tousled, but she'd never been this radiant in the morning. Her normally calm gray eyes were only one shade away from blue, and her complexion glowed. Like Noelle, she possessed several tiny bruises and red areas from those moments when they'd become especially passionate.

She carefully brushed her fingertips over a nipple, which felt skinless. She gasped between her teeth. She'd never experienced a night like the previous one, either physically or emotionally. Helena's defense mechanisms hit the red-alert button, and she stepped into a scorching shower, trying unsuccessfully to rinse the feel of Noelle off her body.

❖

The mood in the kitchen was chilly. Helena had made coffee and prepared eggs and bacon for herself, while Noelle insisted on having only some fruit and a large mug of chamomile tea. Currently, she concentrated on peeling, so Helena could try to gauge her mood. *She can feel that something's off. That* I'm *off.*

"Noelle," Helena said, clearing her throat, "I have to go to the office in half an hour. Can I drop you off somewhere?" Only when the words left her lips did Helena realize that she sounded terribly dismissive, like she couldn't get rid of Noelle fast enough. It was true, in a sense, but only because Helena needed time to think, to regroup and examine why she was feeling this way.

"No, thank you." Noelle gazed up from the orange. "I called Morris when you were in the bathroom. He'll be here in…" She checked her cell-phone clock. "About five minutes, depending on traffic."

"Oh. I see. Good." Helena sipped her coffee. "Going into the studio today?"

"That's the plan."

"Excellent. I've left a memo for the producers regarding our agreement. They contribute half the songs, and you pick the rest."

Noelle's eyes warmed marginally. "Fine." Her cell phone beeped twice. Reaching for it, she pressed a button. "That's Morris. He's here." She rose and grabbed her notepad and baseball cap. "Guess it's time for me to go."

"Yes." Helena's heart twitched painfully as she walked Noelle to the door. "Take care, Noelle."

"Sure. You too." Noelle grabbed the door handle, but stood motionless, as if unable to open the door. "Helena…"

"Yes?" Concerned, Helena stepped closer.

"Helena." Noelle looked at her with profound sadness. Suddenly she wrapped her free arm around Helena's waist, pulled her close, and kissed her, without finesse, with feeling. She let go just as quickly, opened the door, and exited. She strode over to the elevator and stood there, her back rigid. Helena couldn't stop looking at her, but Noelle didn't turn her head even once.

Helena returned to the kitchen and emptied what was left of her coffee into the sink. When she turned around she saw Noelle's orange sitting on the kitchen table, perfectly peeled but otherwise untouched, and somehow the sight of the naked, vulnerable fruit made her want to cry.

❖

Noelle experienced an eerie feeling of déjà vu as she again sat in the backseat of the limo, feeling like an eighteen-wheeler had run over her. *Ha. Last time it was over a mere kiss, and now…now I'm really in trouble.* Her heart was in jeopardy of being seriously broken. She'd written enough self-exploratory love songs to know this pain was like nothing she'd ever felt before. The night with Helena had been the most amazing, tender, and passionate lovemaking she could have hoped to experience.

She shuddered. Helena's behavior this morning had been singularly painful. Noelle recognized cold feet when she saw them. Helena regretted last night just as passionately as they'd made love. *Or perhaps the making love was just on my part. Helena was probably just having sex.* Pushing the button that raised the privacy screen between Morris and the backseat, Noelle gave in to her aching heart and cried. She had definitely lost her footing. What should she do now?

❖

After Helena stepped out of the elevator, she muttered greetings to her staff and they scurried out of the way, which confirmed what she'd seen in the elevator mirror—her face was like carved stone and her eyes stormy gray. It was a huge relief to finally enter the inner rooms of her office and close the door. Wanda and Elise had given her looks revealing something between apprehension and concern, which made Helena wonder just how much her expression gave away.

She put her briefcase down and walked over to the window. Far below her, people strode along the sidewalks, car horns honked, and life in the city carried on as if her life hadn't been altered and challenged by one big mistake. It had been many years now since Helena swore to always be the one in control, the one who initiated the breakup, and if that made her a control freak, so be it. Even her mother had commented that it was impossible to be in full control of every aspect of your life all the time. Helena had tried every day to prove her mother wrong.

When Noelle had embraced her on her fortieth birthday, in front of everyone she knew, Helena had glimpsed the fear that haunted her now. Of course, she hadn't known then what she knew now, that Noelle posed the most danger to her peace of mind and also could break her heart irreparably. Helena simply couldn't let that happen. She hadn't been super-careful all her life only to land in this mess; that just didn't make sense.

Helena carried out her phone conferences with London and Rome without a single glitch, but she was running on autopilot. As long as she encountered no real challenges, she'd be fine, but she hoped she could snap out of this weird mood quickly if she had to. After lunch, which she spent sorting through her three hundred unread e-mails, she suddenly had the urge to call Manon. If anyone would understand, it was her. After asking Wanda to hold all other calls, she dialed her friend.

"Belmont Foundation, Manon Belmont."

"Manon, it's Helena."

"Goodness, Helena, what's wrong?"

"What?" Helena winced, wondering how the hell she sounded if Manon picked up on it over the phone.

"You sound like you're about to cry. What's happened? Something wrong with Noelle?"

"How…how could you know?" Helena could hardly believe how she stuttered.

"Is she all right? Is she hurt?"

"No, no. Noelle is all right. I mean, physically."

"What do you mean, she's all right physically? You're not making sense, Helena. Why don't you start from the beginning? I have plenty of time."

"I screwed up. I made such a mistake." Helena blinked at the annoying tears that clung to her eyelashes. "And I hurt her."

"What happened?"

"I made love to her."

"Oh. I see." Manon was quiet for a moment. "I don't mean to pry, you know that, but how did she react?"

"She—" Helena closed her eyes, her voice softening. "She was on fire. Noelle was wonderful. Trusting, responsive."

"So you made love to *each other*." Manon spoke slowly, as if piecing a puzzle together in her mind.

"Yes."

"You didn't 'have sex.' You *made love*. Your choice of words."

"Yes." Helena shivered. "God. Yes."

"And now you're in cut-and-run mode, afraid this will be too much, too soon, and that she'll bow out just as you're beginning to care."

"Your guess is as good as mine. I had to talk to someone before I drive myself insane." Helena pivoted, keeping the chair's back between her and the door. "You're a good friend, Manon, and you know me well by now."

"And I was even more of a chicken than you are, just two years ago."

"I'm not a chicken!" Helena sat up straight.

"In another way than I was, but yes, you're afraid. You want Noelle, you might be falling for her, and you, who are fearless in every other situation, don't do well with rejection. Not even potential rejection." Manon spoke kindly, but candidly, as always. "It takes one to know one. I was so closeted about being gay, I was *buried*. It took Eryn, and the fear of losing her, to bring me out. I'm wondering if the fear of losing Noelle will help you or destroy any chance of happiness."

"Either way, I'm screwed." Helena sighed. "If I pursue this, she'll end up leaving me. If I don't, then—"

"Then you'll always wonder," Manon said softly. "You'll always have that nagging little thought in the back of your head that keeps insisting you might have been living happily ever after if you'd only tried."

"That's right, twist the knife."

"Oh, Helena, you didn't call me because you needed someone to agree with your every word."

"I suppose. And if I did, I barked up the wrong tree, didn't I?" Chuckling ironically, Helena covered her eyes and slumped back in her chair. "Basically, I'm screwed."

"Before I answer that, I want you to describe how Noelle acted around you."

Helena gave it some thought. "She was terribly nervous at first, but to be honest, she initiated the incident. She'd written a song about a woman who falls for another woman for the first time, and that song… well, it led to some intense kissing."

"During our weekend in the Hamptons, it was clear that she's smitten." Manon sounded as if she was still piecing together a puzzle. "That doesn't say anything about the depth of her feelings, of course, but she was completely enthralled. Nobody else in the room really mattered when you were around."

"I think she may have, you know, a crush on me. Like a student can have on a teacher." Helena disliked her own example, since it stirred unwelcome feelings.

"Crush, you say? From where I was standing, it looked like more than that. Noelle is a deep individual, wouldn't you agree? No one superficial wrote those new songs of hers."

"Are—are you saying she's in love with me?"

"I would never say that, only Noelle knows what she's feeling, but I find that much more likely than the idea that she's about to do a number on you."

"Ah." It *was* out of character for Noelle to be shallow. In fact, as Helena thought about it, she couldn't remember Noelle ever showing any such signs. She groaned and hid her eyes again. "I'm just at a loss, Manon. I don't know what to do. She's gotten under my skin in a way nobody ever has. I mean, I usually make sure the person I'm seeing doesn't even begin to harbor such ideas. I go out of my way to date women who know that 'no strings attached' means just that."

"And Noelle has no idea about this, and you're falling hard, aren't you, Helena?"

"I...I guess so. And that can't happen."

"Before we hang up, I want you to think about one more thing," Manon said slowly. "You are about to, or have just recently, hurt Noelle, much like you were hurt once. We've never talked about what happened to you, but that's the only possible thing that could cause someone to be as calculating and careful as you are. Just think. You might be doing to Noelle what was done to you. I'm not saying it's *necessarily* so, but from my point of view, and not knowing all the details, that's how it looks."

Helena found it hard to breathe. Manon was probably more correct than she realized. "I don't want to hurt anyone."

"But?"

"I'm just hoping she hasn't invested anything in me, emotionally, I mean. That way she can go back to her old life. I mean, dating those hunks, partying."

"So you're not only using her as a one-night stand, but you're telling her to resume the shallow existence that the media built up around her? She's been herded into that type of life, with her agent's approval, no doubt, and now she's trying desperately to get away from it by writing those songs. Noelle shows us all so clearly with those songs what's in her heart. The way you're acting doesn't make sense. The Helena I knew would never do that to another person. You may have ruled the boarding school, but you ruled benevolently and fairly."

Helena cringed at Manon's disappointed and disapproving tone. No, it didn't make sense, but it was the only solution as far as she could see. If Helena allowed Noelle to inevitably break her heart, she would never recover.

"I'm sorry, Manon. Thanks for listening. I've taken up far too much of your time."

"Helena, don't hang up." Manon obviously wanted to keep Helena talking.

"I'll call you back in a day or two. Give Eryn my best." Helena said good-bye and disconnected the call before Manon could object again.

Helena furiously wiped a few renegade teardrops as she pulled a folder from the desk and moved over to the couch. Burying herself in papers and folders had worked before and would do so again.

CHAPTER SIXTEEN

Noelle stood patiently as Reba circled her, scrutinizing the low-cut black dress she was wearing to the opening night. Claudia and Laurel wore similar dresses in pastel colors, and Reba had chosen a black-and-white dress that flattered her full figure.

"Happy?" Noelle raised an eyebrow when Reba circled her a fifth time. "We'll be late, you know."

"And Morris is tapping his watch. Never a good sign," Claudia said. "Traffic is a bitch on Friday evenings."

"Language, Ms. Claudia," Reba cautioned. "And yes, I'm very happy. My three girls will be the most beautiful there."

"Thanks, Mom." Noelle kissed her mother quickly. "Let's go."

The limousine was freshly stocked with champagne, but Noelle only took a sip of mineral water on the way, knowing she had to be fully alert tonight. She hadn't seen or talked to Helena for almost two weeks, and she would be at the movie theater tonight.

Her youngest sister chatted happily about being included, and even Claudia was impressed. Noelle recalled her recent conversation with Brad Haley, her agent, who was discontented when she refused to go to the opening night of the second Diana Maddox movie with any of the male performers he'd suggested.

"You need to be seen with the right people," he'd insisted. "There isn't a guy alive that wouldn't come running to escort you."

"And there isn't a guy alive I would want to be escorted by, unless I chose him. I won't agree to any of your stable of the latest rappers, ballad crooners, or sports stars." Noelle had towered over Brad. "I choose my own company from now on. No more fixed headlines in the tabloids about my 'latest lover' or anything like that. I'm taking my mother and my two youngest sisters. Period." She had left his office, furious to have wasted her time. Feeling liberated, she kept convincing herself that everything was still good. She'd finally put her foot down, even if Brad didn't realize it for a while. And if he balked, well, plenty of other agents would line up just like Brad's boys, if she spread the word she was shopping around for a new one.

The limousine moved lithely through the Friday Manhattan traffic despite its size. Morris stopped at the red carpet and rounded the car to open the door. Reba and the girls exited first, and Noelle could hear the crowd begin to roar when they realized who was in the limo. Taking a deep breath, she stepped out, making sure she beamed at her fans. Thousands of people filled the sidewalk on both sides of the ropes, calling her name.

"Oh, my God," Claudia shouted. "This is awesome. Absolutely awesome, Noelle."

The impressed look in Claudia's eyes warmed Noelle after all the harsh words between them lately. Laurel gripped one of her hands and Reba walked just behind them, looking as regal as always.

"Noelle, may we ask you some questions?" a reporter from one of the entertainment channels said. "We're streaming this feed directly to our Web site, is that okay with you?"

"Why not, Glenn? It's Glenn, right?"

Glenn looked flattered. "Sure is. Who's with you tonight?"

Noelle introduced her family, knowing this would make Claudia and Laurel's day.

"I can see the family resemblance," Glenn said, "although I was certain you were four sisters out on the town tonight."

"Hear that, Mom?" Noelle winked at Reba, who studied the young reporter with a look that said, *I know who you're trying to impress, and it ain't workin'.*

"I do."

Glenn coughed nervously. "Anyway. You sing three of the songs on the soundtrack, which is already climbing the charts, so I'm told. One of the songs is called 'Diana's Theme' and it's sung from Erica's point of view. What was that like for you? Singing about love between women?"

Noelle's anger rose but she quickly harnessed it. It wasn't obvious where Glenn was going with this, but she could think of two possibilities. Either he wanted to embarrass her, or he was waiting to see if she'd say something controversial. Noelle donned her sweetest smile and made sure the TV camera caught her expression.

"You know, Glenn, it comes perfectly natural to me."

Glenn stuttered, obviously struggling for something witty or intelligent to say, but came up with nothing. Resorting to coughing, he signaled a woman standing to his left, probably his producer, to cut the feed. She spoke quickly into her mike, and the small light on the camera turned off. Noelle turned to continue along the red carpet, but before she did, the producer winked at her. Not sure how to respond, Noelle merely nodded.

Inside, celebrities holding glasses of champagne mingled before they found their seats. Reba and the girls sat farther back, while Noelle was included with the VMP crowd. She'd tried not to think about this the entire day. Helena would be here, of course, since VMP was so involved with the movies as well as the production of the Diana Maddox audio books. When Noelle found the chair with her name on it, to her dismay, Helena was seated to her left. Noelle sighed as she sat down, adjusting her dress. This was going to be pure hell.

❖

Helena walked into the VIP section of the movie theater, checking the name tags for her seat.

"I believe this is yours, Helena." Noelle's voice made her stop so suddenly, the person behind her bumped into her with a quick apology.

"Thank you." Helena sat down, glancing longingly at Noelle. She wore a skintight black dress that glittered in an understated way, and her hair was piled loosely top of her head with long, curly tresses caressing her neck. Less than two weeks ago Helena had licked that very neck, and the thought made her squeeze her thighs together.

"You all right?" Noelle asked politely.

"Fine. Thank you." In fact, Helena's heart hammered so fast in her chest, she was certain her white silk blouse was fluttering. "You here alone?" She hadn't expected to find Noelle without an escort.

"No. My mother and my sisters are about ten rows behind us.

Since I brought Claudia and Laurel, they couldn't fit them in this row."
Noelle turned and waved to her family. "The girls are in heaven. I think
the red-carpet experience gave me points even in Claudia's book."

"At that age, I don't doubt it. I hope they end up in the columns.
That should go over well with their friends."

"For sure." Noelle didn't elaborate.

"Noelle—" Helena wanted to say something that would bring
back a glimpse of the Noelle she'd held in her arms so recently.

"Helena, don't. Not here." Noelle's eyes darkened. "Please."

"All right." Swallowing, Helena directed her gaze forward. "Here
are our stars."

Carolyn Black entered from a side door at the front of the cinema,
walking up the aisle with Annelie Peterson. Behind her, Helen St Cyr,
who played Erica, Maddox's love interest in the movie, walked next to
others in the cast. People rose from their seats, cheering and applauding.
Carolyn smiled back and waved, and Helena saw her cling to Annelie's
hand.

"They look amazing together," Noelle said.

"Yes, they do." Carolyn and Annelie, one auburn, the other blond;
one average height, the other tall; one in her mid forties, the other at
least ten years younger. There were many parallels to Noelle and her.
Except that I'm even older, and she's not really gay. She ignored the
small voice that reminded her that Carolyn Black had seemed to be
heterosexual before she met Annelie.

The introduction to the movie began and the lights dimmed. Her
senses heightened by the darkness, Helena smelled Noelle's perfume
surround her like invisible fingers. She inhaled, only to regret it
immediately since she recalled how her bed had smelled for two nights
before she let her housekeeper change the sheets. *Oh, damn, this is
going to be a long evening.*

❖

"Noelle? Are you hiding?" The fantastic, famous voice of Carolyn
Black jarred Noelle, who was deliberately staying out of sight behind
a large display of palm trees in a corner of the ballroom. The cocktail
party was well under way, and after having had to escape overzealous

fans twice already, Noelle was reluctant to return to where they were supposed to conduct the meet-and-greet.

"I'm sorry, Carolyn. I didn't see you." Noelle shuffled out from under a tree, picking two fragments of a palm leaf from her hair.

"Tell me the truth. Are you hiding from a stalker-fan or from Helena?"

"What?" Noelle winced. "Oh, well, a bit of both, I suppose."

"What's poor Helena done now?"

"'Poor Helena' hasn't done anything at all." Noelle cleared her throat. "Congratulations on another wonderful performance. This movie was even better than the first one. I knew the storyline and I was still on the edge of my seat, actually holding my breath."

"Thank you." Carolyn looked genuinely happy. "It was great to work with the cast again. We're comfortable in our roles by now, and I think it showed."

"It did. The relationship issues were so real, they were tangible. I just wanted to smack you over the head at one point!" Noelle gasped. "Oh, God. I didn't mean that literally."

"At what point?" Carolyn laughed, which attracted even more attention from the people around them. At first, Noelle wondered why the other guests didn't try to intrude on her conversation with Carolyn. The famous actress seemingly kept them away with just a glance.

"When Erica wanted to tend to your wound after you fought off that guy with a knife, and you were too stubborn to let her see you in a weakened state."

"Ah. I see." Carolyn tilted her head. "In my experience, that reaction usually happens because a scene triggers a memory."

"That could be."

"And would Helena be this person you're so frustrated with?"

"Carolyn, please, let's don't discuss anything so personal here." Noelle looked nervously around. Paparazzi had a way of sneaking in unannounced or bribing someone to let them snap a few pictures when you least expected it. She'd even had someone place a long-range spy microphone that caught every word she said to a friend.

"Point taken, Noelle. Can't be too careful." Carolyn positioned them so nobody could see their faces unless they were standing right next to them. "I just want you to know that you can always turn to me or

Annelie. We're practically your next-door neighbors in Miami. Please, remember that."

"All right. Thank you, Carolyn. I appreciate it." Noelle clasped her hands, not sure what to say next.

"Oh, come here. You look so forlorn." Carolyn pulled Noelle into a friendly embrace. "Thank you for lending your fantastic voice to our soundtrack, darling. It gives the movie yet another dimension. Everybody says so."

"Noelle?" A young-sounding voice interrupted the exchange, yanking Noelle back into the present.

"Laurel." Noelle lowered her arms, but Carolyn kept a protective arm around her waist. "This is Carolyn Black."

"Hello, Ms. Black." Laurel blushed and glanced around, looking relieved when Reba and Claudia caught up with her. Several introductions later, everyone was chatting easily, Laurel and Claudia basking in Carolyn's presence. Annelie joined them after a while and soon they were chatting amicably. Noelle began to relax.

"There's Helena," Annelie said suddenly, and waved. "Helena. Come join us."

Noelle flinched and immediately felt Carolyn's hand against the small of her back. Grateful for the wordless support, she adjusted her expression before Helena joined them. To her surprise, Helena looked almost dazed. Squinting, Noelle realized something must be very wrong.

"Please, you must introduce me to your family," Helena said, extending a hand to Reba. "We spoke on the phone a while back."

"Yes, right before you and Noelle worked on her music all night. She looked so tired when she came home, I made her stay in bed all day." Reba faltered when Helena winced.

"Yes, Mom is such a worrier." Noelle spoke fast, trying to salvage the situation. She didn't dare look at Carolyn, but felt her hand make comforting little circles on her back. "She actually gave me chicken soup."

"Well, you looked like you were getting a cold," Reba said defensively. "All red around the eyes."

Noelle wanted to groan, but stood ramrod straight and kept a light tone. "I was fine, Mom. No cold, no nothing."

"Mom always fusses over us when she thinks we're sick." Claudia snickered, but stopped when Laurel smacked her upper arm.

"It's because of losing Dad, you idiot."

"Okay. Sorry." Claudia studied her shoes.

"I'm sorry Mr. Laurent didn't get to experience Noelle's success and see all his daughters grow up." Annelie looked sympathetically at Reba.

"Me too." Reba looked a little sad, but in full control. "It's been more than ten years now, and I do miss him still, but I have my girls and perhaps I worry, but that's because I have to be both mother and father for them. Of course, Noelle is sometimes a parent to the younger ones too."

Claudia huffed, making everybody laugh at her funny expression.

Noelle kept studying Helena surreptitiously. Her face was pale and she looked like she had used a lot of concealer to cover up dark circles under her eyes. Part of Noelle wanted to stick out her tongue, thinking it only fair that Helena was suffering too. Another part of her wanted to find out exactly what was wrong and make it right.

"Annelie and I plan to go out to dinner after the cocktail party. I'd love for you all to join us," Carolyn said.

"Oh, the girls and I can't, but thank you for asking," Reba said. "We have an early-morning flight to catch tomorrow. We're going down to Austin to visit my parents."

"But Mom, we can still do that—" Claudia said, whining.

"No. We can't. It'll take a forklift to get the two of you out of bed in time as it is." Reba pursed her lips. "But you go ahead, Noelle. I'll have Morris on standby for when you want to go home."

"Mom, no, I'd rather—"

"Please, Noelle," Carolyn said, "it wouldn't be the same without you there."

"And you, Helena." Annelie looked quizzically at her. "Feel like joining us?"

"I really should be heading home, but I don't think you'll take no for an answer." Helena turned to Reba. "I'll make sure Noelle gets home safely."

"Thank you," Reba said. "She's a big girl, but I worry when Morris or any of the other bodyguards aren't with her."

"Understandable," Carolyn said. "So it's settled, then. When can we get out of here, Annie?"

Annelie checked her white watch. "In about twenty minutes. Let's just do a quick tour around the VIP sections of the room first. I'll have them bring the limousine up for us."

Carolyn gave Noelle a light squeeze before she let go and started mingling once more. Annelie left, and so did her mother and sisters. Standing there, so close but miles away, Noelle felt, was Helena. Noelle didn't know what to say, and she certainly didn't *want* to talk to her. She would just endure dinner, then go home and live her life. Noelle was sure she would be able to pull it off.

CHAPTER SEVENTEEN

Helena knew the restaurant Mother's Hat well. A small place with about ten tables, it offered gourmet cuisine from around the world in a luxurious setting. Two award-winning chefs, Elspeth and Vanessa, who owned and ran it, also happened to be iconic lesbians who had written several bestselling cookbooks. Key Line published them, and the authors had become good friends with Annelie and Carolyn, even catered their wedding.

"Ever been here, Noelle?" Carolyn asked as they entered the inconspicuous door that led into a room decorated mainly in green and gold.

"No, never. I didn't even know it was here. I mean, I've heard of their books, but that's it."

"Their waiting list is insane," Annelie said. "If it wasn't for our friendship and working relationship, we couldn't eat here every time we're in Manhattan."

"And we're so glad you do, Annelie." A petite woman wearing a crisp white chef's outfit stepped up to them. "Good to see you again."

"Elspeth, these are our friends, Helena Forsythe and Noelle Laurent."

"Nice to meet you, Ms. Forsythe." Elspeth lit up as she saw Noelle. "Ms. Laurent needs no further introduction, of course. I'm thrilled to have you pay us a visit, both of you. Ah, here's Vanessa, my better half." Another woman in chef's clothes appeared, and Elspeth introduced her. "And now that we all know each other, I have a surprise," Elspeth added. "I've arranged the rooftop especially for you."

"You haven't!" Carolyn exclaimed, kissing Elspeth's cheek. "I've been dying to dine up there."

"And now you will, with your friends."

Helena had no idea what they were talking about. She'd dined at Mother's Hat once before, when her mother still ran VMP, but had never heard of rooftop dining.

"Follow me. And don't worry, there's an elevator." Vanessa showed them through the kitchen over to the delivery elevator. They rode eight floors up, the elevator making worrisome squeaking sounds.

"Is it safe? It sounds like we may crash anytime." Noelle looked nervous and held the small rail.

"It's safe, and now we're here." Vanessa stepped out and held her hand up to the door sensor to keep it open. "Over to your left, ladies."

Helena stopped as she rounded a corner, staring at the beautifully set table surrounded by multicolored lights and gas heaters.

"It's a perfect evening to dine up here," Vanessa said, and showed them to their seats. "No wind, still not too cold, and a starry sky."

"It's stunning," Annelie said, sounding a bit out of breath. "I love it."

"Thank you. Your food will be up soon. I took the liberty of putting together a menu for you that I think you'll enjoy."

"Thanks, Vanessa. This is fantastic." Carolyn took a seat next to Annelie, softly kissing her cheek. "Isn't this incredibly romantic, darling?"

"Yes." Annelie returned the embrace. "What a night. I'm so proud of you. The movie will be another hit, and it's because of you and how you've inspired the rest of the cast."

Carolyn colored faintly, and Helena could tell how Annelie's appreciative words hit home. A winner of several Emmys and nominated twice for an Academy Award, Carolyn had received her share of accolades, but Helena knew she considered Maddox the role of a lifetime. Somehow, Helena suspected Annelie's praise meant far more to Carolyn than that of the movie reviewers.

Noelle slowly sat down next to Helena, moving the chair marginally away from her. Helena didn't think any of their companions noticed, but to her the small gesture, whether deliberate or not, was obvious. So was the quick stab of pain in her chest, which Helena did her best to ignore. She remembered Manon's words and how her friend had clearly disapproved of how she'd treated Noelle. *And thanks to Reba's innocent remarks about swollen eyes and working an entire night, Annelie and Carolyn have probably guessed what happened.*

Helena wanted to groan, but deep down she knew she deserved their disapproval. She had acted like an idiot, and even if she had her reasons, she still was in the wrong. Dreading the blank look from Noelle she'd received all evening, Helena braced herself before she spoke.

"Isn't this something?" Helena knew her question was almost as lame as *Do you come here often?*, but she needed to say something.

"It's beautiful." Noelle didn't give her the cold stare, at least not yet, which made her inhale a little easier.

"What did you think about the movie?"

"Hey, don't put the poor girl on the spot like that, Helena." Carolyn grinned, holding Annelie's hand between hers.

"I loved it. I forgot everything and everyone around me, and toward the end, I didn't breathe properly for the longest time."

"Me either, and I'm the producer, for heaven's sake. I've seen every single daily at least five times, and still the scenes toward the end got to me." Annelie shook her head. "After a while I stopped seeing Carolyn as the woman I love, and she was Diana Maddox, madly in love with her Erica, kissing her and making love to her all over the place—and I wasn't even jealous!"

They all laughed, and Carolyn playfully pinched Annelie's earlobe. "I'm not so sure that's flattering."

"It is. You're a great talent, but the fact that you can make me not mind you kissing someone else…that's almost scary, you know."

"Annelie." Carolyn gently kissed her wife. "It's a fantastic compliment."

"And Noelle's ballad emphasized that alluring scene when Maddox and Erica make love behind the curtains." Helena spoke fast, not wanting Noelle to interrupt.

"I was just thinking that." Carolyn nodded eagerly. "I hadn't seen that particular part with the soundtrack added. It made the scene into something so much more—well, I guess, sensuous."

"Thanks. I'm glad you think so. I love that ballad. Wish I could write something like it one day," Noelle said.

"Your songs have the potential to become just as good." Helena knew she was right. "Once you've edited them some, you'll reach people just like you did with that ballad."

"Yes, whether you have a half-naked Carolyn Black to lure people in or not," Annelie deadpanned, and for a moment the other three stared at her. "Oh, God, you should see your faces." Annelie burst into a bubbly laugh, something Helena had never heard from her until she began living with Carolyn. *Loving Carolyn certainly changed the perpetual bachelorette.* Annelie, so private and serious, had fallen for her complete opposite, the ambitious, presumably straight, Carolyn.

Helena had watched it happen from afar, and for the longest time, she'd expected them to admit they'd made a mistake. When they married nine months ago, Helena knew they were among the rare ones who truly loved each other. Fighting her unbecoming envy, she was now truly happy for them and glad they counted her as one of their friends. Helena joined the amusement—it was impossible not to—and Noelle echoed Carolyn's sexy chuckle.

A quick glance at Noelle stole all of Helena's oxygen. Noelle's eyes were nearly amber, with a golden glitter catching the reflections from the multicolored lights. Her dress was like a second skin, and Helena wondered if Noelle would get cold, despite the gas heaters. She thought she saw small shivers travel through her upper body. Stealthily, Helena took off her suit jacket and wrapped it around Noelle's shoulders.

"Helena? That's not necess—"

"Hush. You looked cold."

Helena saw that Carolyn had paid full attention to the exchange and now nodded approvingly. *They love her already.* The thought warmed Helena as she saw the obvious. Noelle had a way of getting under your skin, and she'd already done that to Carolyn, who'd seemed very protective several times during the evening.

"Thank you." Noelle sounded courteous, but there was a question in her eyes and in the way her eyebrows wrinkled and rose at the same time.

"Here we go, ladies." Vanessa arrived with the food and started placing small bowls of starter dishes on the table. "We have blankets if anyone feels cold. Are you all right, Ms. Laurent?"

"Please, call me Noelle. And yes, I'm quite warm, thank you."

Noelle tugged the lapels closer around her, inhaling deeply as she did. Helena wondered if Noelle could smell her perfume on the jacket, and, as if Noelle had read her mind, she raised her gaze, looking embarrassed.

The innocence in her eyes, coupled with her strong charisma, was like a blow to Helena's abdomen. If Noelle was merely stunningly beautiful, Helena could've tuned her out or replaced her with some other beauty in her bed. The torment Helena felt went much deeper and would be much more painful to extract. It had nothing to do with beauty and everything to do with how Noelle affected her. Helena realized she was in trouble because she actually *liked* and respected Noelle.

❖

Helena's jacket lay around her shoulders like a warm caress while Noelle ate her way through one gourmet dish after another. Vanessa and Elspeth offered different wines with every course, but Noelle declined most of them. Somehow it felt important to stay sober.

Carolyn put down her fork. "I can't eat another bite. I honestly wish I could, but it's impossible."

"I can't either." Annelie wiped her mouth on the napkin. "Maybe some coffee?"

"Sounds terrific." Helena looked regal where she sat, still chewing, looking basically unattainable in her silk shirt over an above-knee-length skirt. "When does the restaurant close?"

"Usually at midnight, I think," Annelie said.

"How about coffee at my place?" Helena asked.

"Thanks, but we're heading back to our hotel. We have a long day tomorrow with interviews and so on." Carolyn tipped her head back and sighed. "Need to get a few hours in. I'm not seventeen anymore."

"I see." Helena was clearly not offended. "Your hotel is just two blocks north of here, right?"

"True." Carolyn made a funny face and yawned discreetly. "Within walking distance, but I think I want a cab."

"Why don't you and Annelie grab one and go to your hotel. I can share with Noelle. We're practically neighbors."

Noelle nearly jumped up and screamed no, but managed not to. *A cab ride. We can do that. I can do that.* "Thank you, Helena, that's very kind."

"Anytime."

Carolyn and Annelie insisted on picking up the check, despite objections from both Helena and Noelle, and relented only when they promised to let them reciprocate soon. Vanessa rode down with them in the elevator, and Elspeth stood by the front door to say farewell. She had already called two cabs, and one of them stood by the curb.

"Carolyn, you and Annelie take the first one." Noelle motioned for the car. "Helena and I will be fine waiting for the other."

"Are you sure?" Carolyn wrapped her arms around Noelle and whispered, "Don't forget what I said. And don't sell Helena short. There's more to her than meets the eye. Try to be patient and you might just see a Helena that you thought was lost." Carolyn pulled away, replaced by Annelie, who repeated the embrace, but not the cryptic words.

Soon, only Noelle and Helena stood on the sidewalk. A few couples strolled by, but since it was a reasonably safe area with several restaurants, delis, and galleries, Noelle felt safe. When she glanced furtively at Helena, who stood in the light of a street lamp. Noelle thought she saw new lines around Helena's eyes. Had their last exchange gotten to her too? Noelle doubted it. She wanted to believe that Helena harbored some sort of feelings for her, but she'd made it pretty clear that she never entered any type of relationship for the long haul. *Perhaps I'm just too romantic, too naïve.*

"Here's our cab now." Helena raised her hand. "I'll drop you off first."

"Thank you."

They got into the backseat and Noelle gave the driver, a young Hispanic man, her address. He seemed to need to use the accelerator and brakes simultaneously. Helena reached for her seat belt, only to be tossed against Noelle during the next turn.

"Ow!" Noelle pressed a hand to her temple and held on hard to Helena so she wouldn't fall onto the floor. "Hey, you! Can you slow down?"

"Sure thing, ma'am." He slowed marginally, but they still had to cling to each other.

"Are you all right?" Noelle looked at Helena's face where she'd slammed into her shoulder.

"Yes. How about you?" Helena gently touched Noelle's temple. "I'm afraid you'll have a bruise here. I'm suing the bastard."

"No, don't worry about it. Unnecessary headlines. I've been through worse with cabdrivers, trust me."

The cabdriver must've heard them and tried to outdo the other drivers, because he made a U-turn, which sent them skidding as far as the seat belts would allow.

"God Almighty," Helena muttered. "No wonder you go by limo most of the time."

"Exactly."

They sat in unexpectedly comfortable silence until they reached Noelle's apartment. "Wait here a minute," Helena ordered the cabdriver, who looked far too young to drive at all. After insisting that she walk Noelle to her door, Helena stood there studying her hands before she raised her gaze to meet Noelle's. "I had a nice time tonight. I—I just wanted you to know that." She licked her lower lip. "I also wanted to say I'm sorry for how I treated you that morning after we—I mean, it wasn't fair to you—"

"Helena, don't. It's okay." Noelle didn't want to hear all the excuses why she was all wrong for Helena.

"No. No, it wasn't okay at all. You deserve so much more, and the sad thing is, I mean for *me*, that I'm not the one able to give you that." Helena did look distressed. In fact, unless it was a trick of the streetlights, she had tears in her eyes. She smiled tremulously and patted Noelle's arm. "Good night, Noelle. Good luck with your recording sessions."

Nothing of what Helena said made sense to Noelle. First of all, her words sounded suspiciously like a farewell, which made Noelle nearly panic. Secondly, why did Helena sound like she *wished* she could have been right for Noelle? *You felt so right to me that night. You still do.* Breathless, like struck by a nameless deity, Noelle realized the truth. *I love you. I love you, Helena Forsythe.*

"Thank you." Noelle managed by some miracle to sound casual when she responded to Helena. She took off Helena's jacket and handed it to her. "Thanks for lending this to me. You were right. I was a bit cold. So…see you around?"

"Sure. Sleep tight." The wistful sound in Helena's voice was gone and she looked her normal dynamic self as she strode back to the cab.

"Buckle up," Noelle called out after her, suddenly remembering the kamikaze driver.

"Absolutely. Go inside now." Helena waved and climbed into the cab.

Noelle stood at her door until she couldn't see it anymore.

CHAPTER EIGHTEEN

Seen the morning paper, Noelle?" Reba retied the belt of her bathrobe, her movements jerky. "Lots of stuff from the opening night."

"Uh-oh, Mom. You have that look on your face." Noelle sighed inwardly. Her mother had a foreboding way of frowning. Noelle picked up the paper from the kitchen counter and sat down to have some hot green tea. Her voice was huskier than normal, because of the cool night air from the rooftop dinner. Green tea always seemed to help.

A full spread about the celebrities attending the opening night of the Diana Maddox movie included one of her and her family. The photo byline said, NOELLE LAURENT WITH MOTHER AND SISTERS. "We look good, Mom." Noelle peered over at her mother.

"Uh-huh."

Another sign of her mother's discontent. Noelle kept turning the pages until she reached the gossip columnists' page. "What the…" A photo showed her and Helena clinging to each other in the cab, Noelle with one arm around Helena's shoulders and the other around the back of her head. "A heated embrace in a New York cab. Noelle seems to have found a new love after all." Another photo revealed them standing together by her door, Helena gazing intensely at her. "Smoldering exchange at the door. Ms. Helena Forsythe is apparently a gentlewoman, since this reporter saw her leave shortly afterward."

"Oh, God." Noelle thudded her forehead into the counter. "I was so busy holding on for dear life with that cabbie driving like a madman, I didn't even see the paparazzi."

"And you looked quite occupied while talking to Ms. Forsythe at the door too." Reba sat down next to her. "What's going on, sweetie?"

"Mom, I'm not ready to talk about this. Not yet. Trust me. Nothing is going on in any of these pictures."

"But things have been going on, haven't they?" Reba looked increasingly concerned. "That night you stayed over at her place. Noelle—"

"I'm almost thirty, Mom." Noelle clenched her jaw. "Yes, we live together here. You take care of the household most of the time, but that doesn't mean I have to report everything I do."

Reba didn't budge. "You have to set a good example for your sisters."

"I do. When have I *not*?" Noelle was angry now. Mostly at the invasion of her privacy, but also at her mother. "After almost twelve years in the spotlight with me, you should know better. The paparazzi will do anything to get a shot, even chase a taxi all over the city, endangering both me and themselves. No wonder the cabbie drove like a maniac. Helena and I nearly got a concussion. Look here." Noelle raised her hair and showed her black-and-blue temple to Reba.

"Oh, my God. I'm sorry, sweetie." Reba's eyes filled with tears. "I didn't know—"

"And you should never assume." Noelle quieted. "Mom, I'm discovering things about myself that you might have a problem with, but I haven't done anything wrong. I'm just finding out who I am, and though it's mainly through my music, it also has to do with Helena." She took a deep breath. "You can relax. She's not interested in me."

"And you wish she were?" Reba took Noelle's hand and rubbed her thumb across it.

"Yes," Noelle whispered.

"Sweetie." Reba pulled her into a fierce embrace. "She's a fool."

"Do you hate it, Mom?"

"Hate what, sweetie?" Reba pulled back, looking at her.

"I think I'm gay, Mom. Do you hate that?"

"I don't pretend to understand, but I could never hate anything about you."

"Really, I don't want to talk about it, dissect it, right now. It's still so new, and I don't understand everything." Noelle buried her face in the collar of her mother's robe. "Later, Mom, please?"

"Later is fine. I'll be here. When I saw the pictures, I called and canceled our tickets to Austin. I called Grandma and told her we'd visit in a few weeks."

"I'm so sorry, Mom. Was Grandma upset?"

"I told her the media was up in arms again. She understood."

"What's going on with Noelle?" a sleepy voice asked from the doorway. Laurel entered, dressed in an oversized T-shirt. "Something wrong?"

"Nothing's wrong," Reba said. "Help yourself to the French toast staying warm in the oven."

"Thanks, Mom." Laurel glanced sleepily at Noelle. "You don't look too happy."

"And you don't look quite awake." Noelle rose and kissed the top of her sister's head. "I'm going to my study to make a phone call. We'll talk more later, Mom." As Noelle left the kitchen, Laurel was complaining that something secret had to be going on since they wouldn't talk in front of her.

Her study, connected to her master bedroom suite, had cherrywood shelves and desk. Noelle had installed sound protection and a small music studio that hooked up to her stationary computer. She sat down and flipped through her contacts on her cell phone. Finding Mike's number, she hesitated only briefly before she pressed the Talk button. *Please, be there. Please.*

"Noelle! Hi. How are you?"

"Hello, Mike. Am I calling at a bad time?"

"Not at all. I'm walking to my Saturday shift at my coffeehouse right now."

Noelle knew of Mike's popular coffeehouse, the Sea Stone Café, but hadn't realized that Mike still actually worked there.

"Do you get a New York morning paper up there?"

"We do, but I haven't had time to look at it yet. I normally read some of it to Vivian."

"I see." Noelle pulled her legs up underneath her and pressed the phone closer to her ear. "There were some paparazzi pictures of Helena and me today, taken in a way that makes it look like we're… like we're…" Tears began to stream down her cheeks. "She's going to hate me, Mike."

"Hey, hold on. What's happened? Tell me everything."

"We made love last week, just one night, and she regrets the whole thing, and last night, she...she sort of said good-bye, or that's how it felt, and now with these stupid pictures, she's going to regret ever knowing me."

"Oh, Noelle, seems like a lot has happened since the Hamptons. Please, don't cry. I've got plenty of time to listen to the whole thing. Right now you're not making much sense." Mike's warm voice made it nearly impossible for Noelle to stop crying, but she forced herself to swallow her tears and try again. She told Mike about Helena kissing her at her house in the Hamptons, how Helena found her in Central Park, and that they'd made love the entire night. Noelle cried quietly as she recounted the way Helena brushed her off the next morning.

"And last night, you felt she was rejecting you once and for all. How did she seem?"

"Sad, in a strange way. She kept saying it was *her* loss. Carolyn Black said I should give Helena another chance to show her true self. Was that what she did last night, do you think, Mike? By pulling back altogether?"

"I don't presume to know Helena as well as Manon does," Mike said, her voice gentle. "In a sense, Helena's this larger-than-life person who's continued her mother's legacy and broken new ground in the media world. I don't think either of us can understand all the hard work and responsibility that come with her position."

"So I just have to fumble in the dark here? Or should I cut and run like her?"

"I'm not saying that. If you did, you'd always wonder." Mike sounded infinitely sympathetic. "You know, I went through a similar thing with Vivian. She was so certain that her going blind was something insurmountable, something she'd have to deal with on her own, she was prepared to withdraw from humanity altogether at one point."

"But you managed to convince her."

"I was scared, but love found a way. That and the fact that we both dared to finally take the leap. I think *honesty* was the key. We ultimately could be completely honest with each other, and by that I mean we told each other just how much we loved and cared."

"Are you telling me I should ask Helena if she loves me?" Noelle had never dared to think about the word *love* and Helena's name in the same sentence, and the prospect made her dizzy.

"No, not at all. I'm suggesting you examine your own feelings. What you feel for Helena, why she confuses you. Are you prepared to ignore your pride and fear of losing face, not to mention the professional ramifications? I'm aware Helena and you have a business agreement, as she does with us, but if you ask me, you'll never be able to move beyond this point unless you bring what's between you out into the light and examine it."

"I'm not sure it's a matter of pride. I'm not even sure it's fear of rejection. Or maybe it is. I'm not used to letting my guard down." *And I only realized I love her last night.* Noelle couldn't bring herself to tell Mike, no matter how good a friend she was becoming.

"That's my point. Only when I did let my guard down, told Vivian everything about my sordid past, did I help create the basis for a relationship. You can't just stick to your guns and hope that some divine force will wield its wand and resolve things. There's always a risk, Noelle. Only you can decide if it's worth it." Mike's kindness made Noelle realize just what an unusual treat it was to have someone dependable tell her the truth. No sucking up to the mega-celebrity. Mike had no personal agenda, merely tons of experience from her relationship with Vivian.

"Thank you. I sure needed a voice of reason." Noelle attempted a smile, but felt herself grimace.

"Voice of reason? And you called me?" Mike chuckled. "No joking, I did tell you to call whenever you want. I'd never share what you tell me with anyone."

"I know that, and I appreciate it, Mike." Noelle was quiet for a moment. "I'll think about what you said. Maybe you're right. Not being candid with Helena might be the biggest mistake. It's just such a daunting thing, you know, to bare it all."

"It's up to you."

"I'm trying so hard to make my music authentic, I'd be a hypocrite not to do the same with someone I care about, right?"

"Yeah, well, when you put it that way. I wouldn't call you a hypocrite, though. You're being far too hard on yourself," Mike said gently. "Been there, done that."

"I'd like to hear more about that, and about you, when we have a chance." Noelle hadn't had a close friend in a long time. Mike's offer to be one was a true gift. *I've been all work and no play for more than a decade.* "Mike, thank you for talking to me. I really needed a friend, and I won't forget how you've treated me."

"As I said, anytime, Noelle."

After they said good-bye and hung up, Noelle kept her cell phone tight in her hand for several minutes. Mike had a point, but the thought of facing Helena, especially after the whole paparazzi mess in the gossip columns, was beyond intimidating. The fact that Helena had also sounded so final didn't exactly encourage Noelle to seek her out.

Helena usually started her Saturdays cooking breakfast. Having Mrs. Baines in her house in the Hamptons spoiled her in many ways, but cooking had become quite a pleasure. She rarely ate lunch or dinner at home in the city, but her breakfasts were sacred. Today she lacked both the urge to cook and the appetite to eat, so she made a pot of Darjeeling tea and two slices of toast with apricot marmalade. Then she grabbed the morning paper and headed off to the couch instead of the kitchen table, curled up, and turned on the TV above the fireplace. *The Today Show* was on, but she paid it little attention as she started to read.

There seemed to be a bit of a news drought, and once she reached the entertainment section, Helena was bored with the recycled news. She nodded approvingly when a well-known reviewer gave one of her new classical artists a nod. Turning the page, she began to read about the Maddox movie's opening night. She recognized most people in the "who's who" among the celebrities attending the movie theater. The picture of Noelle and her family kept her interest for several minutes, and before she realized what she was doing, she'd traced the outline of Noelle's jaw. Yanking her hand back, she quickly turned to a page where a columnist had received a full spread with "news" that was actually gossip. Noelle's name glared at her, and when Helena suddenly saw a grainy, but unfortunately clear enough picture of herself and Noelle in a cab, she felt sick at her stomach.

She and Noelle seemed to be locked in a passionate embrace, when they were really holding on to each other so they wouldn't fall onto the floor. The second picture, which was much better quality, showed her looking up at Noelle with a smoldering expression. Helena tossed her head against the backrest and groaned. *This isn't happening. God, she must be even more fed up with me. Furious.* Helena was steaming. The paparazzi had gone too far. Again. Usually, when a person wanted to break into the entertainment business, the paparazzi might be helpful. But when someone was an established celebrity, the paparazzi too often turned to locusts that disregarded the sanctity of private life.

Helena squinted at the picture, trying to gauge Noelle's expression. She looked sad and confused. *I've done nothing but treat this woman like…like I've treated every woman since college.* Shuddering, Helena recalled Noelle's face the morning after their passionate, wonderful lovemaking. Before Helena had shot her down with her casual behavior, Noelle had stared at her like she was everything. Her eyes had radiated a sort of shy happiness that had sent Helena into full reverse. *And I sure rained on her parade.* Helena tossed the newspaper away. She couldn't bear to look at Noelle anymore. And still she would have to, soon. They needed to discuss potential fallout from this gossip.

The sudden ringing of her cell phone made Helena jump. She fumbled for it in her robe pocket and saw Noelle's name on the screen. Her mouth instantly dry, she answered.

"Helena here. What can I do for you, Noelle?"

"Seen the morning paper yet?" Noelle said, clearly not about to aim for small talk.

"I have."

"I'm sorry, Helena."

Was there a small catch in Noelle's voice? Helena rubbed the back of her neck. "Not your fault, Noelle. Those leeches just won't quit. I've never been much of a target before, but surely you know they'll invade your privacy without a second thought."

"Yes. I've dealt with them for a long time. I've just never risked anyone else's reputation." Noelle sighed. "And as if things aren't strained between us as it is."

"I'm sorry. That's my fault." Helena's cheeks burned.

"I just don't know what I did wrong." Noelle's voice sounded unusually small. "Guess I'm not cut out for casual one-night stands."

It was obvious to Helena that Noelle was trying for some gallows humor. As flat as the joke fell, the attempt spoke volumes. She was trying to make Helena feel less self-conscious. *Why would she do that, when she could blame me for being a total bitch?*

The answer to the question was such a far reach, Helena quickly backtracked in her mind. She spoke hastily, before she had a chance to second-guess herself.

"Can we meet to discuss this? Please?"

"Um…Sure. Where?"

"Would you be uncomfortable coming to my penthouse?" Helena instantly regretted her invitation, but couldn't think of another private place. The office was never empty and Noelle's condo housed her family, making it far too crowded.

"I suppose that'd be fine." Noelle spoke slowly, as if judging the potential risk while she spoke. "When do you want me there?"

Helena gasped inaudibly at the double entendre, wondering if Noelle had chosen her words deliberately. "Half an hour, an hour?"

"All right." The tremor in Noelle's voice betrayed her nerves. Helena took some comfort in the thought that she wasn't the only one with her heart tearing around in her throat.

"See you then." Disconnecting, Helena opened the paper again. She looked at the way Noelle was cradling her in the cab, trying to keep Helena from banging her head against the window. Noelle's unreadable expression reminded her of the rare tenderness her mother could show her. All-protective and strong. Helena ran a hand over her face. She needed to take a quick shower and get dressed before Noelle arrived. The urgency in Noelle's voice told Helena she would be there in thirty minutes rather than an hour.

CHAPTER NINETEEN

Her heart pounding, Noelle rode the elevator up to Helena's penthouse. As she clutched the shoulder strap of her favorite Prada bag, she thought back to the brief phone call. It had taken every ounce of her courage to call, and she had tried to determine Helena's mood by the sound of her voice. It was impossible, and Noelle suspected that Helena was a master of concealing her emotions because of her position in the business world. Was it possible to ever get close to such a guarded woman?

The elevator stopped and Noelle stepped out onto a small landing where one door led to Helena's penthouse and the other to her neighbor's. Preparing to knock, Noelle jumped when Helena's door suddenly opened.

"Hello. Doorman told me you were on your way up." Helena was dressed in her trademark chinos and a short-sleeved button-down shirt. Her hair was slightly damp, forming waves rather than arranged in its usual perfectly coiffed style. Noelle wanted to run her fingers through it, but entered the penthouse with more confidence than she felt.

"Hi." She stopped by a chair next to a full-length antique mirror and took off her Diesel jacket. "So...all right if I put it here?" She placed her jacket and bag on the chair, trying her best to look casual.

"Sure. Can I get you something to drink?"

"Oh. Some ice water, please?"

"Coming right up." Helena hurried into the kitchen. "Make yourself comfortable on the couch," she said over her shoulder.

The cushions engulfed her like an embrace. The room was bright with the light streaming through the windows. Sitting there alone, Noelle couldn't suppress the memories of their night together. Her breasts responded, and she squeezed her legs, trying to prevent any more reactions.

"Here you go." Helena joined her, placed a tray on the coffee table, and sat in the leather armchair. She had made herself some tea, and Noelle took a deep gulp of water, feeling parched, probably from an onset of nerves. Putting the glass back, she noticed the offending newspaper on the coffee table next to the tray.

"I didn't spot the paparazzi. Guess that cabdriver did and that's why he drove like a madman."

"My thoughts exactly."

"So you didn't see them either, huh?" Noelle couldn't judge what Helena was thinking. She was sipping her tea and seemed to hide behind the large mug.

"No. I was busy holding on to you, to keep you from hitting your head again—oh, my God." Helena suddenly put the mug down and joined Noelle on the couch. She lifted a thick tress of Noelle's hair and examined the bruise on her temple. "Oh, honey, does it hurt?"

Noelle had tried to cover up the bruise, but knew it was visible if you looked closely enough. "No, it's not too bad."

"I didn't know you were hurt this severely." Helena gently touched the bruise with her fingertips.

"What about you?"

"I'm sore, but no bruises."

"Oh, good." Noelle didn't know what to do with her hands. She just wanted to wrap her arms around Helena and hide her face in the soft, smooth skin of her neck. Trembling, she tried to appear encouraging. "Well, as long as you're all right."

"I am, but you're not." Helena's usually steady gray eyes were dark with concern. "And I worry about your reputation."

"What?" Noelle tried to follow Helena's reasoning, but failed. "What about my reputation?"

"They're suggesting you're having a lesbian love affair." Helena spoke slowly. "With a much older woman."

"In the past, I've had the press pair me off with at least twenty guys, if not more, and that did hurt my reputation. Some people think I'm a slut and a man eater. Some even think I'm connected to organized crime since the press insisted I was dating that rapper who went to prison. None of it's true. The guys I actually dated were never interesting enough for the tabloids."

"I understand. I do. But this is different."

"Like Lindsay Lohan different?" Noelle sighed. "You mean, because they've paired me off with a woman, with you, that will hurt my career more?"

"It might."

"Same goes for you, in that case."

"I'm not a household name, and besides, my being gay is no secret even if I don't broadcast it from the rooftops." Helena took Noelle's hand, looking pleadingly at her. "This isn't about me. Trust me, I'm fine. Neither the article nor the photos have hurt me, but you're breaking new ground, musically speaking, and you need to bring as many of your fans with you as possible. If being connected with a woman happens at the same time, you may lose some listeners. People aren't as tolerant as we'd like them to be, Noelle."

"I know. I'm not as naïve as you seem to think." Noelle's anger rose, born out of frustration since they were discussing only what was best outwardly for her...Was Helena talking about what was best for her or for VMP? She talked about bringing fans with her when she introduced her new type of music. What else could that be about if not money? Noelle freed her hand and stared intently at Helena. "What do you really mean, Helena? Are you concerned for me, personally, or are you worried this could hurt your business?"

"Noelle! Of course I worry about you first." Helena flinched. "I know I've been acting, well, like a bull in a china shop, to be blunt, and you deserved something better after our night together. I'm not proud of myself. That said, I'm naturally concerned that one of my biggest stars might run into trouble."

"Like I thought." Noelle's stomach began to hurt. "Money. That's what it always boils down to, isn't it? I came here concerned for you, worried how this would affect you, *us*, but I could have saved my time and breath, couldn't I? You're already over it." Noelle wasn't sure if she meant their night together or the photos in the paper. "You don't need me."

Helena clasped her hands on her lap. "It's not true."

Noelle blinked. *Which part?*

"It's not true that I don't need you." Helena gestured vaguely with one hand before she laced them tight again.

"I don't believe you." Noelle looked down at Helena's hands. Why was she so white-knuckled?

"I don't blame you."

Noelle took a deep breath. She was letting her frustration get the better of her. "So we just ignore this? Or are you saying I should allow my agent to hook me up with one of the guys he lines up for me every time I have to make an appearance?" Noelle nearly startled herself when she heard the venom and pain in her own voice.

"Noelle. No." Helena held Noelle's arms gently. "I'd never suggest anything like that. Who you allow to escort you, or date, is up to you. I just don't want you to worry that today's pictures will have any impact on me personally. I really don't care about that. I do care what happens to you. I know you regret that night, but—"

"What?" Noelle could hardly believe her ears.

"It couldn't have been very romantic for you." Helena stroked Noelle's arms with slow movements. "And I'm sorry about that."

"What are you talking about?" Noelle's thoughts were racing now.

"About the night we made love."

"You didn't find it romantic?"

"I..." Helena faltered, clearly taken aback. "I meant, for you. Your first time with a woman and everything." She let go of Noelle's arms, but before she could move her hands, Noelle took them in hers, needing to know the truth.

"What was it like for you?" She didn't take her eyes off Helena and kept her hold.

"It...It was wonderful." The words left Helena's lips like they were painful to say.

"It was wonderful for me too. I loved how you made me feel. And you said it just now. We were making love. You could've chosen other words, like 'having sex,' or 'slept together,' or something like that. You said we made love. And that's what I felt we were doing."

Slowly, Helena relaxed. "You're right," she whispered. Clearing her throat, she continued in a normal voice. "You're right. It was special. Very special. That scared the living daylights out of me because I'm not used to it. I haven't been with anyone in a very long time, Noelle, and when I made love to you, well, I was overwhelmed and I reacted badly afterward."

"You panicked." It wasn't a question. Noelle knew it was true.

"Yes." Helena pressed her lips together. "Which I'm not prone to do either."

"Oh, I know that." Noelle tried to sort all this new information. "I guess I don't have to tell you that I was shocked at the difference in the way you acted the next morning. I was sure I had done something wrong or been such a lousy lover you just couldn't get rid of me fast enough."

"Oh, God, Noelle. It was exactly the opposite." Helena slid up to Noelle and cupped her cheeks with both hands. Her eyes fell on the bruise on Noelle's temple. "I just can't bear that you got bruised so badly last night. I wish I'd known how hard you hit your head. I would've gone up in the elevator with you."

"I'm fine." Helena's nearness was making Noelle's head spin. "Maybe you shouldn't sit so close."

"What?" Helena looked bewildered.

"You're making me dizzy."

"I'm making you—oh." Helena didn't back off. Instead, she placed her arm around Noelle's shoulders. "Why don't you relax a little? I know we both have tons of questions to answer, from both sides, but I'd really like to just sit here for a little while."

Noelle thought Helena was crazy at first, talking about unwinding when her entire body was aflame. Eventually, she did let go against Helena's shoulder. Finally closing her eyes, Noelle inhaled Helena's scent of soap and faint musk, so familiar by now. Unable to resist, Noelle buried her face in the softness of Helena's neck, sighing in contentment. Helena held her close with her arm still around Noelle's shoulders.

"There. Just kick back," Helena whispered in Noelle's ear. "Let's just be quiet."

"All right," Noelle replied against Helena's neck. She was tempted to kiss the silky skin, but she didn't. She was so comfortable right now, and it felt right being here, being this close and finding strength in Helena's closeness. Noelle closed her eyes, hummed almost inaudibly, and within minutes she dozed off.

❖

Helena wasn't sure holding Noelle as she slept was the smartest thing she could've done, but it was definitely the most tender moment she'd ever experienced. Had Dorcas had ever held her like this? Though she recalled herself at age four or five years, she had no memory of ever sitting on her mother's lap or falling asleep against her.

Looking down at the curled-up Noelle, Helena wanted suddenly to weep, but pressed her tongue firmly to the roof of her mouth, a technique that had proved useful many times.

"You didn't find it romantic?" Noelle's sexy voice reverberated within Helena, and even if she'd tried to answer as truthfully as possible, she still couldn't confess so many things to Noelle. Yes, it had been a most romantic, wonderful night, and she had devoured Noelle in more ways than one, probably because she thought this would be their only night together. *Did part of me want more nights? More of that all-consuming passion?*

Helena closed her eyes briefly and didn't groan only because she didn't want to disturb Noelle's sleep. She wasn't cut out for this. *Love 'em and leave 'em.* Helena shuddered. That method of operation had worked so well, ever since college. After the fiasco with Ms. Johnson during her freshman year, she had vowed to never put her heart on the line like that again, and soon the actions that her wounded heart adopted became a lifelong habit.

Did I ever realize I would never gain anything but loneliness? Noelle stirred and wrapped an arm around Helena's waist. *I simply can't bear to hurt her anymore.* Helena had most likely hurt several women with her rules over the years, but she tried to always seek out her peers, the ones with similar rules. Occasionally, though, she'd come across someone who wanted a commitment, which Helena had never been even close to giving.

What about Noelle turned everything on its head? Helena stealthily pressed her lips to Noelle's hair and kissed the outrageously white-blond strands several times.

After fifteen minutes, Helena's arm was painfully asleep and she woke up Noelle as she moved it.

"Oh, I'm so sorry. Your poor arm. Here. Let me." She massaged it, despite Helena's protests.

"You don't have to." Noelle's touch reverberated throughout Helena's entire system. "I'm fine, Noelle."

Noelle kept massaging a minute more, then slumped against the backrest. "How long did I sleep? Half an hour?"

"Not even that. Maybe fifteen minutes." Helena tried to control her breathing.

"I see."

"Feeling better?"

"Yes. A little less confused."

"So what are you thinking now?" Helena tucked an errant strand of hair behind Noelle's ear.

"That you're right. Let's just ignore the paparazzi and move on."

"What do you mean by 'move on'?"

"Just what I said." Noelle gestured emphatically. "Move on. Live our lives the way we planned, the way we want."

"Good point. You're right."

"I'm just not quite sure how to handle it, if moving on means never being able to sit like this again." Noelle studied her laced-together fingers. "You know? This part of it."

Helena wanted to cry or howl at the moon and let all her frustration out. "I—I know." She was desperate to find a way for Noelle to not look at her that way, with those soulful, pleading eyes. "We should focus on your music, your new songs, first. Have them orchestrated." Noelle seemed surprised as Helena changed the subject deliberately. "Your songs are beautiful and we need someone who can do them justice. David and his crew will know."

Noelle looked like she wanted to object, either to David still being the producer or to the change of direction their conversation took. "They weren't very motivated last time," she said. "In fact, they bordered on being condescending."

"They were following the terms of the contract."

"And being condescending is in the fine print?" Noelle's eyes, no longer soft or pleading, shot sparkles, virtually singeing Helena's skin. "You want me to put my trust, and my music, in their hands?"

"They're professionals. They might not be very sensitive, but they know what they're doing."

"I can tell you haven't worked with them up close and personal."

"Why are you acting this way all of a sudden?" Helena squinted as a headache began in her temples. "I thought we had a deal."

"We did. You and I. In my naïveté, I thought I would get a whole new set of producers, someone with a fresh view of my music. Not this gang of three who've only done dance and pop music, as far as I know."

"Noelle—"

"I wish you wouldn't sound like that." Noelle folded her arms across her chest. "I wish you'd give me some credit that I know what I'm talking about, that I've gathered a lot of experience over the last decade. Or are you like so many of the other people I run into in this business, convinced that I'm just a pretty face, unable to fend for myself?"

"Of course not!"

"From where I'm standing, that's how it looks."

"You're angry. That colors your judgment. I'm not quite sure why you're this furious all of a sudden, but I'm starting to realize why David and the others thought you've become more difficult to work with." Helena wanted to take the words back as soon as they left her lips. Granted, she was angry too now, but their frustration over personal matters fueled their irritation. Noelle had a point when it came to David and his crew. They were brilliant in their genre, but hadn't quite proved themselves when it came to singer/songwriters. The fact that Noelle had thought them condescending worried her. If Helena had learned anything, it was that singer/songwriters, which Noelle was developing into, had to be handled with finesse.

"I'm sorry you see me that way. I don't see how we can gain anything from continuing this conversation." Rigid, Noelle began to rise from the couch.

"Wait. Please." Helena took Noelle's hand. "This is insane. I don't think that of you. That was my anger talking. Please, don't go."

"Give me one reason." Noelle slowly sat back down. "You don't want me. You don't particularly like me, and you seem to think I'm more trouble than I'm worth, professionally."

"Stop." Helena's mind whirled. She couldn't blame Noelle for coming to several of those conclusions. "Listen to me. I do like you. I like you very much. You're the most extraordinary young woman I've ever met, and I'm not talking about your beauty, which is obvious. I mean your talent, your kindness, your unspoiled nature. Don't you think I didn't notice how you carried luggage with Mike, how friendly you treated Mrs. Baines, or how you were sweet to your spoiled little sisters and how you respect your mother, even if you're the breadwinner?"

Noelle looked surprised, her lips parting in a small *O*.

"And yes, I have entertained the idea that your desire to break into a new genre, to become a singer/songwriter, is more trouble than it's worth, but ultimately it shows growth and courage, where stagnation would have been easy money. I'd be dumb not to admire you."

"Really, Helena? You do?" Noelle covered her mouth with a trembling hand, her eyes suspiciously shiny.

"And while I'm confessing, yes, I do want you. Not a day goes by when you're not on my mind, and if you think it's easy to sit here with you on this couch and keep my hands off you, then you *are* a fool. But I'm not right for you. You're better off without me complicating things for you. I'm definitely not relationship material. I never have been. But you'll make a man or a woman very happy once you fall in love."

"Oh." Noelle flinched. "So you're not going to even give me a chance, are you?"

"A chance to do what?"

"You're making this decision for both of us, without letting me show you how wrong you are."

"I'm wrong about you?"

"No. About you."

"What do you mean—Noelle…" Helena gasped and tried to back away when Noelle gently grasped her shoulders and held her close. Cupping the back of Helena's neck, she massaged the tense muscles with long fingers. "Noelle, don't."

"Don't what?"

"Don't touch me." Helena spoke in spite of the pain in her throat. The feeling of Noelle's fingers against her skin and in her hair made her scalp tingle.

"All right." Noelle's fingers stilled and she captured Helena's lips. Noelle kissed her softly, with hardly any intrusion but with an insistence that completely shook Helena. Helena moaned, and Noelle seemed to take that as permission to slip her tongue inside Helena's mouth and caress its counterpart repeatedly.

Helena whimpered now, overcome with desire and her body on erotic red alert. She cupped one of Noelle's breasts, not surprised to find her nipple as hard as a stone through several layers of clothing. Helena caressed Noelle in slow circles, reveling in the touch as she pressed closer. The sweetness of her lips and the seductive scent of something entirely Noelle broke down Helena's defenses.

"Yes. You do want me." Noelle kissed a hot trail down Helena's neck. "And I don't think you can mistake how I feel. I can't stop thinking about you either. You doubt me and don't think I can judge if I'm gay, but I can. I'm as certain as it's humanly possible to be. This is right for me. This is who I've been all along. I just didn't know. It took meeting you, kissing you, to make me understand. That should tell you something."

It did. Helena knew that even if she had awakened Noelle and helped her realize she was sexually interested in women, she was not necessarily the one Noelle would fall in love with. Everything was new and wonderful for Noelle right now, but when that wore off she would see Helena in another light. Sobering from the onslaught of emotions, Helena took Noelle's face in her hands and kissed her gently.

"Honey, I'll hate myself in a little while for saying this, but we have to stop."

"Helena?" Noelle's glittering eyes, dark with passion, looked confused.

"We can't make love. It wouldn't be fair to you, and it would be very hard for me."

"I don't understand."

"You will, I promise." Helena smoothed Noelle's hair back. "You have songs to record, and you need to be able to focus solely on that. I'll send the producers my final PM regarding my decision on how many songs of each genre I'm sanctioning. They'll get it Monday and will be ready to start working with you on that project when you're up for studio time."

"So this is it? You won't give me a chance to prove you wrong." Noelle withdrew, and the void she left behind was tangible.

"I'm not wrong. I have a lifetime of experience with myself, which .

is proof enough." Helena smiled joylessly. "Go and record beautiful songs, no matter the genre, Noelle."

Noelle rose, and this time Helena didn't stop her. She watched Noelle gather her things and leave the penthouse without saying good-bye. The condo had never felt emptier, and Helena curled up on the couch, tugging a small pillow close to her chest. She closed her eyes, forcing herself to breathe evenly as she tried to convince herself that she'd done the only possible thing. The right thing.

Helena squeezed the pillow closer, running through her options repeatedly. Perhaps it was a big mistake to allow Noelle to record the deeply personal songs. What if her fans recoiled rather than took them to their hearts? And the press…those damn paparazzi. It wouldn't be far-fetched for them to connect the dots between some of Noelle's lyrics and the pictures in the newspaper. Revealing herself through her lyrics might make Noelle too vulnerable and a target for cheap shots from the usual stand-up comedy crowd. Noelle was courageous enough to brave all of it, but it might harm her and her career.

"So, I did the right thing to let her walk out of here." The echoing loneliness contradicted her. Helena dug her teeth into the pillow. It might have been the right thing to do, but it certainly felt wrong. Now she would have to decide whether to sanction the recording of Noelle's own songs—or not.

CHAPTER TWENTY

Noelle pushed her cell phone closer to her ear as she strode to the elevator in her building with Morris in tow, trying to understand what Brad Haley was raving about. Noelle had never heard her agent raise his voice until it actually cracked.

"For the love of God, Noelle, what were you thinking? A simple denial probably won't matter in the long run, but it would be a start."

"Denying what?" Noelle wanted him to say it out loud as anger simmered under her skin.

"You have to deny this damn gay rumor, of course." Brad sounded completely exasperated. "I don't know what that Forsythe woman thought she was doing, but it's hit the tabloids and all hell's broken loose here."

"God."

"Exactly. I've prepared a statement—"

"No."

"What?" Brad spat.

"I said no. You don't talk for me, and you don't put words in my mouth. If I decide to speak to the press, I will, but you don't say anything I haven't agreed to."

"Noelle, you're a sweet kid, but—"

Noelle exited the elevator, but stopped just outside it. "Listen to me, Brad. I'm not a kid, and you work for *me*. I've told you before, if you don't show appropriate loyalty or act with my best interest at heart, you don't work for me at all."

"Noelle! How can you say that? I *am* acting in your best interest. That's exactly what I'm doing. You obviously haven't seen the message boards online or the commentaries in the papers from everybody and their damn dog. Mothers of teenage girls, the conservatives, Christians—you name them. They all have an opinion and, trust me, it'll affect sales."

"So this is about money."

"It's about your career. Your livelihood and your future. Until now, everybody has connected you with hot studs or even clean-cut mama's boys. *Now* you're in league with Lindsay Lohan and Jodie Foster. People will always wonder." Brad suddenly stopped talking as if something had hit him. "You would've told me if you were a lesbian from the get-go, wouldn't you?"

"Why would I even discuss my sexuality with you in the first place?" Noelle asked, incredulous. "You're out of line, Brad."

"You'll regret it if you don't listen to me now." Brad raised his voice. "You're my favorite client and I have devoted practically all my time to your account, letting my partners deal with our other stars. Please tell me I haven't been wasting my time."

"I'm beginning to think I'm wasting my money." Noelle was fuming. "And now *you* listen, Brad. My personal relationships, whether they may be with men or women, are none of your damn business. Your job, what I pay you top dollar for, is to look out for me in contractual situations, help promote my work, and make sure no record company, commercial director, or TV company rips me off. What you don't do is call me, lecture me, and treat me as if I were five years old. Do what I keep you around for and don't even bring up the other issues, or I'll start interviewing new, more modern-thinking agents."

The silence at the other end spoke volumes. Noelle figured Brad was probably gnawing off his lower lip or perhaps his mustache.

"All right," Brad said, finally. "We'll lay low for now and see if this media frenzy burns out on its own." It was pretty obvious he didn't think it would. "If you aren't ready to deal with it, don't watch E! or any of the celebrity gossip programs tonight."

"It might come as news to you, but I never do." Noelle spoke the truth. She had learned early in her career that they only sidetracked and upset her in a game she could never truly win, since the reporters always had the last word no matter what. She played possum and just ignored tabloids and any gossip online or on TV. Until now. This time she was freaked out because of Helena. *Wonder if they're going after her too or if she's just an excuse for them to write about me?* "Okay, Brad. We'll touch base later. Bye."

Noelle nodded at Morris, who stood next to her, waiting for her instructions. "See you this afternoon, around four?"

"Sure thing, Noelle."

She waved to him as he left. Her penthouse was quiet and the thin linen window treatments dimmed the light. The air-conditioning made it nice and cool, which felt wonderful after the heated argument. Though she knew better, she flipped on the large TV in the media room and surfed a few channels. After about ten of them, she'd seen the slightly grainy pictures of her and Helena twice. The comments ranged from "Noelle and her May-December love affair" to "Why has Noelle Laurent kept her true identity a secret from her fans?" to "Is this a photo manip?" Noelle groaned and turned off the TV. Tossing the remote on the couch, she stomped into her room, still reeling from her confrontation with Brad and the emotional exchange with Helena.

Noelle sank down on her bed, suddenly bone tired. *If I live two hundred years, I'll never figure that woman out.* Helena was hot and cold, stubborn and compliant, kind and stern, and most of all, she was apparently less affected by Noelle than Noelle was by her.

What would happen if I told her I love her? Noelle snorted. Helena would declare her incompetent to judge her own feelings, because obviously, according to her, you were supposed to own some sort of gayness badge that entitled you to certain feelings. But Noelle loved Helena, despite how infuriating and overbearing she could be.

Noelle wanted nothing but to call Helena now and tell her everything that was going on, but Helena's dismissive attitude when they parted made it impossible. Noelle's first experiences of unrequited love in her teens couldn't compare to the agony of her yearning for Helena. She longed for Helena's touch, her attention, and the way she looked at Noelle as if she was her reason for living.

Noelle sat up, frowning. When had Helena looked at her that way? It was such a vivid memory, surely it couldn't be her imagination? Helena's eyes were beautiful, and normally so calm, even distant. How could they suddenly become so warm, so voracious, when they rested on Noelle? That they had on so many occasions was puzzling. Helena kept saying she wasn't relationship material, almost like a mantra. Was it possible to reach that part of Helena she occasionally glimpsed, the part that let her in and allowed Noelle to feel the depth and range of Helena's emotions?

❖

"Forsythe." Helena answered absentmindedly as her phone rang. Her home office was scattered with papers and folders, and the list of unread e-mails scrolled by forever on her laptop screen.

"Ms. Forsythe, this is Wanda. I hate to bother you on a weekend, but I've just talked to Gus Wilder, who's minding the office. He and his staff have been inundated with calls today. Papers, magazines, network news desks, e-zines, you name it, they want to ask questions about Noelle Laurent and…and you, Ms. Forsythe. The pictures in the paper today? They're all over the Internet and the bloggers are having a field day, I'm afraid."

"God damn it." Helena closed her eyes and stretched far back in her chair. "You've got to be kidding me."

"Ma'am?"

"Sorry, not you, Wanda. What's the bottom line here? Do I need to make a statement?"

"Honestly, I don't think that matters at this point." Wanda sighed. "They're eating this piece of news, if you can call it that, with a huge spoon and sugar on top. And to be brutally honest, it's not you they're interested in. It's Noelle Laurent."

Helena knew how vicious and persistent the press could be once they smelled blood. They milked every drop from any hint of a scandal or rumor, and this was huge in their eyes. Noelle Laurent, the brightest star on the pop sky, potentially gay?

"Thank you, Wanda. I'll be in the office within an hour."

"Thank you, ma'am. I'll meet you there."

Hanging up, Helena slammed a fist onto the desk so hard her arm hurt all the way up to her elbow. Ignoring the pain, she stalked to her bathroom. The mirror reflected the image of a woman with thin, pressed-together lips, stormy eyes, and a pale complexion. Helena dismissed her own glare and headed for the shower. Switching back and forth between icy cold and scorching hot, she felt her body and spirits come alive. The method never failed, and yanking on her favorite power suit, chocolate brown with a cream silk shirt, Helena felt ready to deal with anything. It was high time to go do damage control.

❖

"Mom, listen to me. It's nobody's business. I'm not going to comment, and I'm not going to deny it." Noelle gestured emphatically toward her mother, who was preparing dinner. "I thought you were more broadminded than this."

"I'm not asking you to comment to the press, though if you decided to, there are enough members of that 'noble profession' down on the street to choose from." Reba turned around and placed one hand on her hip. "I just want you to talk to me. I know, I know, you're not a kid anymore, but I'm your mother. You can be honest with me. As for broadminded, you know I have no problem with people's sexual orientation."

"Yes, but talking about it with you, when I'm trying to figure things out for myself, it feels like...too soon. Premature." Noelle pushed her hands into the pockets of her hoodie. "Honestly."

"Are you in love with Helena Forsythe?" True to form, Reba cut to the heart of the matter while regarding her with a mixture of tenderness and pain.

Tears welled up in Noelle's eyes and she wiped hastily at them. She didn't want to cry in front of her mother. She hadn't done that more than once or twice since her father died. "It really is a moot point."

"How could it be?" Reba strode over to her and cupped Noelle's cheeks. "How can it be a moot point when it's tearing you apart? Don't you think I know my own child? My firstborn?"

"Mom." Noelle relaxed into her mother's touch for a moment, then straightened up. "I do love her. I'm not sure how it happened, or what I can do, since she clearly doesn't love me back. Or won't allow herself to. I just don't know." She managed to speak without her voice failing.

"Oh, darling. Nothing hurts more than loving someone who doesn't show any love in return."

"You don't understand." Noelle gazed at her mother intently. "Helena shows a lot of love, tons of affection. But when it comes to words, she clams up and backs off."

"She's afraid? Or is she thinking of you, your career?"

"All of the above."

"I see." Reba hugged Noelle and rubbed her back. "You are in a jam, aren't you, sweetie?"

"Big one, it feels like."

"So what do you plan to do?"

"Well," Noelle said slowly as she thought out loud, "what I set out to do from the beginning. Write more songs, record the best of them with some of the pop songs, and go on with my life. Helena isn't prepared to let her guard down, and I sure as hell don't know what I can do about it."

"Don't be bitter." Reba caught Noelle's chin with two fingers, making her meet her gaze. "I can hear it in your voice, and if you let that fester, you'll regret it later. Bitterness is an ugly emotion, however human, and it's like a leech. It attaches itself, drinks your blood, depletes you."

The analogy was accurate, but it was hard not to slip into self-pity. Only Noelle's strong dislike for this type of self-indulgence made it possible not to. "All right, Mom. Point taken." She relaxed into her mother's soft frame again. "You sure you don't disapprove? It seems too easy, somehow."

"What does?"

"Coming out to you."

"Oh." Reba pursed her lips. "You mean that."

"I do."

"And what did you expect? That I'd throw you out of your own house?" She stroked Noelle's hair. "Sweet girl. You're my baby, my daughter, and I love you." Reba suddenly grew serious. "Now don't get me wrong, I do worry about the reaction these pictures received in the press. I mean, they're innocent pictures, but the way the media is blowing them out of proportion, I'm concerned how they'd hunt you if they got their hands on even more intimate shots, or if you, um, came out publicly."

"I know." Noelle drew a trembling breath. "That worries me too." She jerked as a sudden thought hit her. "That's what this is about. At least part of why she's pulling back, Mom. Helena knows this. She knows the press, the media, and how they operate. She's trying to steer me toward work, to stay focused on that, to save me from the media posse."

"That sounds like she really cares, Noelle."

Could it be true? Noelle desperately wanted to believe it, but so many thoughts and impressions whirled through her mind, she couldn't pin them down. "I have no way of knowing unless I talk to her."

"Exactly."

"But she doesn't want to."

"Oh, sweetie." Reba smoothed Noelle's hair away from her flushed face. "Why don't you call her? You'll drive yourself insane this way. You two need to sort this out, no matter what. You've worked too hard for too long to let the tabloids rule your life."

"Brad says—"

"Brad." Her mother spoke his name with a world of contempt. "He hasn't exactly proved himself lately, has he?"

"No."

"So listen to your mama and call Helena. I'd trust her rather than Brad any day."

Noelle flung her arms around Reba's neck. "I love you, Mom." How could she have feared telling her mother about her self-revelations? "I will. I'll call her."

"Good." Reba kissed Noelle's damp cheek. "You'll work it out."

Noelle inhaled her mother's familiar scent of Chanel No 5. She hoped Reba was right.

CHAPTER TWENTY-ONE

Helena had used every means available to counter the media storm. Before she was even in her office, Wanda had rallied the major players from the department responsible for all media relations. After an hour of brainstorming, they presented Helena with a suggestion for a press release. They didn't need to simply perform damage control regarding Noelle, even if that was the main goal. They also had to make sure VMP didn't appear homophobic or intolerant.

Helena read the press release and was finally happy with the wording. They explained the factual circumstances behind the photos, but didn't deny anyone's sexual preference. She doubted that the worst of the tabloids would pay any attention to it, but the major news and entertainment channels should get the message.

"Ms. Forsythe?" Wanda's voice startled her via the intercom. "Ms. Laurent for you on line one."

"Thank you. Hold any other calls for now, please." Helena took a deep breath and unbuttoned the top button of her shirt. As she gripped the receiver, refusing to talk to Noelle over the speaker phone, she found her palm was damp. "Hello, Noelle."

"Helena." Noelle sounded a little strained. "Seems things have gone from bad to worse."

"Yes, I'd say so." Helena knew she sounded curt, but her nerves had tied her vocal cords in a knot. "How are you holding up?"

"I'm...I'm okay." Noelle cleared her throat. "I talked to my mom."

"Oh. You did."

"Yes. I had this rather unpleasant call from my agent, and I needed to discuss things with someone. I couldn't trust anyone else."

"I see."

"Are you mad?"

Helena sighed and rubbed the back of her neck. "No, of course not. How could I be?"

"I've sort of come out to her. She knows how I feel."

Helena could hear Noelle breathing faster now. Was she crying? "Noelle. It's all right."

"She suggested I call you, since things seem to be going to hell pretty fast. Every paper I pick up, every damn Internet blog or e-zine seems to be about this, about me. At least you're not plastered across the pages as much as I am."

"Small consolation." Helena thought fast. "Listen, honey, I've prepared a press release with my staff that will take care of the factual errors. The pictures are innocent enough, no matter what outlook you have on this."

"That'll be a drop in the ocean."

"It will still matter. It'll show the major players that this is our stand. We won't play nice with the ones that cross the line, nor will any of VMP's stars, and we represent a lot of them. Members of the press won't get many interviews or free tickets if they don't clean up their act. We can always find ways to lean on the media, so even if our press release doesn't level the playing field entirely, it shows our intent."

"Playing field. Interesting choice of words when it's my life, my career, we're talking about."

"Sorry about the jargon, Noelle, force of habit. And just so you don't misunderstand, this is very much on your behalf, but on mine as well."

"Tell me, do you have network vans and paparazzi crowding your condo?"

"I don't think so. Are they outside your place now?"

"Yes."

"Oh, God. I should've realized." Though Helena wanted to rush over to Noelle's condo and get her out of there, it was better for her to stay where she was. "Listen, I'm on my way home in a bit, so I'll see if they're swarming my place too. If they are, I'll spend tonight in a hotel."

"I wish I could be with you." Noelle spoke so quietly, Helena nearly missed her words.

"This isn't a very good time," Helena said, hating every word. "I wish the same thing, though." *Why did I let her know that? It's only making things worse.*

"Are you going home now? Right away?" Noelle asked.

"In about half an hour. Why?"

"Since we can't actually see each other, maybe we can…eh…talk, later, in private. I'd really appreciate it, Helena."

Helena closed her eyes and suddenly images of Noelle's naked body, satiny and the color of latte, stretched out beneath her own, flickered behind her eyelids. The blond-black hair spread over half the bed and her eyes glittered with passion as she gasped with full, red lips, half open, as she came.

"Yes. Of course. I'll call you when I'm either home or at a hotel. All right?" Cutting the conversation short, this time to chase away the images that made her ache for Noelle, Helena said good-bye and hung up. Her heart pounded so hard in her chest, her ribs ached. "What the hell am I going to do?" she muttered. "Talk about a rock and a hard place." Would she be able to put memories like the one she'd just experienced out of her mind?

She had so many of them already, and they engaged all her senses. She had smelled, tasted, listened to, touched, and looked at Noelle that night, over and over. Helena pinched her eyes closed. Hard. But the images kept flooding her, as did the memories of how miserably empty her bed had felt since then. *I have known Noelle in every sense of the word, even the biblical one. Now I have to break her heart in yet another way. Damn it to hell.*

Helena composed a memo to e-mail to Noelle and her producers. She chose her words as carefully as always, but the bottom line was the same. This wasn't the time to let Noelle pour her heart out to her fans via the beautiful songs she'd written. That would have to wait until the media had all but forgotten their reason for chasing her this time. For now, the bouncy soul-pop would have to do, and if Noelle refused, Helena would have no choice but to sue her for breach of contract.

Helena kept typing and didn't realize the back of her hands were wet from tears streaming down her cheeks until she was done. *Oh, no. Oh, please, no.* Helena wiped furiously at her face, then pulled out a small mirror from her top drawer. Her makeup was intact, but the look in her eyes made her groan. "Damn." She pressed the mirror to her hot forehead as her chest constricted from the sobs she refused to release. *I can't believe this. I must be out of my mind, but…I love her. I'm in love with Noelle.*

❖

Noelle had a hard time waiting, maybe because of her artistic nature, but she was born impatient, her mother insisted, though she had painfully learned to fake patience. Usually she was able to, but now she drummed an increasingly rapid beat on the armrest of her chair, waiting by the phone for Helena to call like some schoolgirl.

She had to snort at the preposterous idea. Hordes of schoolgirls thought being a star, a celebrity, meant you had it made. They thought you had guys lined up to choose from and that everyone was waiting to take you on fancy dates, such as jetting to Paris for dinner on a whim. Noelle chuckled. If they only knew how many evenings she spent at home, when she wasn't on the road. Sure, she'd been on glamorous dates—almost all of them set up by Brad and his team of hunks. Some of the more handsome guys were decidedly gay, but that meant they actually had a great time together. No pressure.

"Noelle?" A small voice from the doorway broke through her reverie.

"Laurel? You okay?"

"Yeah. On my way to bed. I just wanted to say that, well, Claudia and I talked." Laurel looked like a little kid, barefoot and in an oversized T-shirt. "Just so you know, we think the things they're writing about you are wrong. I mean, you should be able to see whoever you want without the paparazzi breathing down your neck. It's just not fair."

"Thank you, Laurel." Noelle rose and wrapped her arms around Laurel. "It means a lot to hear you say that."

"Are you gay, Noelle?" Laurel looked up at her with golden-speckled eyes nearly identical to hers.

"Yes, I think so."

"Okay." Just that. Okay. Laurel hugged Noelle hard for several moments. "Night, Noelle."

"Good night, sweetie."

Laurel padded back through the hallway to her room, and Noelle resumed her restless vigil in the chair. After another hour, she felt cold and stiff from being in the same position too long. She took her cell phone and, after checking for the third time that it was fully charged, she stepped into her bathroom.

After running the large tub full, she undressed. The hot, lemon-scented water soothed and rejuvenated her. She sank until her chin touched the water, inhaling deeply. Ever since she was a little girl, her mother had used a hot bath to soothe colds, aches, pains, and sadness. It seemed to work now, at least to a degree, but still it didn't reach a part of her, something cold and trembling at the center of her being.

Her cell phone rang, playing the first notes of a tune from her latest CD, and Noelle was in such a hurry to get it that she nearly dropped it. She glanced at the screen as she pressed the button to answer. *Helena.*

"Hello?"

"Noelle? I'm sorry it took so long. I'm at the Shoreham Hotel."

"Where's that?"

"On West Fifty-fifth street. Not far from Central Park. Far enough away from the paparazzi, though."

"Oh, God. They were waiting for you?" Noelle clung to the cell phone, loath to miss any word from Helena. Her voice seemed to be able to do what the bath couldn't as it warmed that last part of her.

"They certainly were. The major networks seem to have gotten the message, however. I'm sure they'll be doing their share of reporting, but I don't think they'll make any more outrageous comments." Helena sounded exhausted.

"Thank you." Noelle reached for a sponge with her free hand and ran it along her neck. She had piled her hair on top of her head to keep it from getting wet, but a few strands floated among the soap bubbles like little water creatures.

"What's that sound? Are you in the tub?" New energy in Helena's voice sent tingles across Noelle's skin.

"Yes. It's my favorite pastime when I'm not feeling so good." A naughtier part of Noelle wondered if Helena was picturing her naked in the bathtub.

"Great idea. The bathrooms here are gorgeous, so I think I'll join you, in a manner of speaking. I'll talk to you la—"

"No, please, Helena. Don't hang up. I don't want to be alone." *I need you.* "Have your bath with me."

"Noelle…" Helena sighed. "Oh, all right." Something resembling relief in Helena's voice made Noelle's toes curl. "Hang on, I'll put you on speakerphone while I, er…undress." After a silence some clothes rustled. A clunking sound, then a roar as Helena apparently filled the tub.

"Mmm, this'll be great. I like tubs too. I normally shower before work, but in the evenings I sometimes indulge myself." After a few minutes, Helena switched the faucet off and Noelle heard a blissful "Ah. Great."

Now Noelle was picturing Helena naked in the tub at the Shoreham Hotel. Had she pulled back her hair or did the edges graze the surface? Did she have soap bubbles, or was the water completely transparent?

"Noelle?"

"I'm here." Noelle coughed, embarrassed. "Just thinking."

"About?"

"Oh, just stuff. You know, letting my mind wander. Sometimes a song is born that way."

"Really, out of thin air?" Helena sounded genuinely interested.

"You call my brain 'thin air'?" Noelle teased.

"God, no. I meant…ah, you're being facetious." Helena gave a low chuckle that did nothing for Noelle's peace of mind.

"Yes." Noelle knew her voice was breathless. "Kind of."

"So, how's the family taking this?"

"Amazingly well. My mother was less conservative and more understanding than I ever could've hoped for. Laurel came before bedtime to give me a pep talk, I think. She was pretty sweet. And you? I mean, your staff, your friends?"

"Most of my friends are gay women, as you know, and I haven't really had the chance to talk to any of them." There was a brief pause. "I have to confess that I did talk to Manon earlier, though, about us. I apologize, Noelle. I didn't mean to be indiscreet, but I had to confide in someone. I was so upset, and you know I felt I took advantage of you."

"And what did Manon say?"

"She was very frank, telling me how horribly I'd treated you the next morning. I deserved it."

"Helena, we've been over that. It's water under the bridge." Noelle didn't want to go down that pessimistic route again.

"Yes, I know. Well, apart from that, Manon didn't seem shocked or even surprised. I wonder what she saw between us that weekend in the Hamptons."

"Probably the same as Mike did." Noelle wished she could see Helena's expression. "Hey, is your phone a 3G model?"

"What?" Helena sounded nonplussed. "Yes, it is."

"Can we hang up and switch to videoconference?" Noelle was eager now.

"Eh, sure. I'll call you back in a minute." Helena disconnected and Noelle stared at the cell-phone screen. It lit up right away, asking for her permission to start a conversation with video. Noelle pressed yes, and within seconds, Helena's face filled the screen.

"There you are," Noelle said, knowing she sounded a little too cheery.

"And so are you." Helena smiled, but Noelle could see the unmistakable signs of fatigue. The clear resolution on her screen showed the deepened lines around Helena's eyes.

"I just needed to see you." Noelle placed the phone on the side of the tub and turned a little on her side to face it. "I've felt so alone, despite having my family and Morris here. I don't know what to do about my agent. He's changed over the last couple of years, and I have no idea why. He's being very pushy, and nothing makes me rebel faster than someone trying to control me."

"I hear you. I can't tell you how sorry I am that my sexual orientation has caused such hoopla over those pictures." Helena closed her eyes and stretched back against the edge of the tub.

"Hey, that's not your fault. You were just being polite and walking me to the door. I'd never blame you for that, ever." Eager for Helena to understand, Noelle rose a bit in the water. "It's in their eyes, you know, what's ugly. You know the expression, 'in the eyes of the beholder'? It says more about them than us, that they'd consider this wrong or something worth gossiping about. I've learned the hard way, during my decade in the public eye, that it's only what I and my immediate family and friends think that matters. I can't afford to let any other thoughts in, or I'd lose sight of what makes me, me. You see?"

Helena's expression changed from one of listening intently to something entirely different. Confused, Noelle tried to figure out what she'd said to cause Helena to lose cohesion in her jaw, and when she glanced down, she realized that her breasts had floated to the surface among the soap bubbles. She dipped down to her chin and felt a blush creep up her cheeks. "Sorry. Got a bit carried away."

"Oh, don't mind me." Helena, her eyes now half-lidded, kept gazing at her, and her parted lips looked fuller somehow.

"Don't look at me like that, Helena." Noelle's legs parted of their own volition and a surge of something hot and silky gathered between them.

"Like how?" Obviously Helena was teasing, but it didn't make Noelle less out of breath.

"You know how. Like you want me." Noelle's breath hitched and she pushed her hands, palms pressed together, between her thighs, squeezing her legs around them.

"I'm sorry, honey. Guess I'm more tired than I realized." Helena shook her head as if to clear her thoughts. "I shouldn't tease you, I know. My only defense is that you're so beautiful, and, God, the way you look at *me*, Noelle…" Helena's eyes looked so vulnerable.

"I don't know how I look at you." Noelle honestly didn't. She definitely had problems taking her eyes off Helena's face—the austere, straight eyebrows, the clear eyes, and the thin, but right now suddenly so luscious lips, but this was nothing new. Noelle had felt that way ever since she sang to Helena at her birthday party.

"You look at me with those golden eyes like you can't stop. All that desire combined with confusion is enough for me to forget about anything and everything else. I may be reading things into your gaze, but—"

"You're not." Again Noelle moved halfway out of the water to emphasize her words. "That's exactly how I feel. I don't understand it, because I've never felt this way about anyone else."

"Oh, honey." Helena's eyes devoured her. "You're so beautiful. I know just how those dark nipples of yours feel, how they taste." Helena adjusted her phone, and Noelle could see the woman she loved from the waist up. "Can you still hear me?"

"I—I hear you fine." Noelle could hardly believe her eyes as Helena cupped one of her breasts, gently pinching the plump pink nipple. "Oh, God."

"Just for you." Helena spoke throatily. "For no one but you, Noelle." She briefly closed her eyes, only to open them again, searching for Noelle's. "Tell me how this makes you feel."

"Hot. Wanting you." Noelle moaned helplessly. "A little frightened."

"What of? Me?"

"No. Myself. It's like I have no control. My body reacts, and it has everything to do with you." Noelle sighed and was so tempted to spread her legs again, to allow her hands to help satisfy the deep ache within her. "And last time I was with you, you ended up being all business. That hurt."

"I know, honey. Trust me, I know." Helena arched into her own touch. "This is the quintessence of guilty pleasure. I should leave you alone, but like you say, it's as if I have no control when it comes to you. If it's any consolation, I hurt just as bad for having to reduce what's between us to merely business." Helena's lower lip trembled. "It kills me," she said, her voice barely audible.

"Oh, Helena." Those words, and the way Helena whispered them, made it impossible for Noelle not to respond. She pulled her hands free and cupped her full breasts, and as she stared at Helena, she began to caress them. Unprepared for how intimate it would feel, like Helena was doing the actual touching, Noelle moaned again.

"Pinch your nipples. I want to see them ready for me. Soon enough my mouth will be on them."

Noelle complied, pinching her nipples hard enough to elicit a whimper.

"Yes. Like that, honey. Just like that." Helena mirrored Noelle's caresses, tugging at her own nipples while biting her lower lip.

"Helena, caress your stomach." Noelle needed to take things further; she was burning up. "Lower. That's right." She followed Helena's progress down her stomach, and even if her hands disappeared out of sight, Helena's expression signaled when she found the source of her pleasure. Noelle spread her legs wide, and in a moment of complete trust and desire to share, she nudged her cell phone sideways until she saw her body from her thighs up to her face, on the smaller of the two screens. Helena's groan echoed between the bathroom walls as she hungrily followed Noelle's movements.

"Oh, Noelle. I can feel what you feel. I really can." The water around Helena sloshed in rapid waves. "And I can feel your hands on me. Inside me."

"Helena," Noelle gasped, touching herself fiercely, but waiting for Helena to join her. "Take me."

"Noelle!" Helena raised out of the water, and Noelle pressed her fingers inside herself just as she began to twitch from her impending orgasm. Squinting, she kept her eyes locked with Helena's, and together they shared stroke for stroke, heading for the ultimate bliss.

Helena came first, and her hoarse cry, combined with the way her face contorted, created new sensations inside Noelle. She felt like she was igniting all over. Her sex was so swollen and sensitized, she could barely touch herself, and one stroke later, she cried out, the fingers inside her Helena's, the fingers strumming her clitoris Helena's. Noelle sobbed Helena's name, over and over, and to her amazement, her own name echoed back.

"Oh, honey, sweet baby," Helena whispered as her body slowly seemed to relax down into the water. "Are you all right? Did you come?"

"Yes." Noelle moved the phone, suddenly a little shy. Apparently Helena did the same, as she could see only her shoulders and her face. "Very hard and very long."

"Me too." Helena looked dazed. "I don't have to tell you that I've never done this, with anyone."

"Neither have I." Noelle was trembling and she blinked at the stinging sensation behind her eyelids.

"Don't cry, honey. Please." Helena reached for her phone, looking concerned. "I'm sorry, I—oh, no!"

There was a faint crackle and the call disconnected. Noelle tried several times to call Helena back, but only reached her voicemail.

The tears she'd fought turned to bitter laughter when she realized what had just happened. Unless she was mistaken, Helena had dropped her cell phone in the tub. *With her list of contacts, including my number.* Noelle groaned. Unless Helena had decided to avoid her, the fact she wasn't trying to call Noelle back meant she hadn't been able to get to her backup copy of her contacts.

Debating whether she should try to call Helena at her hotel, Noelle decided against it. She had no idea which room Helena was in, and she suspected Helena had requested complete anonymity at the desk because of the paparazzi, so they wouldn't just let her call through.

Besides, Noelle thought as she reluctantly, and on wobbly legs, rose from the bathtub, what was left to say? Nothing had really changed. She showered quickly and rubbed herself dry with one of the Egyptian cotton towels her mother favored. She would just focus on her music, on recording what mattered, and one day she would be able to be in the same room as Helena without having her heart shattered. *Someday.*

CHAPTER TWENTY-TWO

The studio was buzzing with activity when Noelle and Morris entered. David and his crew were crowded around the mixer table, a steady, hot beat thundering from the speakers. David didn't even notice Noelle was there until she tapped him on the shoulder.

"Oh, hi, Noelle. Great." He yelled to drown out the music. "Finally time to get started again."

"Is that track four?" Noelle asked when they'd turned down the volume.

"Yup. I've added some extra percussion, and when we edit it, it'll sound fantastic. Like the Pointer Sisters mixed with Timbaland."

"Sounds fun." Noelle was eager to get started, and the fact that half her record would hold her own songs made it possible for her to enjoy the more lighthearted tracks.

"Here's the song list, and you'll see the changes at the bottom half. I'm glad you and Ms. Forsythe reached an understanding. We'll get back to that stuff of yours another time." David patted her on the shoulder.

"What?" A sharp twitch blasted the center of her stomach as she read the list of titles. "This is the original list. The one you showed me weeks ago. What's going on, David?" Her eyes prickling, Noelle refused to feel betrayed.

"You didn't get Helena Forsythe's memo?" David looked confused. "I have it right here." He handed her a printed document.

Noelle didn't want to read the paper, but she glanced at the message. Short and to the point, it shattered her heart. Noelle had never anticipated such pain, and she couldn't allow it to show. Her chest constricted, but when Morris took a step toward her, Noelle put up her hand. Her eyes burning now, she noticed the time stamp. Two hours before Helena had called her from the Shoreham Hotel. Two hours before they shared the most intimate of moments.

"This is unacceptable." Noelle was relieved to hear her own voice carry, sounding casual, even. "I was under the impression that half of the songs on this album would be my own."

"Well, so was I, but you know, it's not the right time. The audience wants to dance, especially when everybody's struggling financially. It's like those glitzy Hollywood movies they made during the Depression." David sounded enthusiastic as he spelled out his personal theory. "People want to have fun and forget, they want the *beat*, you know."

"Really." Noelle looked at Morris and saw true sympathy in his eyes. He jerked his head toward the door, wordlessly asking her an important question. Noelle stood motionless. *If I leave now, it's for good. I'll burn my bridges, not only with VMP, but with Helena.* Straightening, she handed the memo back to David. "Well, there seems to be a misunderstanding. I had a verbal agreement with Ms. Forsythe, which I now consider violated." *Violated. Yes, that's exactly how I feel.*

"Noelle?" David looked horrified. "Don't start this again. Whatever you and Forsythe have going together—"

"Stop talking. I strongly suggest that you—stop—talking."

Morris pushed himself between Noelle and David, towering over the frail man. "Back off."

Noelle walked past them and entered her username and password into the computer. "I'm deleting any recordings I've made since the last CD I was contracted to do, as well as any of my own songs."

"Hey, you can't do that!" David motioned for his assistant to stop her, but a step in his direction by Morris stopped the assistant cold.

"All purged." Noelle had not taken any pleasure in deleting her files. She had copies at the house, but it had been important for her to show Helena and her goons that she refused to back down and comply. "Ready, Morris?"

"Noelle, you're breaking your contract." David reached for her arm as she passed him. "They'll go after you in court. You know that."

Morris stopped David with one glare. "You must've misunderstood. Ms. Laurent is leaving."

"Thank you, Morris." Noelle hoisted her Prada bag and slammed on her sunglasses. Relieved to be able to hide her eyes, she turned to walk out the door.

"Get that gorilla of yours off me," David said, raising his voice.

"Bye, y'all." Noelle left the studio with Morris right behind her. It took all her strength to maintain her casual demeanor, but after she was in the limousine she curled up in the backseat and hid her face in her hands.

"Home, Noelle?" Morris's gentle voice penetrated her pain.

"Yes, please, Morris. Home."

"Good." He nodded solemnly and closed the door.

Noelle heard her cell phone ring in her bag, but she didn't even check it. She would never be able to talk to anyone without crying. She turned off the phone, but the silence was just as unnerving. As Morris drove into the garage beneath her building, Noelle saw the gathered reporters mixed with fans calling her name and people waving signs. The police kept them far enough away for Noelle to be unable to read them, but the frenzy of the crowd left her feeling sure the messages weren't very supportive. The fans were easy to spot because they were shouting at the ones carrying signs, and their "We love you, Noelle" drowned out everything else.

Noelle couldn't take it anymore. The media, the broken promises, and...Helena. Thinking quickly about her options, she had figured out everything by the time the elevator she was riding in reached the penthouse level.

❖

Helena knew exactly what the knot in her stomach was about. Noelle had to be in the studio by now. When they'd shared that magical time last night she obviously hadn't read the memo. Of all her actions, Helena thought with self-contempt, this was her most cowardly. Sending out memos made it easy on herself but not on the recipients.

She'd tried to blame dropping her cell phone in the bathtub for not calling Noelle back and discussing her decision. She'd rationalized her action with the fact that she'd decided to stick with the original contract. Legally nobody could hold that against her. *They don't have to. I hold it against myself.* Helena honestly did believe she was sheltering Noelle, as well as VMP, by not recording her deeply personal songs. If Noelle recorded a song like "Never Before," the one she'd sung to Helena at her condo about loving a woman, she would reignite the media interest.

"Sir, you can't go in, you just—" Elise's frantic voice escalated, making Helena snap her head up. The door to her office flew open and David Boyd stormed inside, waving a piece of paper.

"I've fucking had it with that little bitch," he yelled. "She's played Miss High-and-Mighty Diva one time too many with me. I won't work with her when she comes back with her tail between her legs."

"I'm so sorry, ma'am," Elise said from the door, her hand pressed against her chest. "He just stormed by me—"

"I'll handle it, Elise. It's all right."

Elise nodded quickly and closed the door.

"David. Calm down. Sit down."

"I'm so frustrated—"

"*Sit* down." Helena made sure she stood, towering over him. "What's going on?" She had a vague idea and it made her nauseous.

"Noelle Laurent saw your memo and stormed out."

"What do you mean, she saw my memo? I sent it to her as well."

"Clearly she hadn't seen it. When I explained your standpoint, she pitched a fit. I expected her to start throwing things at me, but instead she set that gorilla of hers on me." David looked affronted, his goatee moving constantly in a circular motion as he energetically chewed gum.

God. Noelle had gone into the studio, happy to start recording her songs. Having to find out from David, of all people, that Helena had changed her mind, was horrifying. The memo she had sent Noelle explained more of the personal reasoning behind her decision, something she wouldn't share with David and his crew. To think Noelle had only that callous explanation... Helena slammed her fists on the desk.

"And when she became upset, did you urge her to talk to me?"

"Eh, no, not really." David coughed violently, but stopped chewing.

"What did you say?" Her threatening voice, which had kept

unruly, far more seasoned board members in check, and it made David push back farther in his chair.

"I...uh...I tried to reason with her, you know, telling her I could care less about who she was into or anything, but the time wasn't right to change genres. My crew and I have worked damn hard to find the right songs. She's among the best of her generation when it comes to performing, but as a song writer, she's a newbie. She's like those supermodels who think they can act," David said, grinning nervously, "or the actors who think they can sing, or direct."

Helena was fuming.

"You're fired."

"Wha—"

"Fired. As of now. And your 'crew.'"

Opening and closing his mouth like a fish, David had a but-what-did-*I*-do look on his face.

"You want reasons? Fine." Helena sat down on the side of her desk, and it didn't escape her that he eyed her stocking-clad legs despite his distress. *Figures*. "One. You referred to Ms. Laurent as a bitch. Two. You presumed to know and passed judgment on her, and on me. Three. You failed to reassure her in a professional manner, which I expect of the producers I have on contract. You'll find that the fine print in that contract handles all these offenses."

"I see." David's expression slowly turned from shocked to sly. "So it's all true, isn't it? Your attempt at damage control backfired, huh? The little hot chick's got it bad for you, and you're trying to keep her fan base intact."

Fury rose inside Helena like the lava inside the mountain that had shared her name so many years ago. She pressed a button on her intercom. "Wanda? Alert security. I need them to escort Mr. Boyd out of the building and divest him of his key card."

"Yes, ma'am."

"Wait outside. I'm done with you."

Perhaps her glowing wrath frightened David, because he nearly tumbled out of the visitors' chair. "You owe me money."

"All that will be taken care of before you leave the building." Helena's anger dissipated and she heard her voice become utterly bored. She focused on her paperwork, her mind already preoccupied with how she would approach Noelle. When she looked up a minute later, David was gone and the door closed behind him.

Wanda's voice interrupted Helena's thoughts. "Manon Belmont for you on line one, ma'am."

"Thank you." Helena wasn't sure if this was good timing or not. "I take it security has dealt with David Boyd?"

"He's being escorted out as we speak, ma'am."

"Good. Thank you." Helena pressed the button for line one. "Manon. What can I do for you?"

"All business today, Helena?" Manon's well-modulated voice soothed Helena's frayed nerves a bit. "I just wanted to check on you, see if you need anything after all the tabloid crap."

To hear Manon use such unsophisticated language made Helena laugh, if a little bitterly. "Eryn's had a great influence on you, I can tell."

"Yes, I know. I find cursing quite liberating."

"Thank you for thinking of me, but Noelle's bearing the brunt of the media interest. I'm just their means to an end, so to speak." Helena sighed and rested her aching head in her free hand.

"How is Noelle holding up? This has to be tough on her, even if she's used to this type of attention."

"She's probably hating my guts right now, apart from the fact that she's the tabloids' favorite prey." Helena took a deep, trembling breath.

"Why would she hate you? She's infatuated with you. Mike hasn't been gossiping about what they talked about, but she's convinced that it runs even deeper than infatuation."

"If that's true, then she has all the more reason to loathe me." Helena winced. "I wish things could be different. I really do."

"How do you feel about her, if it's all right for me to ask? You know nothing you tell me goes any further, not even to Eryn."

"Manon—" Tears rose in Helena's eyes and she covered her mouth. "I'm in trouble. I'm in big trouble."

"Oh, Helena. You love her."

The kind words broke the dam. Helena whispered, "Yes," then bent over the desk and cried. Manon didn't speak, but Helena could hear her breathe, and her friend's presence made the tears nearly bearable. "I don't know what to do."

"Take my word for it, Helena, you have only one choice, or you'll regret it for the rest of your life. You have to tell her. If you don't, you'll always wonder."

"She won't listen to me."

"Why not?" Manon spoke kindly in a low voice.

"Because I went back on my word, and something went wrong with the memo I sent, and she had to hear it from someone else…the last person I'd choose to tell her."

Manon was quiet for a moment, and Helena knew her friend was less than impressed with her conduct. "Helena, I don't have to say it, do I?"

"I'm a coward."

"Hmm. I know you'll hate hearing this, Helena, but you've always been a coward. I think you're afraid. Why did you go back on your word and what was it about?" Manon's nonjudgmental tone made it possible for Helena to not balk at her choice of words.

Helena told Manon, without making excuses, how she'd reasoned when she decided this was the wrong time for Noelle to record confessional and deeply personal songs. Manon chuckled when Helena described how she had just handled David Boyd.

"I can picture it. And to sound like a broken record, no pun intended, you need to talk to Noelle. If nothing else, you need to come clean about your motives for going back on your word, and you owe it to both of you to at least try and tell her you love her. She may be too upset to listen right now, but she'll calm down eventually, and she'll remember what you said and how you said it. I nearly screwed it all up with Eryn. I could have lost her if I hadn't listened to a good friend. It's my turn to be that frank friend to you. No matter what you think, you would make someone a great wife and lover."

"Me? The serial girlfriend, the hit-and-run lover?" Helena snorted and blew her nose. "You've got to be kidding."

"Don't sell yourself short." Manon spoke sternly, sounding every bit the business tycoon, used to assuming command. "You've never really been in love, I believe, and I'd also wager that you thought yourself incapable."

"You wouldn't lose that bet." Helena tipped her chair back and closed her eyes. "I thought I was, once, and the rejection was horrible."

"And with a mother like Dorcas, who used rejection as a method to bring up a child, that added insult to injury."

"True." In fact, the experience had colored her entire future... *No. I let it shape my life.* "It doesn't exactly place me in a favorable light, does it?" Reaching for another tissue and a small mirror from her drawer, Helena wiped her eyes and checked her makeup.

"Isn't that beside the point? Your image is the least of your problems, isn't it?" Manon was brutally honest, but Helena found her candor soothing and supportive. She always did appreciate the hard facts because she knew how to work with them.

"Yes, you're right."

"What matters right now is Noelle, isn't it? How she's feeling? Go to her."

"All right. I will." Part of Helena couldn't wait to see Noelle, to try to set things right, but she dreaded it immensely. She could imagine Noelle's pain and disappointment only too well. "Thank you, Manon. I'll call you later, all right?"

"Anytime, Helena. I mean it."

"All right." Helena said good-bye and hung up. She shouldn't waste any more time. She had to go to Noelle.

CHAPTER TWENTY-THREE

Noelle closed the second carry-on bag, pleased that it had taken her only half an hour to pack. She didn't need much, for she had a complete wardrobe in her house on Star Island in Miami.

"Running doesn't solve anything," her mother said from the doorway.

"Maybe not, but I've had enough of so many things. I need some space. I need to think." Noelle jerked on her leather jacket and pulled her wild hair back with a black velvet scrunchy. "I'll call when I get there. Take care of the girls and keep them away from the press."

"All right, sweetie." Reba hugged her. "I still wish you'd talk to Ms. Forsythe and sort things out, but maybe you'll have time to do that when you get back."

Noelle knew she wouldn't be talking with Helena any time soon. Merely thinking about her made her heart ache so badly, she felt like it would never heal. "Sure, Mom." She looked over her mother's shoulder when Morris showed up to get her bags.

Morris grabbed her bags like they were empty. "We have two hours."

"They do have wheels, show-off," Noelle said, trying to sound casual.

"Got to stay in shape, you know." Morris looked completely unfazed. "Ready?"

"Yes." Noelle hugged her mother again. "I'm sorry the girls aren't here. I'll talk to them when I get to Miami."

"Be careful, Noelle. Be safe."

"Bye, Mom. Don't cry. You and the girls can fly down for the weekend whenever you want. You know that."

"Yes, I do. I'm just being silly."

"You're being my mom." Noelle stroked her mother's arm. "Bye."

The ride to the airport took nearly an hour, which wasn't bad, considering the traffic. Morris had chartered a small plane to take them to Miami, and the pilots and flight attendant were already waiting. Noelle had used this charter company several times before and vaguely recognized the captain. She nodded civilly and took her seat in the luxurious plane.

Morris sat down farther back, and Noelle appreciated him giving her some space. She wore her largest, darkest sunglasses, hiding from everyone, and she couldn't wait to be behind the walls of her Miami house. Star Island was the home of many celebrities, and even if it was a public subdivision, a manned gate kept the curious visitors to a minimum. Noelle had bought her house from a movie star who was even more private than she was, and she felt safe when she engaged the elaborate alarm system he had installed.

Morris loved Miami and came out of his shell when they stayed there. He was a great cook and didn't mind doubling as a butler of sorts, taking care of the details when it came to employing other people required to take care of Noelle's property. She was eager to arrive and delighted that she could get there quickly.

She closed her eyes behind the sunglasses, and once the plane was in the air she dozed off. Drifting in and out of sleep, she thought of Helena. Instead of dwelling on the fact that Helena had betrayed her, Noelle kept seeing her half-naked body, slick with bath oil and soap bubbles. Noelle jerked awake. When would it be possible to think or dream about Helena without feeling such excruciating pain? Ever?

Noelle curled up in her seat and wrapped a blanket around herself, suddenly cold. So this was love, this strange mix of indescribable hurt and strange longing? *It's too much.* Her chest ached so she could hardly breathe. She tried to focus on being angry, but the fury that had filled her at the studio and prompted her actions eluded her. Instead, she had to repeatedly take deep breaths to keep from crying. She refused to show any sign of what she perceived as weakness, even around strangers.

Miami greeted her with warm, humid weather. Morris had arranged for an anonymous cab service to collect them at Miami International, so Noelle managed to dodge the press entirely. Some paparazzi were always at the airport, especially in a city like Miami, which held its fair share of celebrities. Not using a limo was one trick Morris had taught her when she wanted to arrive incognito.

The ride to Star Island was uneventful and Noelle sat lost in thought, constantly reviewing the morning's turn of events. She couldn't shake her numbness. She had arrived at the studio excited about work. She'd even hoped that her phone session with Helena might have sparked more of Helena's interest in her. *She did want me. She was just as much on fire as I was.* Noelle wasn't kidding herself. Helena wasn't ready to be serious about anyone, least of all someone who wasn't in her league. That hadn't stopped Noelle from hoping she'd have some more time with Helena, though.

"We're here," Morris announced as the cab drove across the bridge leading to Star Island. The guard recognized them on sight and nodded as they drove through. At the house, Morris opened the gate to the house with a remote control and the cab drove up to the white Mediterranean-style structure. Noelle stepped out and inhaled the sweet scent of Miami, paired with the salty air from the water around them, then grabbed one of her suitcases and rolled it up to the door. Pressing her index finger to the pad, she unlocked it and stepped inside, where she repeated the procedure to turn off the alarm.

"Home," Noelle said with a sigh, kicking off her sandals. She loved the feel of the smooth tiles under her feet. After going to her master suite with Morris just behind her carrying the second bag, she unpacked quickly.

"Please, Morris, take the day off. Kick back, watch sports, whatever. I'll just do the same. Well, perhaps not watch so much sports. You've been great throughout all this. I appreciate it, buddy."

"Anything, Noelle. You know that. Anything, anytime." And she knew he meant it.

"I hope I never do anything to make you leave me," Noelle said, suddenly feeling as if her throat was swelling. "I don't know what I'd do without you."

"Hey, kid," Morris said, clearly disregarding the fact that he was only eight years older than her. "Don't you worry about that. I'm privileged to work for you *and* to be considered a friend of the family. You, Reba, the girls, you're my family. You've treated me better than anyone else ever has, and nothing can change that."

"Thank you, Morris." Noelle flung her arms around the tall, burly man she'd sometimes taken for granted over the years. "Thank you."

Morris patted her back. "Well, I'm going to take you up on your offer. There's a football game tonight." He grinned. "We calling for takeout?"

"You bet. No cooking for you today, but tomorrow we should get our hands on some stone crabs, don't you think?" Noelle tried to keep it casual, and she seemed to have succeeded because Morris lit up.

"Ah, great idea. Stone crabs it is." He kissed her forehead and left.

Eager to go outside to the pool area, Noelle tugged on a black swimsuit. She showered poolside and threw herself into the water. Lap after lap, she swam with powerful strokes, as if some water demon were chasing her. Eventually her arms couldn't keep up anymore and she barely managed to pull herself up on the edge. Gasping for air, she discovered that not even complete physical exertion would purge thoughts of Helena. She slowly wrapped a towel around her shoulders. With time, she'd learn to handle this, to rationalize it and tuck it away, but for now, she had to face the fact that her heart was broken.

Noelle rose on trembling legs. Walking back to the house, she thought of Carolyn Black's words at the opening-night party. She and Annelie lived on the other side of Star Island, and as far as Noelle remembered, this was their permanent residence. Carolyn was probably busy promoting the latest Maddox movie, but Annelie might be around.

After another quick shower, Noelle dressed in shorts and a T-shirt. Poking her head into the entertainment room, she told Morris where she was going. Though he offered to escort her, she declined.

Noelle met only two dog walkers. In fact, Star Island seemed deserted in the late afternoon. Carolyn and Annelie's house had a wall around it similar to Noelle's, with a cast-iron gate. She rang the bell and soon heard Annelie's soothing voice over the speaker.

"Noelle? Come on in."

Noelle looked up, spotted the surveillance camera, and waved. "Thanks. Sorry for showing up unannounced."

"Don't worry about it." A small part of the gate opened, and Noelle walked up to the peach-colored art-deco house. Framed by different types of palm trees, it was spectacular.

Carolyn and Annelie stood in the doorway, Annelie with her arm around Carolyn's shoulders. The sight of their apparent happiness sent an unexpected stab of envy through Noelle, and she blinked at the tears that welled up.

"Oh, darling, come here." Carolyn opened her arms and hugged Noelle close. Burying her face in Carolyn's hair, Noelle knew she'd done the right thing.

"Annelie, let's go to the Floridian in the back?" Carolyn kept her arm around Noelle. "And you, Noelle, are going to tell us everything and we'll brainstorm. I'm sure we'll come up with something."

"I don't think so, but I just had to see you. I couldn't think of what else to do."

In the backyard, the Floridian, a net structure, covered half of the patio, keeping mosquitoes out. Noelle sat down with Carolyn on a wicker couch, and Annelie retrieved some cold drinks from a refrigerator in their stainless-steel outdoor kitchen.

Annelie placed the bottles on the coffee table. "Orange juice, soda, water?"

"Orange juice, thank you." Noelle accepted a glass and drank thirstily. "Mmm. It's hot today, isn't it?"

"Sure is." Carolyn helped herself to some ice water. "Now, tell us what's happened. We've seen the tabloid covers, of course, and we were worried."

"It's been kind of rough. Not so much because the reporters… Well, it's never nice. I'm sure you had your share of harassment by the tabloids."

"We sure have," Carolyn said. "And Helena, how's she taking it?"

"She's…we've…" Noelle found it impossible to continue. She sipped her juice, but it went down the wrong way and she began to cough.

"Oh, my." Carolyn stroked her back. "Easy, easy. Breathe."

Eventually Noelle stopped coughing and managed to take another sip without choking. "I'm sorry. I just had a bit of a rough day. I…" As the day's events caught up with her, she began to cry.

Carolyn held her gently. "Poor thing. That's it. Get it out. Just let it out."

Annelie sat down on Noelle's other side and put her arms around them. They remained like that until she stopped crying. "There," Annelie said. "Better?"

"Better." Noelle accepted a tissue and blew her nose. Calmer now, she told Carolyn and Annelie what had happened earlier in the day. "So I came here," Noelle said, finishing in a low voice. "I just had to get away. I'll most likely be sued for breaking the contract, but I'll cross that bridge when I get to it. I just couldn't stay."

"Talk about trauma," Carolyn said, flinging a hand in the air. "Terrible."

"Have you talked to Helena?"

"No." Noelle shuddered. "Not since Sunday evening." Her cheeks warmed. "Our conversation then made me think we had a chance, but I was obviously wrong."

"You need to talk to her, sooner or later. Maybe you can still sort things out." Annelie tugged gently at Noelle's hair. "She'd be a fool to let you slip away."

"Really." Noelle shook her head. "Helena is incapable of loving someone. No, wrong choice of words. She doesn't dare to love someone. I don't know why, she hasn't told me, but it's clear."

"Then that should tell you something." Annelie cupped Noelle's chin. "You mentioned that the two of you were intimate, more than once. She realizes she was the first woman you've ever been with. She could have stayed away after the first time. You know, kept the contact to a minimum, but she couldn't, could she?"

"Annelie's right." Carolyn kept her arm around Noelle's shoulders. "For a woman like Helena—proud, austere, and with a tremendous workload—to keep showing her vulnerability when it comes to you, and the way she looked at you when we were at that rooftop, having dinner. Whatever is between you, and only the two of you know that, it's *strong*."

"Overpowering," Noelle whispered. "Some people would call

it pure lust, physical obsession, but that's not true, Carolyn." Noelle kicked her sandals off and pulled both legs up, hooking her arms around them. "You're right. She doesn't want to want me. She's afraid. I think she may even resent me for evoking any such feelings."

"And yet she does care."

"Not enough to keep her promise. Not enough to inform me of her decision herself. She let David Boyd do that, and I can't understand why. I just can't."

"Darling." Carolyn wrapped both arms around Noelle and held her tight. "We'll help you figure it out. At least you're here now. Granted, Star Island is a public place and we do get our fair share of tourists and paparazzi here, but the gate leading into the place deters some. So far, the press is...wait..." Carolyn quieted, frowning. "Wait a minute."

"She's onto something," Annelie said, winking at Noelle, who had to laugh. "She's into her Maddox mode."

"Very funny." Carolyn wrinkled her nose in an uncharacteristic way. "Listen. I just thought of something. The press has been going crazy over those pictures, and so has the Bible Belt, the moms of teenyboppers, and the tabloids. Now, here's what I'm thinking. Annelie, if I was in Noelle's shoes, being hunted by the press, and I insisted on writing my own manuscript about my life, about every aspect of my life, even the details that were deeply personal, what would you do?"

"Hey, I'd ask you to postpone that idea until it calmed down... oh."

Noelle stared at them. "What?"

"Think about it. Your songs. Confessional, deeply personal, and honest." Annelie held up three fingers. "Add Helena's persona to that. Protective, professional."

Noelle tried to follow their train of thought. "You mean she thought I'd be in even more trouble with the press if I shared my songs with my fans?"

"And the rest of the world. You wouldn't have any privacy left, since the tabloid posse is out to get you. At least that's how I think Helena might have reasoned. That rhymes better with her personality from what I know of her." Carolyn caressed Noelle's cheek. "It's a possibility."

"Then why didn't she tell me?"

"She's afraid, remember." Annelie spoke quietly. "If I'm not mistaken, Helena doesn't trust herself around you. She's acted out of character on more than one occasion. Unheard of for a Forsythe."

Noelle's heart hammered. What did all these speculations mean? Was there still a chance if she talked to Helena? Would Helena lower her guard enough to listen? *And most important of all, would I dare to talk to her?*

Noelle wasn't able to wrap her mind around all of it at once, but it felt good to sit with such friends as Carolyn and Annelie. She closed her eyes, exhausted.

"I'm sorry," she murmured.

"Don't be. Just relax. It's all right." Annelie's voice soothed her.

Noelle couldn't resist giving in to sleep. She curled up between Carolyn and Annelie and let herself drift off.

CHAPTER TWENTY-FOUR

Please, Mrs. Laurent." Helena stood just inside the front door of the Laurents' Manhattan penthouse. In front of her stood a discontented Reba Laurent, her arms folded across her chest.

"Noelle has had enough of everything, especially you, Ms. Forsythe." Her Texas accent even more pronounced, Reba wouldn't budge.

"I know she's upset, but that's the reason I need to talk to her. Make her understand."

"You don't have to *make* Noelle do anything." Reba nearly spat the words. "You've caused her nothing but heartache lately. I've never seen my girl that upset. She's her father's daughter, so dutiful, so dedicated. I don't think any of you people have ever realized what an unusual jewel you had in Noelle."

"I do realize it." Determined to explain to Reba, Helena raised her hands in a pleading gesture. "I've known all along that Noelle is special, and I don't just mean her voice. She's one of a kind."

Reba suddenly looked tired, rubbing her neck with one hand, holding up the other, palm forward, as if to stop Helena. "You hurt her."

"I know. I'm trying to make things better."

"I'm not convinced that you can. I've never seen Noelle look like she did when she packed her bags. Not even when her father died."

Reba's words made Helena shiver. "She's never really talked about her father."

"She worshiped him. Even when he pitied himself and drank too much. Eventually, when she had her breakthrough and was starting to become famous, we found out he was dying. He refused any life-prolonging measures and died when Noelle was eighteen. She's the oldest."

"That much I know." Helena pushed a hand through her hair. "Please, Mrs. Laurent—"

"Call me Reba." Reba's eyes softened marginally, but Helena had no idea why.

"I'm Helena." After an awkward pause, she continued. "Reba, I really need to see Noelle. I know she's upset, and she has a right to be, but I can rectify part of it. She must think I blew her off, but I didn't, at least not in the way she thinks."

"So if I tell you where she is, you'll make everything all right?" Reba looked doubtful. "Somehow that sounds too good to be true."

"I can only fix what Noelle allows me to. I can promise you that I'll try, though." Helena took Reba's hand. "She may not want to talk to me, but I have to try. I have to."

Reba studied Helena for several moments. Her eyes, darker than Noelle's, but with the same almond shape, didn't reveal any of her emotions. "Do you care about my daughter, Helena?"

"Very much."

"Enough to do the right thing and help her reach her true potential, rather than what's best for VMP?"

"Yes." Helena didn't miss a beat. She had to face her own fears and misgivings and think about was what was best for Noelle.

"And can you walk away from her, on a personal level, if that's what she wants?"

It will kill me. "Yes."

Reba looked down at their joined hands. "She's in Miami, at her house on Star Island."

Relief flooded Helena. "Thank you. I won't let her, or you, down."

"I take that as a promise."

"Please don't tell her I'm on my way." Helena cleared her throat. "She may be so angry at me that she'll run before I have a chance to explain."

"All right." Reba surprised Helena by kissing her cheek. "Maybe you're right for my daughter after all."

The company Learjet was available, and two hours after her talk with Reba, Helena was on board as the plane left for Miami.

❖

Morris had cleaned up after their takeout dinner and then gone to his rooms. Noelle stayed on the couch, holding a barely touched glass of red wine. She turned off the TV, unable to focus, as she tried to sort her thoughts. She had felt self-conscious, waking up after sleeping an hour on Annelie and Carolyn's patio, but they had quickly reassured her that they didn't mind. They'd arranged to have dinner together tomorrow, and Noelle prayed keeping busy would help keep her mind off Helena.

The Miami night came on fast. Noelle pressed a remote and lit a few lamps around the living room. The pool lights illuminated the garden, and though it was beautiful, Noelle couldn't appreciate it. She had the beginnings of a headache. Glancing at the wine she made a face, put it on the coffee table, and rubbed her temples. It was too soon to think of where she would go from here, but she kept thinking about her options, over and over. She tried to focus on practical matters, like which new record company among the many she'd received offers from over the years she'd choose, but images of Helena kept appearing. It hurt every time a new vision surfaced, and though she refused to cry, she kept swallowing to try to alleviate the pain that constricted her throat.

Noelle rose and sat down at the grand piano on the other side of the room. Instead of selecting one of her own songs—she felt far too raw to sing something written from her heart—so she chose a Billie Holiday song, "Lady Sings the Blues." It seemed fitting, and her voice carried the famous song with all the emotions that welled up inside.

At first Noelle wasn't sure what the buzzing sound was, but then she realized someone was at the front gate. Her first reaction was to call Morris, but she walked into the home office where the surveillance monitors were located. Noelle saw a cab, its driver, and the outline of someone in the backseat. She pressed the button to zoom in the camera and used the small joystick to direct it to the passenger.

"You sure they'll buzz you in, ma'am? Folks on Star Island are pretty paranoid about who they let inside, you know." The cabdriver's voice sounded blasé. The microphone gave away Noelle's visitor's identity before she could zoom in completely.

"Not sure at all, as a matter of fact. How much do I owe you?"

Helena. Noelle stared at the screen as Helena stepped out of the cab and paid the driver.

"Shouldn't I wait, ma'am?"

"Not necessary. Thank you."

The cab drove away and Helena pressed the buzzer again. Noelle wanted to close the monitors and pretend she didn't hear or see anything from the front gate, but she pressed the opener. After Helena walked through the man-gate, Noelle closed it behind her and went to the front door. Opening it slowly, she watched Helena approach, rolling an overnight bag behind her.

"How did you find me?" Noelle knew she sounded as accusatory as she felt.

"I talked to your mother."

"Mom? She'd never—" Noelle shook her head. "What lies did you feed her?"

"No lies. Only the truth." Helena stopped just outside the door. "Please, Noelle, let me come in. I need to talk to you."

"I let you in the gate. Some people would say that's way more than you deserve."

"I'd probably agree with them." Helena's laconic words caught Noelle off guard.

"You would?"

"Yes. Please. Can I come in?"

"All right." As Helena walked past, her familiar scent engulfed Noelle, who had to pinch her left thigh not to inhale too obviously. Helena would've looked the part of a successful CEO if her business suit weren't wrinkled and her hair disheveled. When Helena stepped into the light from the living room, Noelle saw other telling signs. Helena had dark circles under her eyes, clearly visible through her makeup.

"Don't blame your mother. I promised her I'd set things right."

"More empty words. Well, Mom doesn't know you the way I do." Noelle felt as if she'd stepped out of her body and could talk to Helena without her emotions overwhelming her.

"Can we sit down? It's been a long day for both of us."

"I think you should go. I'll call another cab."

"Please, Noelle. Listen to me." Helena raised both hands, palms toward Noelle. "I know you're upset. I don't blame you one bit, but please let me have my say."

"I don't know what you could possibly say that would make things all right." Noelle stepped closer to Helena, anger simmering under her skin. Helena actually swayed where she stood, and only now did Noelle realize how exhausted the other woman really was. "God, don't fall over." She braced herself and took Helena by the arm, guiding her to the couch. Helena momentarily slumped as she sat down, but then she squared her shoulders.

"Can I get you something to drink? Some wine?" Noelle felt awkward resorting to courtesy.

"Some water would be great, thank you." Equally polite, Helena thanked Noelle when she brought her some ice water from the bar. She drank it in a few large gulps.

"More?"

"No, thank you. I was thirsty, though." Helena placed the glass on the coffee table, next to Noelle's unfinished wine. "Would you mind sitting down? You're making me nervous."

Good. Noelle wanted to remain standing, preferably at a safe distance from Helena, but sat in one of the leather armchairs. "All right."

"Thank you." Helena took a deep breath. "I'm sorry you had to find out through David. I sent a memo with my decision, but obviously you never got it."

"No. I didn't."

"David showed up at my office, ranting and raving. I fired him for how he treated you."

"Good." Noelle felt no joy over David losing his job, but she was happy not to have to work with him again.

"He and his team are off the VMP payroll." Helena pressed her palms together. "As for my decision to stick to the original contract—"

"You mean, go back on your word." Noelle was shocked at how cold she sounded. She saw the impact on Helena, but she couldn't, or didn't dare, sound any other way. Her tone of voice was the only thing shielding her heart. "It'll be interesting to see how you try to weasel your way out of this."

"I have no intention of weaseling, now or later." Helena looked down at her hands. "I'm almost done. Please hear me out."

"All right."

"I was wrong when I wrote that memo. I was acting like a coward and I was so very wrong."

"Really?" Noelle tried to gauge why Helena would do a one-eighty on her again. The answer came easily. *Money.* Helena had been very clear about that from day one. VMP was a business, with stockholders to consider. It was all about the money.

"Yes. Really. Noelle, you should record your songs. You should sing what's in your heart. Screw the rest."

Noelle laughed, a thoroughly unhappy sound.

"Noelle." Tears rose in Helena's eyes. The tormented whisper together with the teary glance made Noelle recoil. *No. I won't feel sorry for her. I just won't.* If she did, this manipulative woman would only break what was left of her heart.

"I was worried about you. I still am. I thought if you postponed the recording of your own songs, you wouldn't give too much of yourself over to the tabloid vultures. Those beautiful, confessional songs come across as being ripped from your personal diary, Noelle. So close to the whole hoopla about the photos of us…I figured I could spare you that unwanted attention."

"Noble." Noelle looked contemptuous. "But bullshit."

❖

The uncharacteristic foul language showed more than anything how upset Noelle was. She was clearly trying to look casual and unaffected, but Helena knew Noelle's expressions, and most of all, she was able to read Noelle's eyes. A quick glance at her slender hands showed the faintest of tremors. Noelle was angry and sad.

"It's not bullshit. Why would you say that?" It was time to push Noelle just a bit, so Helena knelt on the floor next to Noelle's chair.

"Don't, Helena. Get up." Noelle looked horrified, but remained seated.

"You said you'd listen." Helena took one of Noelle's hands, like she'd done with Reba. "If you still want me to leave you alone afterward, then I'll never bother you again."

Noelle shuddered slightly, but she nodded.

"All right." Another deep breath later, Helena began again. "The first time I fell in love, I was completely humiliated, and I promised myself that it would never happen again. I had no one to talk to, and the woman I had fallen for looked at me with nothing but pity. *Pity*. Talk about adding insult to injury."

Noelle looked at her, but didn't comment.

"So I became a serial dater. I'd go out with a woman for two, three weeks at the most, then bow out. I always made sure she knew what she was getting herself into, but I stomped on some hearts along the way."

"Including mine." Noelle's voice was a mere whisper, and Helena wasn't sure if she knew she'd spoken aloud.

"Including yours."

"Yes." Noelle flinched.

"I was so sure that first woman loved me, that she was as infatuated and obsessed with me as I was with her. I caught her looking at me, smiling at me, and my hormones ran wild. I was eighteen, and I ruled the school. Actually, I was only thirteen when I took over the unofficial leadership of the boarding school my mother sent me to. It was that or miss her so much I'd die, or so it felt at the time. I never knew until then that I was a born leader, but once I asserted myself, all the other girls fell in line behind me."

"How old were you when your mother sent you to boarding school?" Noelle's eyes had softened marginally.

"Eleven. Almost."

"That's young."

"Yes." Helena closed her eyes for a moment before she continued. "Anyway, you know my MO over the years has been to get involved only with women who knew what they were getting into."

"Then what the hell did you ever see in me?" Noelle's anger flared.

"Don't you think I've asked myself that question a million times?" Helena raised her voice too, fear and frustration making her even more nervous.

"And?" Noelle suddenly stared down at their joined hands as if she had only now noticed Helena was holding on to her. She didn't pull back, and Helena clung to a faint hope.

"Remember the first time we met in person?"

"Your fortieth birthday."

"Yes." Helena's knees were beginning to ache and she allowed herself to slide sideways until she sat on the floor with her legs folded. She leaned against the left side of Noelle's chair, careful not to let go of her hand. It was easier to talk when she didn't have to meet Noelle's eyes. "I'm not very fond of surprises, and surprise parties are definitely not my forte. Still, my staff and some of my friends had gone to a lot of trouble, so I decided to try to relax and enjoy myself. I had only been at the helm of the company two years and I thought some goodwill would be clever on my part. I assumed there'd be some performances, and it was fun, until you entered the stage."

"I was that bad?" Noelle's voice didn't give anything away.

"Are you kidding? You were like an exotic flame. You burned and sizzled your way along the catwalk, all animalistic sexiness, and my entire system went on red alert. The other girls were sensual and sexy too, but next to you, they were lukewarm." Helena lost herself in the memories of that evening. "Then the three of you paraded down the catwalk and walked up to me. The other two kissed me like they were posing, but you, you hugged me. That hug was such a contrast to your sexy radiance, because it was friendly and warm. You kissed my cheek and whispered happy birthday, and I freaked out."

"I don't believe you." Noelle suddenly slid off the armchair, ending up on the floor next to Helena. Her hair broke free from the gold clasp that had controlled it and fell around her like a blond and black cloud. She pushed it back with impatient movements, scrutinizing Helena. "You looked at me with such indifference, I've never felt so small in my life."

"But that's just it. I couldn't show in front of everybody that you caught me so off guard. I guess I overcompensated." Helena tried to explain, knowing everything depended on making Noelle understand. "Here I was, the CEO of the company, the center of attention, and there you were, the biggest pop star of your generation. I had to fight hard to keep my composure. I couldn't afford to let anything show."

"What? I mean, what couldn't you let show?"

"You're joking, right?" Helena looked into Noelle's eyes, but saw only honest confusion.

"No. I don't get it."

"First it was sheer and utter lust." Helena cringed, but it was time for the truth, no matter how it made her look. "Your performance, your touch, your scent—they all set me on fire."

"Helena..." Noelle looked shell-shocked.

"I was beating myself up the whole time," Helena said, rubbing the back of Noelle's hand with her thumb. "According to the press, you were a diva who changed boyfriends every week, practically, and partied like a woman possessed."

"Hmm, that's what they like to think."

"I knew my own reputation. The company bitch, a corporate shark that eats and breathes money and power." Helena shrugged. "True to some degree, but as for your reputation, I know the rumors couldn't be more wrong."

"Thank you."

"But I wasn't aware of that fact then. I mean, I surmised it was exaggerated, but I also thought, 'no smoke without a fire.'"

"Who can blame you? My agent has done all he can to cultivate that image." Noelle looked somber. "Isn't it funny how some people have a bigger problem with me being gay than me being portrayed as a partying, drinking, smoking, promiscuous man-eater?"

"I hear you."

The mood changed. Suddenly the hostility seemed to dissipate. Noelle's hand relaxed in Helena's, and Helena scooted closer, resting her back against the front of the chair next to Noelle.

"So I kept my distance, but followed you closely, if that makes sense, until David and his crew called me, telling me you were being the diva and impossible to work with."

"And I was called into the principal's office, so to speak." Noelle shook her head, making her hair float, only to land on Helena's arm, its fragrance spellbinding. "I was so nervous that day. I dressed to the teeth and wore more makeup than I do onstage sometimes."

"You were beautiful, and I had such a problem trying to connect the image of you as a spoiled diva with the withdrawn, gracious girl I saw before me."

"You had me trembling," Noelle whispered.

Helena's heart stopped beating for a moment, only to race moments later. "In what way? Did I intimidate you that badly?"

Noelle tipped her head back on the chair, sighing softly. "You sure did. You sat there behind the desk, so stern and austere, and spoke to me in that husky voice. I was ready to bolt, but you mesmerized me."

"Noelle." Not wanting to move Noelle's hair where it rested on her, Helena carefully wrapped her arm around her. Half expecting Noelle to move out of reach, Helena could hardly believe it when Noelle's head rolled to the side, ending up on her shoulder. "And we both know what happened as soon as we were alone in the Hamptons."

"Yes. We kissed."

"I kissed you."

"And I kissed you back." A mere whisper, Noelle's voice trembled.

"Do you regret it?"

"No."

"Do you regret making love?"

"I know I asked you once before, but is that how you think of it, truly?" Noelle turned her head and gazed at Helena through her wild hair. "Not merely 'having sex'?"

"With you, it was all about making love." Helena didn't waver. "Was it like that for you?"

"It was magical. We connected on so many levels that night, and the next day, when I thought I'd imagined how close you felt…I knew I couldn't trust my own judgment anymore. Whenever it seemed we were getting closer, I reminded myself that I'd been wrong before, when I was so sure."

"That was my fault too." Helena's perpetual guilt weighed her down. How could she even hope that Noelle would forgive her, when she wasn't about to forgive herself anytime soon?

"You did explain that to me already, and I believed you, remember?" Noelle put her hair back into a twist, fastening the clip.

"Yes."

"Can you forgive me for the missing memo, for trying to protect you without talking to you first?" Helena held her breath.

"Life's too short, isn't it?" Noelle said, sounding tired.

"What does that mean?" Helena tried to understand Noelle's monotonous tone.

"It means I understand why we need to pick up the pieces and move on. Life's too short to hold grudges. It was nice of you to stop by and explain."

Helena wasn't sure what lay beneath Noelle's cool demeanor, but something was way off. "Nice. Huh." Unwilling to think about how she might be received, Helena cupped Noelle's cheeks and forced her to meet her gaze. "I'm not famous for being nice or kind. I'm trying to do the right thing here, knowing full well you have the right to loathe me. The thing is, I want you to go to the studio—you can pick anyone you want to produce your album—and record your songs, *any* songs, you want."

"What?" Noelle jerked her head around. "You still want me to record my own songs? On the VMP label?"

"Yes."

"Without restrictions?"

"Yes."

"Can I have that in writing?"

"Yes. I have a contract with me."

"Whoa." Noelle pulled her knees up and hugged her bent legs close to her chest. "You're confusing me. Just when I think I have you figured out, no matter if it's good or bad, you do something like this and turn everything on its head." Noelle looked accusingly at Helena. "It makes it damn hard to keep up."

"I'm sorry."

"Tell me, please, what the hell that woman, or girl, did to humiliate you so when you were eighteen? I mean, we all have crushes that don't work out."

Helena shifted, wondering if she could explain. "You have to know my mother to understand what frame of mind I was in throughout my adolescence. My mother was a ground-breaking industrial leader, for being female and for her success. She believed in diversifying, and she developed my father's thriving company into a complete empire after his death. He died of pneumonia when I was five." Helena pulled her hand back, and to her amazement, Noelle captured it again. "So Mother made it clear that she expected me to excel, to never show any weakness, and to be a Forsythe in every respect of the word.

"Thankfully, it turned out that I was a born leader, and my reputation preceded me, making it easy for me to remain in that position at my school when new kids enrolled. I was always afraid of losing it, of losing face, and thus disappointing my mother. When I fell in love with Ms. Johnson, one of my teachers, I was sure I had interpreted her interest in me correctly."

"Go on," Noelle said quietly when Helena hesitated.

"As it turned out, Ms. Johnson was planning to be married very shortly. I had entirely misunderstood her attention, and to my embarrassment, she even tried to comfort me." Helena looked up at the ceiling, wondering how this experience could have colored her entire life. "Ms. Johnson went through the whole poor-little-rich-girl routine, and I withdrew completely, treated her with cold indifference the last semester. After a couple of failed relationships in college, I fell into my habit of casual affairs, which suited me fine." *Until lately.*

"Which brings us back to the question, why me?" Noelle's voice didn't give anything away. "Sure, I'm perceived to be sexy and all that, but the overwhelming passion, surely you felt it too?"

"I did."

"And the way we were the other evening, in…in the tub." Noelle blushed, which made Helena relax a fraction more.

"That was a first for me. Nobody's ever shown me such trust." Helena couldn't stop looking into Noelle's gold-speckled eyes.

"Same here."

"Truth be told, when you're around, I can't take my eyes off you. It's been like that ever since I met you." Helena was trembling from a bad case of nerves, a completely new feeling that she could have done without.

"Helena." Noelle turned on her knees, staring at her. "You've said that before, but, please, what does it *mean*?"

CHAPTER TWENTY-FIVE

Noelle tried to determine if anything calculating or deceitful was hiding in Helena's eyes, but detected only a shimmer of withheld tears and so many stormy emotions that it was impossible to tell them apart. She was glad they were there, because she'd rather deal with stormy emotions than tears any day.

"It means you're more special to me than anyone else." Helena looked stunned at her own words.

"Special? As a performer? As in more special to you than any other recording artist in your stable?" Noelle wasn't trying to be clever, she simply wanted to understand. She straightened up, placing her hands on her knees.

"Please." Helena tugged Noelle back down. "No. Not as a performer or recording artist. I don't make love to any of my artists, normally. My mother taught me to never mix business with pleasure. In your case, all my good intentions flew out the window." She pressed her free hand to her chest. "You're in my heart. I carry the image of you on the inside of my eyelids, because every time I close my eyes, I see you. Not only that, I feel you too. Your soft skin…" Helena gently tugged Noelle closer. "Your soft, smooth skin." She kissed Noelle's cheek and nibbled down her neck. "Mmm."

"Helena…" Noelle's mind was a blur from trying to keep up. And now, Helena's touch severely impaired her ability to reason.

Capturing Noelle's lips, Helena kissed her gently, a non-intrusive kiss that left her yearning for more. Much more.

"Seeing you touch yourself for me over the phone was such a gift.

Nobody has ever trusted me so freely, shared with me that way, and you turned me on so much that I could barely breathe." Helena took Noelle's hand and raised it to her lips, where she kissed the inside of Noelle's wrist—small, hot kisses right where the blood pulsated under her skin.

"Oh, God." Noelle moaned and her head fell first forward and then back. The heat emanating from Helena's lips lit tiny bonfires across her skin, and she realized she was heading for trouble. "Stop. Helena. We can't."

Helena withdrew slightly and wrapped Noelle in a tight embrace. "Why can't we? Tell me what you need, what you want from me, and I'll make it happen."

Noelle wanted to burst into tears when she thought of what she most wished for. "You don't understand," she managed to say, "it won't happen. It's impossible, you've said so yourself."

"What is?" Helena ran her hands up and down Noelle's sides rapidly. "What's impossible?

"You don't love me. You've said you never could."

"I never meant I couldn't love you. I thought I was incapable of loving you the way you *deserve*. But I do love you, Noelle." Helena raised her voice. "I love you with all my heart, and if you just give me a chance, I can show you. Please, honey. Just one more chance and I'll do my best not to hurt you."

"What?" Noelle tried to stay afloat in the river of words flowing from Helena's lips. "You love me?"

"Yes." Helena was pale, with tears in the corners of her eyes.

"How...when did you...how?" Noelle knew she wasn't making sense.

"I knew a while back, but I finally confessed to myself after the bathtub session." Helena cleared her throat. "Noelle? Will you let me be part of your life?"

"Yes." Noelle found herself suddenly straddling Helena's thighs. "Yes. I want you in my life. I want you in my bed. I want you. Period."

Helena's uncharacteristic whimper told Noelle what she'd inadvertently omitted.

"And yes," Noelle added slowly, "I love you. I've loved you for quite a while." Noelle couldn't breathe. Not because she was overwhelmed by emotions, even if that did play a part, but because Helena hugged her so tight around the waist.

"I can't believe it." Helena buried her face in Noelle's hair. "I can hardly believe you love me. Occasionally I dared to hope, for short, short moments, but then I looked at you and asked myself what I could possibly offer you."

"A lot." Noelle began to unbutton Helena's shirt. "You could start by offering me...this." She kissed her way down from the indentation on Helena's throat to the soft skin between her breasts.

"Anything you want, honey. Anything." Gasping, Helena buried her hands in Noelle's hair, her fingers creating a tantalizing pattern on her scalp. "Just tell me what you want, and it's yours."

"So if I want to do this, it's all right?" Noelle blew hot air through the bra cup that held Helena's right breast, and immediately, Helena's nipple rose under the silk fabric, as if straining to meet her lips.

"It's more than all right." Helena pulled Noelle's head closer. "Open your mouth."

Happy to oblige, Noelle parted her lips, tasting Helena's nipple through the bra. She worked it with her tongue, and the sweet whimpering sounds her actions elicited made her breathe faster. She could hardly believe how fast everything had changed again—from utter unhappiness to ecstatic bliss in minutes. This thought suddenly made her stop.

"Noelle?" Helena rose on one elbow, cupping Noelle's neck with her other hand. "Talk to me."

"I just got scared. What if you change your mind again?" Hot tears stung her eyelids.

"Honey, I won't. I'll never change my mind. Before, I didn't trust in my feelings, and I didn't think I deserved any of this. I still would've had that opinion if it hadn't been for Manon and your mother."

"Mom? I know you talk to Manon, but Mom?" What could her mother have said to Helena to encourage her to fly down here?

"Reba asked me if I cared about her daughter, and that was a no-brainer."

"And?" Noelle pushed her hair behind her ears.

"She asked if I could walk away from you, if that was what you wanted." Helena kept caressing Noelle's neck.

"And?" Noelle felt like a parrot, but she had to know.

"I told her yes." Helena's eyes darkened to a stormy gray. "And I meant it, even if it would have killed me. I think she realized that I meant to fight for you, though."

"You did? I mean, you would? Fight for me?"

"That's what I *am* doing." Helena sat up, wrapping her arms tight around Noelle. "I'm fighting for my life here, because I came so close to destroying every chance I had with you, and for all I know, I may still find another ingenious way to screw things up." She looked so unhappy, Noelle had to kiss her long and deep.

"No, you won't. I won't let you. Now that I know you love me, you're stuck. I can be very stubborn, and remember, I'm the soul-pop diva, used to getting my way."

"Ha. I don't think so. You're humble, generous, and honest. Don't think I don't know. I plan to learn from you."

"Not too much," Noelle said, and wrinkled her nose. "I kind of like the way you command a room merely by entering and how you make men twice your size tremble when you stare them down."

"Oh, really?" Helena's eyes brightened. "That appeals to you, honey?" She slipped her hands under Noelle's long-sleeved T-shirt.

"It turns me on." Noelle gasped as Helena's fingers found her bare nipples. "Oh."

"Mmm, now here's an interesting discovery. Going commando, too, perhaps?" She found the drawstring of Noelle's sweat shorts.

"Um, no, well, not unless you think wearing a thong is almost like going commando."

"Thong?" Helena wet her lips. "Really."

"Uh-huh." Rising on her knees, Noelle allowed Helena to undo her shorts and push them down her hips. "That's it. See?"

"No, but I can feel." Helena cupped Noelle's bottom with both hands. "Yes, I can certainly feel it." She caressed Noelle with strong hands, every now and then dipping in between her legs. Noelle's wetness coated her sex and the inside of her thighs, and she realized Helena must feel it. A little shy about her obvious arousal, Noelle shifted and her cheeks warmed.

"As sexy as this thong is, what do you say we remove it?" Helena tugged at the flimsy material. "I want to look at you."

"Yes." Noelle slid down next to Helena. "And I want to look at you. All of you." She tugged at Helena's suit jacket. "You're wearing far too many clothes."

"And I haven't had a chance to clean up after my flight." Helena trembled under Noelle's hands. "Any chance we could reenact our bathroom session in real life?"

"I have a very nice tub in my bathroom. Come to think of it, less risk of Morris walking in on us there." Noelle laughed at the look of instant horror on Helena's face.

"Morris?" Helena glanced over her shoulder, looking like she expected him to show up any second.

"He has his own suite in the east wing. Though he thinks I'm alone, so he might just venture in to check on me."

Helena jumped up and pulled Noelle with her. "Bathroom."

"Oh, there's that command persona." She guided Helena to the large bathroom connected to her bedroom. "This way. Check this out." She pushed a touchpad to the left of the doorway, and a starry night sky lit up on the ceiling, creating the illusion that they were outdoors.

"Oh, my. Not bad." Helena purred and shrugged off her jacket. She started to unbutton her shirt, but Noelle nudged her hands away, wanting to finish the job herself. She tugged at the shirt and yanked it off, impatient to find Helena's smooth skin underneath. The bra followed, and Noelle knew the image of Helena standing topless in her slacks and pumps would stay with her for a long time.

"My turn." Helena's throaty voice made Noelle shiver. She reached for Noelle's thong and pushed it slowly down her thighs. Leaving it at the level of her knees, she stopped Noelle when she tried to push it off completely. "Not yet, honey. Not yet."

Standing with her underwear at half mast made Noelle feel unexpectedly vulnerable, yet more aroused than she thought possible. How did Helena know this?

"You look so beautiful, so damn sexy, honey." Helena removed the last of her own clothes, and her naked form, slender and compact, was the most wondrous sight Noelle had ever seen. She couldn't remember studying Helena properly that first heated night they'd shared together, when she'd still been so guilt ridden and confused. Now she took her time and used both eyes and hands to explore her lover. *My lover. My lover. Mine.*

"Water." Helena gasped. "As much as I'm loving every second of your attention, I still need to clean up my act."

"Oh. Right." Noelle reluctantly took her eyes off Helena for the few seconds it took to run the faucet and stepped out of her thong. "Tub should be ready in a minute or two."

"How about a quick shower while it fills up?"

"Good idea." Noelle hurried into the shower stall that easily accommodated both of them. The water cascaded on them, and Noelle pressed Helena close while devouring her lips.

"Noelle, oh God, Noelle…" Helena moaned against Noelle's lips. "You drive me crazy."

"Good." Noelle pushed her up against the wall, sliding her wet body along Helena's. "You do the same to me, so that makes it fair." Glancing over her shoulder, she saw the tub was ready for them. "Helena—oh!"

"Sorry, honey, the tub will have to wait." Helena allowed Noelle to turn off the water, then took her by the hand, pulling her with her, dripping all over the floor. "I can't wait a second longer for you."

❖

Helena had never felt such urgency, as if she'd implode if she couldn't feel Noelle's naked body next to hers. In a rush she tried to explain. "I promise we'll have our romantic bath, Noelle. I don't know what's the matter, but I need you. Now."

"I need you too. I want you so much." Noelle pushed the covers off the king-sized bed and climbed onto it. Made of cast iron, the four-poster bed was a beautiful focal point in the bedroom, but Helena only had eyes for the woman she loved with every cell in her body. Water drops glistened over her latte-colored skin, making it glisten like it was covered in a multitude of diamonds. Her hair hung in damp curls around her face and down her back. Noelle now held out her arms, beckoning Helena to join her.

Helena didn't hesitate. She slid her body along Noelle's satiny skin and groaned deep in her throat.

"You sound positively feral," Noelle said, breathless.

"And you look like a feline predator yourself, honey." Helena didn't know which turned her on more, the feel of Noelle under her hands or the sight of her incredible body. "You're so beautiful. I love you so much."

"And I love you, Helena." Noelle seemed to guess what Helena needed. "Here. Touch me." She lay down and spread her legs. "I'm yours. All yours."

Helena gasped as she slid a hand down Noelle's stomach and combed through the small patch of hair at the apex of her thighs. Noelle pulled her legs up, spreading herself trustingly, all the time keeping her eyes locked with Helena's. It was so hot, and yet so endearing, to see the trust she displayed.

Helena made sure her fingers were gentle as she explored Noelle's soaked folds, which were hot and slippery enough to make it challenging to focus on Noelle's clitoris. Helena had never felt such tenderness for anyone else as she caressed the little bundle of nerves, and soon Noelle's moans turned to keening whimpers.

"Please, Helena, go inside. I want you to take me…make me… yours." Her breath came in searing gushes as she tensed. Pushing her feet down into the bed, her knees still bent and spread wide, Noelle met Helena halfway as she entered her with two fingers. Even hotter inside, Noelle engulfed Helena's fingers, pulled them farther in with her strong internal muscles.

"God, you're so tight, so hot." Helena hovered above Noelle, not taking her eyes off her. "You're amazing. Just let go, anytime you want. I've got you."

"Helena?" Something resembling panic flickered across Noelle's face. "Helena?"

"I'm here. Shh. I've got you." Helena kissed Noelle softly as she thrust her fingers in and out. "Just hold on to me and let it come."

"He-le-na…" Noelle arched, clenching her teeth. "Ah!"

"There." Helena pressed her fingers deeper, curling them up inside Noelle. The convulsions continued for precious seconds, until Noelle finally slumped back, trembling. "Hey, you all right there?"

"Never better." Noelle was panting. "No exaggeration."

Helena was shivering, both from the air-conditioning against her damp body and from her own arousal. "Raise your leg, honey?"

"Mmm. No."

"What?" Helena froze.

"I want to watch you." Noelle rose on all fours. "I want you to part your legs and show me. Like you did over the phone. Show me." Her golden eyes were like bright amber now, glittering in the muted light from the bedside lamps.

Another surge of wetness flooded Helena's sex. "Oh, God, honey." She couldn't believe how vulnerable and sexy Noelle's words made her feel. Wanting to please Noelle and desperate for her own release, she complied. Her legs spread wide, she ached for Noelle's touch.

"Touch yourself," Noelle said, her voice urgent. "Show me."

"Yes." Helena touched her sex, using both hands. She slipped the same two fingers she'd used on Noelle inside herself and rubbed her clitoris with the thumb of her other hand.

"You like it like that." It wasn't a question, but Helena nodded.

"Yes."

Noelle took Helena's left nipple between her lips and sucked it deep inside her mouth. Crying out, Helena needed the connection more than anything else. "Noelle, please."

Noelle pressed Helena's breasts together, moving from one nipple to the other, biting, licking, devouring them until Helena felt so aflame, she was barely coherent.

"My turn." Noelle carefully nudged Helena's hands away and replaced them with her lips and fingers. Helena moaned, pulling her knees up to her chest to accommodate Noelle.

"I can't wait any longer, honey. I can't."

"And I don't want you to," Noelle murmured against Helena's sex. "I want you to come for me. Now."

As if the last, single word was all it took, Helena came, over and over, the pleasure bordering on pain. She had never felt more loved and more safe to express her arousal and release. Noelle held her in such a loving way, Helena knew she would never let go.

"God, you burn me, Noelle." Helena pulled Noelle up along her body to hug her close. "That was incredible." She was out of breath.

"Here. Don't want you to get cold." Noelle tugged the sheets up to cover their damp bodies. "The tub is waiting for us when you can move, though."

"Sounds heavenly, but not yet, all right? I'm not ready."

"Me either." Noelle curled up against Helena. "Truthfully, I don't think I want to be away from you or this bed. Ever."

"Really?" Helena chuckled, which seemed to make Noelle shiver. "You may get hungry after a while, honey."

"Only for you." Noelle kissed her slowly, her tongue exploring Helena's mouth. "Just for you."

"Then I won't argue." Helena arranged Noelle's hair like a tent around their heads, shielding them from the outside world. "I certainly could stay here forever."

"Great minds think alike." Noelle nuzzled Helena's cheek and neck. "You're beautiful. I just can't imagine not being able to hold you like this. If you...if you were to change your mind again..." Noelle stopped talking, a faint trace of fear shadowing her eyes.

"I won't. I may have been acting like a complete idiot so far, but that feels like another lifetime, almost. I was afraid, honey." Helena kissed Noelle slowly. "I was stuck in some damn time warp where the only thing I focused on was professional success. When it came to personal relationships, I favored friendships rather than romantic ones, making sure I wouldn't lose face or get hurt. It was like an inaudible mantra."

"Any idea why you felt that so strongly? I don't mean to lessen your girlhood experience, but we all have crushes and get our hearts broken when we're teens." Noelle looked up at Helena, her eyes kind and completely without judgment.

"Oh, I've speculated, trust me. Never gone to therapy, though, which might have been clever, in retrospect."

"From a purely selfish point of view, I disagree," Noelle said, and drew a tantalizing line along Helena's neck with the tip of her tongue.

"What are you talking about?"

"If you'd had therapy, you could've resolved your issues and found someone else a long time ago. Awful reasoning, isn't it?" Noelle gave a one-shoulder shrug.

"I don't think it would've mattered. As soon as you walked into my life via that catwalk, singing and moving to the music like nobody else, I was lost. I could have resisted you as easily as a cat resists a bowl of cream."

"I'm a bowl of cream?" Noelle laughed.

"You're the ultimate bowl of cream." Helena lapped at Noelle's chest, licked her way back and forth between her nipples. "One I'll never tire of."

"I just don't want you to have any regrets."

"No worries when it comes to that. None." Helena tilted her head, squinting as she tried to picture herself as a very young girl being sent off to boarding school. Perhaps that perpetual separation anxiety she had experienced every semester when she went back to school had something to do with her love-them-and-leave-them tactics? Helena didn't really care anymore, as she lay wrapped in Noelle's arms. "You know, I'm not sure how, but I have the strangest feeling."

"You do?" Noelle looked curiously at her.

"I do." Helena stared at Noelle through sudden tears. "I feel like I've just come home."

"Oh. Oh, my love." Noelle held on tight to Helena, her arms around her neck. "You are. I mean, you have. I don't want to be alone again. I've felt so lonely for so long and, well, I had no idea I was waiting for you."

"I'm so glad you did. And I'm thankful you decided to give me another chance." Helena ran her hand along Noelle's body, reveling in the touch. Noelle in turn stretched and returned the caresses in long, languid movements.

"Honestly, I think it was *you* who decided to take a chance. You're a brave woman, Helena. It takes courage to do what you did."

"I'm not so sure, but you might know more about that than I do. You're very courageous to reach for your own happiness, on your own terms, whether by writing your songs or by loving me."

Noelle laughed, a thoroughly happy sound. "Loving you will be much easier now when I know you love me back."

"Agreed." Helena grew serious. "It may prove difficult in other ways, though, honey."

"You mean in the eyes of the public, or the media, or the fans?" Noelle snuggled closer. "I realize that. But for tonight, everything is perfect. I'm perfectly happy."

Helena sighed, contentment and euphoria pushing all negativity out of her mind. "You know something, honey? I'm perfectly happy too."

EPILOGUE

Four months later

"Champagne?" Carolyn Black took two glasses of the sparkling wine and handed one to Noelle. "Are you enjoying yourself?" She gestured toward the large crowd gathered around the pool and the outdoor bar area in Annelie's and her garden.

"It's a wonderful party," Noelle said. "What a great turnout too. You've invited *the* most exciting and diverse group of women in the entertainment and literary industry."

"Yes," an amused voice said from behind them. "I can visualize you and Annelie going over your cell phone contacts one by one." Helena wrapped an arm around Noelle's waist. "Truthfully, this has to be the party of the year in Miami."

"I would certainly hope so," Carolyn said in a mock stuck-up tone. "The time it took to go through those cell phones alone." Her famous voice turned heads around the pool.

"What's so funny?" Annelie joined them, carrying a glass of champagne of her own. "Oh, look. They made it!" She beamed and waved to the four women who just walked out on the patio. "Manon, Eryn, welcome. Vivian, Mike. The four of you look amazing."

Noelle found herself embraced from two directions as Vivian and Mike hugged her at the same time. "Oh, heavenly," she said, winking at Helena, who shook her head and grinned.

"Glad the bad weather in Rhode Island eased up enough for you to fly down." Carolyn made sure everybody had a glass of champagne.

"Now, before you all wander off to mingle, I need to ask you if you have given some more thought to my question? Noelle? Ladies?" She looked expectantly between the four members of Chicory Ariose and Noelle.

"As a matter of fact, we have a surprise for you." Eryn twirled her long red braid around her hand. She craned her neck and looked at something at the far end of the pool. "Your staff is setting up the instruments now, so how about we start in half an hour or so. After we mingle."

"Mingle away." Carolyn swiveled and kissed her wife's lips. "Oh, this is exciting."

"I'll say," Helena said, raising her eyebrows at Noelle. "Care to fill me in on the surprise?"

"No." Noelle found it humorous that Helena frowned at her refusal to share. "It wouldn't be a surprise if I did that, now, would it?"

"True. So when have you had time to work on surprises with these four?" Helena looked suspiciously at the women from Rhode Island.

"Do you *have* to sound like you think we're leading her down the path to the dark side?" Vivian snorted and then broke into full opera-diva laughter.

"Yes, I wonder why?" Helena pursed her lips and tapped her index finger to her chin. "Maybe because you all look like cats who swallowed at least one canary—each."

Noelle could hardly believe that anyone could feel as happy as she did and not have it all backfire. She had worked on her new album, a double CD with both dance music and her own songs, for the last four months, and it was almost done. New producers, a new agent—it was like she had a whole new existence. Also new and exciting was her secret collaboration with Chicory Ariose. It would soon become public knowledge that they had guest-starred on each other's albums, but tonight's particular surprise was especially created with this party in mind.

Gazing down into Helena's eyes, Noelle knew that everything she valued in life would feel empty without the love she shared with this amazing woman. Once the media frenzy calmed down, Helena and Noelle had taken their cue from Carolyn and Annelie by not commenting but not hiding their relationship.

Paparazzi still flocked around them, but even that attention had lessened to some degree. Helena had kept a close eye on Noelle's sales figures, and judging from how the Maddox soundtrack was selling and the outpouring of support from fans on the forum on Noelle's official Web site, Noelle didn't have to worry that they would all abandon her.

Noelle's family had rallied around them, and even her rather conservative grandparents in Austin seemed infatuated with Helena.

"So you won't tell me?" Helena asked, interrupting Noelle's thoughts.

"No."

"All right. Be like that." Helena sighed. "We better mingle then, mystery girl." Helena caressed Noelle's neck and kissed her just beneath her ear. "I'll have to copy your strategy and fake some patience, then."

"Hmm. You can always *try*." Noelle sidestepped quickly to avoid being tickled. "Behave, Ms. Forsythe."

Helena's bright eyes showed she had no intention of obeying.

❖

"Ladies." Annelie and Carolyn stood by the microphone on the small stage at the end of the pool. The night was velvety black, and the lights from the Miami mainland around Star Island made the city look like a huge piece of jewelry. Helena waited at the front of the crowd now moving closer to listen to their hostesses, her eyes never leaving Noelle for long. Her lover, her *love*, was dressed in a deep burgundy dress that reached midthigh. *Trust my girl to flaunt it when she wants to.*

Helena didn't know anyone who could wear a dress that bordered on sleazy and make it look super-classy. Sequins made the dress look like a live entity, and the low neckline seemed to keep her breasts out of plain view by sheer willpower. Helena had heard more than one woman gasp when Noelle turned her back and showed just how low-cut it was.

"Ladies." Carolyn tried again. "I know, I know, you're all excited to see these amazing performers up here. Chicory Ariose, with world-renowned mezzo-soprano Vivian Harding and superstar Noelle Laurent, on the same stage together. We are creating entertainment history, dear friends. Well, we won't keep the surprise for you much longer. Annelie and I just want to thank you again for coming and for digging deep in your purses and wallets to help women, men, and children in shelters throughout our country. Thank you."

The guests applauded enthusiastically and several women hooted encouragement as Eryn stepped forward on the stage, letting her fingers play on her Fender Stratocaster. Helena shivered as silvery tones emanated from the instrument and seemed to touch her skin like rain. Eryn nodded to Mike, who engaged the crash cymbal and hi-hat in a lazy rhythm. Manon and Vivian began to exchange strings of tones—voice and keyboard, keyboard and voice, over and over.

Slowly the music built a pattern, and Helena knew she would never have been able to truly appreciate it, to feel the utter joy at hearing such talents come together in a brilliant jam session, if it hadn't been for Noelle. Helena had taken every opportunity to join Noelle's new producers in the studio when her lover recorded her songs. Eighteen tracks in all, nine of her own songs and nine of her old soul-pop genre, and most of them were potential hits, as far as Helena was concerned.

Noelle now stood next to Vivian, and Manon introduced a new melody, wove it in with their improvisation, and then Noelle began to sing. Her warm, husky voice carried over the pool. As clear as expensive crystal, it conveyed the true feelings behind her words. Recognizing Noelle's style of writing by now, Helena knew this was a new composition. Tears streamed down her cheeks as the words hit home, but Helena didn't care if anyone noticed.

> So sure she would lose,
> So certain she would fail,
> So bound for heartache,
> Yet she still prevailed.

Noelle sang with so much feeling, and she didn't take her eyes off Helena. Soon it became clear to the rest of the audience that Noelle was singing to someone special, and Helena saw out of the corners of her eyes how some turned to look at her. She couldn't have cared less. Noelle's words were universal, but Helena knew the song was about her.

She touched me like no other,
Her soul called out to mine.
I felt her wants, I felt her needs,
As I knew that she felt mine.
So I sang to her of my love songs
And I told her of my soul,
And showed her all my secrets
And together we'll be whole.

Noelle ended the song and the women in Chicory Ariose took a bow next to her before joining in the applause. Noelle smiled through tears, holding out both hands to Helena as she walked toward her. Helena wrapped her arms around Noelle, hiding her wet cheeks in Noelle's hair.

"Thank you." Helena could barely speak. "It was for me, wasn't it?"

"Yes, Helena, all for you," Noelle whispered. "All for you."

About the Author

Gun Brooke resides in the countryside in Sweden with her very patient family. A retired neonatal intensive care nurse, she now writes full time, only rarely taking a break to create Web sites for herself or others and to do computer graphics. Gun writes both romances and sci-fi.

Books Available From Bold Strokes Books

Fierce Overture by Gun Brooke. Helena Forsythe is a hard-hitting CEO who gets what she wants by taking no prisoners when negotiating—until she meets a woman who convinces her that charm may be the way to win a battle, and a heart. (978-1-60282-156-9)

Trauma Alert by Radclyffe. Dr. Ali Torveau has no trouble saying no to romance until the day firefighter Beau Cross shows up in her ER and sets her carefully ordered world aflame. (978-1-60282-157-6)

Wolfsbane Winter by Jane Fletcher. Iron Wolf mercenary Deryn faces down demon magic and otherworldly foes with a smile, but she's defenseless when healer Alana wages war on her heart. (978-1-60282-158-3)

Little White Lie by Lea Santos. Emie Jaramillo knows relationships are for other people, and beautiful women like Gia Mendez don't belong anywhere near her boring world of academia—until Gia sets out to convince Emie she has not only brains, but beauty…and that she's the only woman Gia wants in her life. (978-1-60282-163-7)

Witch Wolf by Winter Pennington. In a world where vampires have charmed their way into modern society, where werewolves walk the streets with their beasts disguised by human skin, Investigator Kassandra Lyall has a secret of her own to protect. She's one of them. (978-1-60282-177-4)

Do Not Disturb by Carsen Taite. Ainsley Faraday, a high-powered executive, and rock music celebrity Greer Davis couldn't be less well suited for one another, and yet they soon discover passion has a way of designing its own future. (978-1-60282-153-8)

From This Moment On by PJ Trebelhorn. Devon Conway and Katherine Hunter both lost love and neither believes they will ever find it again—until the moment they meet and everything changes. (978-1-60282-154-5)

Vapor by Larkin Rose. When erotic romance writer Ashley Vaughn decides to take her research into the bedroom for a night of passion with Victoria Hadley, she discovers that fact is hotter than fiction. (978-1-60282-155-2)

Wind and Bones by Kristin Marra. Jill O'Hara, award-winning journalist, just wants to settle her deceased father's affairs and leave Prairie View, Montana, far, far behind—but an old girlfriend, a sexy sheriff, and a dangerous secret keep her down on the ranch. (978-1-60282-150-7)

Nightshade by Shea Godfrey. The story of a princess, betrothed as a political pawn, who falls for her intended husband's soldier sister, is a modern-day fairy tale to capture the heart. (978-1-60282-151-4)

Vieux Carré Voodoo by Greg Herren. Popular New Orleans detective Scotty Bradley just can't stay out of trouble—especially when an old flame turns up asking for help. (978-1-60282-152-1)

The Pleasure Set by Lisa Girolami. Laney DeGraff, a successful president of a family-owned bank on Rodeo Drive, finds her comfortable life taking a turn toward danger when Theresa Aguilar, a sleek, sexy lawyer, invites her to join an exclusive, secret group of powerful, alluring women. (978-1-60282-144-6)

A Perfect Match by Erin Dutton. The exciting world of pro golf forms the backdrop for a fast-paced, sexy romance. (978-1-60282-145-3)

Father Knows Best by Lynda Sandoval. High school juniors and best friends Lila Moreno, Meryl Morganstern, and Caressa Thibodoux plan to make the most of the summer before senior year. What they discover that amazing summer about girl power, growing up, and trusting friends and family more than prepares them to tackle that all-important senior year! (978-1-60282-147-7)

The Midnight Hunt by L.L. Raand. Medic Drake McKennan takes a chance and loses, and her life will never be the same—because when she wakes up after surviving a life-threatening illness, she is no longer human. (978-1-60282-140-8)

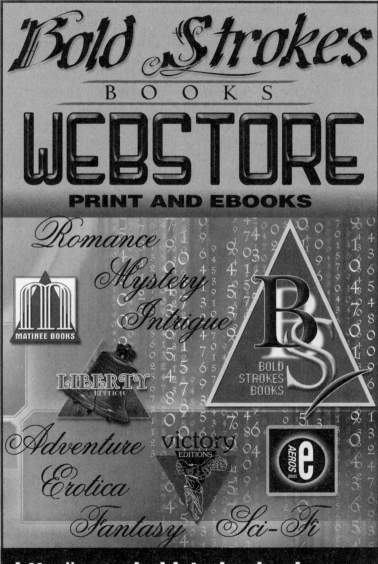